Dead from the Start

KYRA TAYLOR

KISSED PUBLICATIONS

Dead from the Start

ISBN 13: 978-0-9667609-5-8
ISBN 10: 0966760956
LCCN: 2015947664

Dedication

To my family for helping me to stand

Acknowledgments

First and foremost, I would like to honor my Lord and Savior, Jesus Christ, without whom I would not have been able to make it this far. It was the keeping and delivering power of God that allowed me the grace to overcome every rough place. He is my everything.

To my parents, Pastor Leon R. Taylor and Lady "Me" Taylor, thank you for laying a sure foundation. It allowed me to remain rooted and grounded through difficult times.

To my siblings: Kimberly R. Taylor, thank you for the lectures, sermons, critiques and tough love you've so willingly given that caused me to continue to make progress when I felt like giving up. Keisha T. Motley, the advice, support and encouragement you've shared with me will always be appreciated. Sometimes I wondered if maybe you were the older of us. Leon "Kevin" Taylor, Jr, thank you for being there as protector, willing to fight for me, no matter the enemy.

To my children, Ezekiel III, Christian, Zekeira, and Jordan, you are the lights of my life. I thank God for each of you. I do what I do because of you.

To my Aunt Ricky, thank you for being my second mother and for your advice and support.

To my Friends and sisters, Carla Murchison, Joanne Hieskill and Rene Banks. I thank God for you. There is no way I would have made it if it wasn't for your constant prayers, talks, outings and the encouragement given over the years.

To my church family, Elohim Christian Outreach Center, Pastors Leo and Elaine Hackett, Jr. Thank you for wise counsel, sharing the truth in love and never wavering from the word of God. You've allowed me to heal and grow under your watchful gaze.

To my editor and publisher, Kimberly T. Matthews of Kissed Publications, thank you for taking a chance on me and allowing me to take my story to the masses. I appreciate you.

And to everyone who has ever poured into me, believed in me, supported me, encouraged me or loved me, thanks. Without you, this would not have been possible.

As I put pen to paper, I'm in the midst of yet another trial. It seems the longer I'm saved the more junk I have to put up with. Humph---Well, I better get up. It's time for church.

Welcome to My World

As I pull up to the church, I can hear the choir singing already. I hate being late. I glance in the rearview mirror at my kids sulking. They always make me late!

"Come on, y'all," I say. "Don't forget the diaper bag," I tell Gabrielle, my oldest. She just turned fourteen.

"Alright, ma," she grumbles, grabbing her baby sister Mariah and handing the bag to Samuel.

"Tuck your shirt in, Samuel," I fuss. We walk up the sidewalk to the front of the church where the greeters are waiting and holding open the doors.

"Good mornin', Sister Mildred," they say. "Good morning everyone." I smile. I grab the kids and maneuver them into the sanctuary. The usher directs us to a row near the middle, and we sit down. As I proceed to take off my coat and gloves, I look around at all the saints and even some visitors singing along with the choir. I catch my husband's eye. He's sitting on the pulpit with the other preachers and I can tell he's not happy that I'm late. He quickly masks his expression and starts singing again. I take Mariah from Gabbi and remove her snowsuit.

"Stand up for praise and worship." I nudge my kids. We all stand up and sing along. I smile and wave at everyone that I see and try to enjoy myself, but my mind keeps wandering back to last night and replaying it over and over.

"Do I pay you to think?!" he spat. "Now what am I going to wear? You want me looking like a chump?—That's it. You think I should look like you. Like some welfare reject." Jonas paced back and forth, glaring at me like I was the ink stain that the cleaners couldn't get out.

"I'm sorry," I say.

"Shut up!" he yells. "Did I tell you to speak? You don't speak until you're told."

I just look down at the floor and wait for this tirade to end. They usually last about ten minutes. Fortunately, the kids are in bed and not witnessing this scene. Although, he's real careful not to berate me in front of them 'cause he doesn't want it getting back to the pastor. After all, he does have a reputation to uphold. I just stand there trying to hold back tears and tell myself that I can be strong this time and not let him see that his words hurt me.

He goes on and on about how he has to find something else appropriate to wear now that I messed up his best suit. Never mind that he left the pen in the pocket. But because I didn't check the pockets when I dropped it off, I'm responsible.

"You know, the longer I'm married to you the dumber and lazier you get. Sometimes I wish I never met you." With that statement, he goes out of the bedroom to his study. The fight is over and he leaves me to make excuses for him and resolve to do better.

Everybody is taking their seats. Praise and worship is over and the morning announcements are starting. There's a special program this evening and my husband is the MC. *Oh Lord. The show begins. Jonas will be in rare form tonight.* I wish I could just stay home. I hate having to fight with the kids while trying to get into the service, keeping the baby quiet, and trying to look like the happy wife. Suddenly it feels like the weight of the world is on my shoulders. I spend the rest of the service avoiding my husband's eyes and pretending that I'm not. I'm getting good at it. Sometimes even I believe that everything's okay.

After church is over, Samuel and Gabbi run off to talk to their friends and I carry Mariah up to the front to greet Pastor Gilliam and Pastor Evelyn.

"Hello there, Sister Mildred. God bless you," says Pastor as I reach the front. He reaches out and takes my free hand and shakes it.

"It's so good to see you," says Pastor Evelyn, as she kisses my cheek. "And how is little Mariah doing?"

"Oh, she's just fine. Getting big," I reply. Jonas walks up and puts his hand at the small of my back.

"Pastor, that was some blessed word today. You were on fire. And the anointing was so high in here," he says.

"God is good, Jonas. I just let the Holy Spirit have his way," says Pastor Gilliam.

"Yes, sir," Jonas responds. As he talks, he maneuvers between the Pastors and me so now I'm standing behind him. He proceeds to talk with them about the service this afternoon and just like that, I'm dismissed. You would have thought I became invisible at that moment.

While he talks, I walk towards the back trying to decide what to do for three hours until the next service. "Well, first mommy's going to change somebody's diaper," I say, snuggling Mariah. Sometimes I think that if it weren't for my kids I would have lost my mind a long time ago.

I get to the ladies lounge and lay Mariah on the changing table. "Jesus, give me strength," I sigh, as I change my daughter. I remember how excited my husband was when each of our children were born. He was the "proud papa". He carried more pictures in his wallet than I did. I don't know what happened, but one day it just seemed to be a bother to him. He didn't have time for them—or me for that matter. His work at church was more important and he began spending less time with his family. After Mariah was born nine months ago, he seemed happy again, but that didn't last long.

Hey, don't get me wrong. I love church, ministry and all that, but not to the point where my family suffers. I read somewhere that you had to be faithful at home before you could be considered faithful at church. But then, maybe I'm a little biased since I'm getting the short end of the stick. I thought God was giving me His best when I met Jonas and we fell in love. Now I wonder what kind of a sense of humor God has. I thought I was supposed to be happy with my life at this point. We have the best of everything—big house, nice cars, good children, fine clothes, prestige—but I feel like a failure. Like I got more than I bargained for.

"Mill? Is that you?" asks a voice from a stall.

"Yeah, it's me," I answer, smiling as recognition kicks in. "Trish girl, hurry up and come outta there and talk to me."

"Girl, you know womenfolk sometimes need a little extra toilet time. Gimme a minute, I'm coming," she responds.

As I wait for Patricia, I thank God again for putting her in my life. Sometimes I doubt I would have made it this far without her friendship. She's the only real friend I have. I tell her everything. And she tells me things I don't want to hear. But it's because she loves me. We're sisters.

"Here I am," she says, sitting down beside me. "Hey, pretty girl." She gushes to Mariah, and leaning over, she takes her off my lap. "How's my baby?" Mariah laughs and tries to grab Patricia's face as she bounces her up and down. "You planning on staying for the second service?" She asks me.

"You know I am. What would it look like if I didn't show up? And I ain't even trying to hear his mouth."

"Girl, don't get me started on that cause you know I could care less about what anyone thinks and even less about what Jonas says. You need a break!" she fusses.

I can't blame her. I've been going nonstop since Jonas was ordained. With all his meetings and services and classes, I've been responsible for the house, the kids and making sure I'm there to support him. Even when I had surgery, he expected me to be at his initial sermon. I was doped up on pain medicine, but I was there for him. Can't say the same for him, though. When I had to go to the hospital, he managed to get 'hung up' and "why don't you call your sister or dad or somebody to take you". I was in the hospital for a week and the only day he came was when the pastor and his wife came by. How convenient. He didn't even pick me up when I was discharged. His excuse was that it was revival and Pastor Gilliam needed him there to open up the service. Service started at 6:30. I was released at noon.

"Girl, if I've told you once, I've told you a million times, you can do better by yo'self. You're already doing it anyway. Just make it legal," says Trish, still fussing.

"I'm not going there with you," I chuckle. "I've got to figure out what to do with all this time."

"Go feed them children. Matter of fact, we could all use some food. Let's go."

After eating, we all go back to the church for the afternoon program. The worship leader, Sister Joyce, is getting in place to open up the praise and worship portion of the service. We sit in the middle on a row near the front. The youth department is functioning, so the children are in the back. Trish and I are looking around and seeing all the members who stayed back. There are even a few visitors. As Sister Joyce opens up with prayer, the pastor and Jonas come out from the side entrance and take their seats in the pulpit. Jonas looks so dignified and pious. I love my husband. I do. But sometimes I wish that what he shows others is how he really is. The prayer is over and Sister Joyce starts singing her favorite hymn 'What a Fellowship'.

"I swear she sings that song at every service," whispers Trish. "Can't we get a break?"

"Girl, you crazy," I say, covering my mouth as I laugh. I start to relax and enjoy the singing and praise. Trish and I both stand up when she starts singing 'This is the Day'. Next comes 'O Magnify the Lord'. I really begin to get into the praise. My mind starts meditating back on all the good times and everything God has brought me through. I actually start feeling happy. As my spirit starts to soar, I begin really praising and worshipping God. Not to sound too cliché, but my 'soul got happy' and I start shouting. Trish puts her hand on my back to steady me while I praise Him.

"Hallelujah," she shouts.

As the Holy Spirit starts moving over me, I just have to run. I come out into the aisle and run around the sanctuary. My second time around I stop at the side of the altar. The ushers join hands and make a circle around me. I just give God praise. Sometimes God's goodness overshadows my pain, and I just have to give it up. I just wish it was that way all the time. Just to be in that moment of true worship and have time stand still and you live in that moment forever. Wouldn't that be wonderful?

As I begin to contain myself, I feel like something is burning me. I open my eyes and see Jonas looking at me. His face is expressionless, but his eyes are like fire. *Uh-oh, here comes another bad night.*

Jan 8

Man, Jonas railed on me. Told me I acted like some possessed fool running all around the church. I tried to tell him I got caught up in the spirit, but he said I embarrassed him. Then he wanted to know who I've been talking to and what I've been telling people about him. He said Pastor asked him about me and about our marriage, was everything OK. He said he told him we were fine and that things couldn't be better. (Lies!) But if he hears that I've been saying things to people about him, I would regret it. Now what's that supposed to mean? Is that a threat? I'm his wife!

Monday morning. Where did the weekend go? I get out of bed and go into the bathroom to get ready for the day.

"Today you are going to do something special for you," I tell myself, while brushing my teeth. My eyes travel up and down my image in the mirror counting the flaws. "Mmm…maybe thirty pounds less and Jonas'll look at me again."

I finish up in the bathroom and go and get the kids ready for school. Gabbi is already up and dressed, so I go to Sammy's room and wake him up.

"Sammy, get up. It's time for school." I pull the covers back, grab his leg and slide it over the side of the bed. He hates that. But whatever works, right?

Next, I get Mariah and wash, dress and feed her while Sammy's getting ready.

Now that everybody's up I get breakfast ready and put a load of clothes in the washer. Jonas comes down first and I hand him his plate—two scrambled eggs and two pieces of bacon. "Here you are, honey," I say.

"Yeah," he replies. He has the newspaper in front of his face reading while he eats. No 'thank you', no 'good morning', no goodbye kiss. Just eat and run.

I rush the kids through their breakfast and out to the bus stop. I pick up the baby and her bag and get her to the sitter's. Then it's off to work at New Ventures Management Company. Drafting reports, inputting payroll and answering phones for people wanting this fixed or that done.

Or can I pay later, make arrangements, etc. Either way, it boils down to long days.

When I get there this morning the lights on the phone are already flashing, meaning there are messages to be checked. I put my purse down and go over to the shelf behind my desk and get the coffee and filters. As I wait for the coffee to brew, I turn on my favorite radio station that plays all the oldies but goodies and sit down in my chair. I'm usually the first one in every morning, so for the first half hour I pretend that this is my company; that I'm in control. I close my eyes and I visualize all the properties that I manage and how everyone pays their rent on time and my bank account is always in the black.

I open my eyes and see my desk is cluttered with accounts and bills and mail. "Oh, well, back to reality," I sigh. I get my cup of coffee and settle down in my old creaky office chair and check the messages--one leaky faucet, two extensions, a broken lock, and a wrong number. Not bad.

As I go through the mail and start keying in notations on the different accounts, Nora breezes in.

"Hi, Mildred," she gushes.

"Mornin', Nora. Why you look positively radiant today." Nora just got married a month ago, so for her, life is just perfect. Her husband Craig sends her flowers every other day 'just because' and stops in for surprise lunch dates. Sometimes it's just sickening. But I try not to be a hater. I used to have that. Jonas would buy me jewelry and write me poems, and we would hold hands when we walked. He even massaged my feet. And of course, I returned the favor. I just loved the intimacy we had. But over the first few years of our marriage, it just trickled down to barely speaking, except when he was mad about something.

While Nora expounded on the virtues of her new husband—"He really is sooo sweet."—I try to smile and nod in all the right places while gathering my notes and files. I am the one who keeps the books and pays the bills and makes sure money is collected and deposited and payroll is distributed. Nora handles the contractors and dispatches when repairs need to be done. The last to arrive are always Trudy and Judy. They handle marketing, research and real estate. They make coming to work interesting. Because they are twins, they think they are supposed to finish each other's sentences. It can get a little interesting at times. The owner, Mr. Hughes, is into real estate ventures. He buys houses, flips houses, rents houses and even dabbles in commercial properties, hence the name. He rarely comes into the office except to sign papers or see if the building is still standing. I email monthly reports so that he can track the progress of the company from anywhere. He recently got into managing property because the market seemed sluggish and people were more willing to rent than buy.

That worked out well for me because I was looking for work after having Sammy. Jonas didn't want me to work and told everybody that. He said that I didn't have to work if I didn't want to, but when I decided I wanted my own money, you would have thought I sucker punched him. I just didn't want to have to depend on someone else to take care of me. My mother taught me to have my own. I guess somehow I knew things would change. Did they change because I started working or was it inevitable? I don't really know. Anyway, I ran across an ad in the paper for a receptionist at a small startup. I thought it would be perfect to work for a small company and help build it from the ground up. When I went for the interview, Mr. Hughes hired me on the spot. He said it was something about me he liked and asked, "Can you start tomorrow?"

Just like that, I was a professional working woman. And I've been loving it ever since.

Judy was going through the classifieds checking on foreclosures and real estate sales looking for properties that might interest Mr. Hughes. Nora was calling our contractors to get the repair calls left on the voice mail. Trudy was typing away on her computer, and I was trying to figure

out how to get more business for Mr. Hughes. Because I keep the
books, I noticed that the bottom line was flat or that we took losses
some months. We never have to worry about getting paid, because Mr.
Hughes is adamant that I do payroll first and then pay what we owe. I
have to juggle some months, but everybody gets what's due them. That's
why I have been trying to come up with an idea to bring in more money.

As I sit there, I mutter a little prayer under my breath, "Lord, give me
an idea or witty invention to help keep my job."

"What did you say?" asks Trudy.

"Nothing," I reply. "Just talking to myself."

"Uh-oh! That's not a good sign. It's just Monday. If you're talking
to yourself today...," starts Trudy." ...I hate to see what you'll be doing
by Friday," jokes Judy, finishing Trudy's thought.

"Y'all crazy. It ain't that bad yet." I toss a scrap paper ball at Judy,
and she ducks, chuckling. I continue to work and clear out old files and
update reports. Before long, lunchtime is here, and the bell chiming
brings me back to the present.

"Good afternoon, ladies," says Craig, and he enters with a huge
bouquet of yellow roses. "Hello, my darling." He plants a kiss on Nora's
cheek and hands her the flowers.

"Oh, Craig," she gushes. "How sweet!"

"Yeah, how sweet," Judy and Trudy say in unison.

"I just stopped by to take my favorite girl to lunch."

"Okay, let me get my coat," I say. "I didn't think you wanted Nora to
know about us so soon, Craig." I tease as I pretend to gather my
belongings while everybody laughs.

"Mildred," blushes Nora, "you're so silly. I'll be back soon, guys."
And with that, she grabs Craig's hand and pulls him out the door.

"How much you want to bet that she'll still be hungry when she gets
back?" asks Judy.

"Girl, why you think she keeps all them snacks in her drawer? Lunch my eye," I say. We all get a good laugh out of that and go back to our tasks. I usually order in or bring something from home to eat, but today I just snack on some crackers that I keep in my desk and continue working until it's time to go.

On my way home, I pick up the kids from the sitter's. I have the school bus drop them off there so that Gabbi and Samuel won't be home by themselves. That way, I only have one stop to make to get everybody. I'm usually the one who gets the kids anyway. If there is an emergency, and I can't leave work, then Jonas will pick them up, but he acts like it's a big inconvenience. I thought they were our children, not just mine. I've lost plenty of time from work taking care of them, but I love them, and I wouldn't do less for them.

As I pull up in the driveway at home, I see that Jonas is already there.

"Why is he home so early?" I wonder aloud.

"Maybe he wants to help us with our homework before dinner," suggests Sammy. "I like it when he helps me."

"Yeah, baby," I say, distracted. My mind is running through all types of scenarios as I get out and unstrap the baby. "Um, Gabbi, take Mariah." I hand her the baby. "Let me go in first. Y'all wait here."

I walk up to the side door. It is unlocked. I open it slowly and step into the kitchen. My mouth falls open. I think I'm going to faint. Standing in my kitchen wearing my apron is Jonas. He has dinner ready and is setting the dining room table.

"Uh, hi, Jonas," I manage. "What is all this?"

"Dinner," he answers. "But don't touch anything until I tell you. Where are the kids?" He asks, looking past me to the door.

"Oh," I say, remembering they're outside. "Gabbi, Sammy. Y'all get in here!" I holler out the side door.

"We're coming, Momma. We're helping Pastor Gilliam and Pastor Evelyn. They just pulled up," explains Gabrielle.

You sneaky, little weasel. No wonder you cooked dinner, I think to myself as I put away my coat and purse. When the children walk in I send them to wash for dinner. I greet the pastor and his wife and take their coats to hang them up. Jonas leads them into the living room where we sit and make small talk until Sammy and Gabbi come back down.

"Well, let's eat," says Jonas. We go into the dining room where the table is spread. The meal is wonderful! I have to hand it to him. Jonas can cook when he puts his mind to it. There's not a whole lot of talking going on because everyone is enjoying the food so much. There's smothered pork chops, spinach, mac-and-cheese, salad, and rolls. I can get used to this. The cheesecake with cherries for dessert tops it all off. As soon as we finish, I send the kids upstairs to do their homework and put Mariah down for bed.

When I come back downstairs, the pastors and Jonas are sitting in the living room. I sit down in a chair next to the fireplace across from the sofa. Pastor looks from me to Jonas and back again. "Sister Mildred," he starts,"my wife and I have been talking about you a great deal."

"Oh, you have?" I stammer, surprised they thought about me at all outside of church.

"Yes, you see, we plan on elevating Jonas' office and using him more in the ministry. You know, have him going out to other churches more and doing special services at our church, and even Sunday sermons." I glance over at Jonas and he's sitting there looking smug. *As if he ain't gone enough. Now you want to get my permission to have him gone all the time--a built in excuse to be an absentee husband and father. I should have known I was being set up. And he knew all along!*

Pastor continues, "But, and I haven't even mentioned this to Jonas yet, Pastor Evelyn and I want to elevate you as well."

My eyes stretch about as wide as my face. I look over at Jonas and see he's as shocked as I am.

"Pastor," I breathe, "that's such an honor, but…"

"I know you probably want time to pray on it."

"Pastor Gilliam, Mildred doesn't have any real experience or aspirations for ministry or…" Jonas begins.

"Oh, I beg to differ, Jonas," interrupts Pastor Evelyn. "Mildred has been working in the church for years; she has some theological training, and was ordained a deaconess under her father's ministry. She works with the youth department, the outreach ministry, teaches adult bible study and Sunday school. She has a strong grasp of the word and a heart for people and service. She's led praise and worship and testimony service. She volunteers. Remember she's the one who came up with the community fair we do every year and organizes it and makes it a success every time. And the community comes out and supports it. So, you see, she's more than qualified." She turns to me and says, "Sister Mildred, Pastor and I have no doubt that you are called to ministry. You minister to people in so many ways already. This is just the next level for you. You've been on hiatus, but we need to get you active again. This is your season."

"Yes," agreed Pastor Gilliam, "And it makes sense for you two to work together on those occasions when my wife and I can't attend. You can represent us. It only makes sense for couples to minister in tandem, when they're both as involved in ministry as you two are."

Oh my God, I ain't trying to be no minister. And with Jonas?

"Well, thank you, Pastor," I say. "I'm honored and I'll definitely pray on it."

With that they stand up to leave. Pastor Evelyn takes both my hands in hers while Jonas goes for their coats.

"Daughter, God has great things in store for you. Just trust Him. You're stronger than you think. And there are people who look up to you. They need your example. Let your light shine. Don't hide it! God bless you." She kisses my cheek and turns to speak to Jonas. He helps her on with her coat.

"Thank you both so much for your hospitality. Everything was lovely."

"Anytime, Pastors," we say.

"Jonas, you take care of our daughter here," says First Lady Gilliam.

"Yes, Ma'am. Nothing but the best." Jonas grins as he takes her arm and walks them to their car.

I go into the kitchen and busy myself with tidying up the dishes. My stomach starts churning with anxiety. You know how you get that feeling in your belly like something bad is about to happen? Well, I don't have to wait long. As soon as Jonas closes the door, he gets in my face and says, "Sunday, when you greet them after church, tell them you've prayed about it and don't feel like going into ministry is what God wants for you right now. Tell them you have too much going on with the kids and all and now is not a good time. You convince them, you hear?" He says all this through clenched teeth. Then he turns and storms out the kitchen.

I think I'm in shock for a minute, 'cause I just stand there. I can't move. What? Too bad I don't curse, 'cause a choice word would have fit right there.

Jan 10

I can't believe he's just lying here sleeping. How you going to tell me I don't want to be elevated? This ain't even about him. Sure, they want to use him for more things, probably make him an assistant pastor, but they want me to be elevated. Me! A title, recognition. I wasn't asking for that, but they think that highly of me. Of me! God, what do I do? If I don't do what Jonas says, it'll be hell on earth for I don't know how long. But if I accept, I just might like it. I might actually fulfill my calling. Feel like I make a difference in this world. Help somebody. Get rid of this empty feeling inside me. Sometimes I feel like I just exist or I am just taking up space. This may actually be what I need in my life. I'm going to have to pray on this thing for real! I want to be happy, but I'm afraid of making Jonas unhappy. Somewhere along the way that became more important to me. I started making decisions based on how I thought he would react. Or I wouldn't do certain things if I thought it would make Jonas mad. What I wanted didn't seem to matter, or either I would put my desires on hold. I would be angry about it, mad at myself for being weak, upset, sad, but I would still ultimately do what he wanted or close to it. Sometimes I think I fear Jonas more than God. It seems like he gets his way with me more than God does. Lord, please, forgive me!

Jan 16

Oh my God, Oh my God, Oh my God! You won't believe what happened at church today. I can hardly believe it myself. I got up this morning, dreading whatever the outcome was going to be. But, as usual, I acted like everything was okay. I even got to church early. There were only a few people there scattered about the sanctuary. I sent the children with the youth workers and went to the altar. I got down on my knees and just started praying. "God, please help me. I want to do Your will, but I'm so weak. I want to please you and Jonas. I don't know why I get so scared when I try to do what's right and he wants something else. Please take control and let your will be done." Time just flew by and before I knew it, one of the ushers tapped me on the shoulder to let me know it was time for service. He helped me up and escorted me to a seat. I felt a little better, but I was still uncertain about what to do. The choir marched in singing "Celebrate" by TD Jakes and I sang along with them, clapping and rocking to the music. Halfway through Trish came stepping over a couple of toes to stand next to me. We hugged and she squeezed my hand. I had told her **everything**. *And needless to say, she was livid. "Who does he think he is? God or somebody? Puh-lease. Girl, if you weren't still in love with that man, I would make a few calls and 'good-bye Jonas'," she ranted. "Get the insurance straight and give the okay. I'll fix him. Matter of fact, just blink twice and cough and I'll handle it from there. That way they can't implicate you." Funny, ain't she? Anyway, we watched as the pastors came in and took their seats and Jonas followed looking so* *handsome, but slightly uncomfortable. It bothered me because I wondered if it had anything to do with me. Well, I got my answer soon enough. After praise and worship, the pastors came up for a special announcement. They called up Jonas and spoke of his service and dedication, etc, and that they were elevating him to Assistant Pastor. Everybody started clapping and saying "praise God", "it couldn't happen for a nicer guy", "Hallelujah". But hold on, it gets good right here. "Come on up here Sister Mildred and stand with your husband," said Pastor Evelyn. I looked over at Trish and stood up slowly, not knowing what to expect since I haven't given them an answer. So amidst 'amens' and 'Hallelujahs', I made my way to the pulpit. Pastor Evelyn took my hand and smiled at me. I was getting very nervous. She said "Church give a hand for your new assistant Co-Pastors." The church went up. I was shocked. Assistant Co-Pastors. Me, a Co-Pastor? Oh my God! I couldn't speak. I couldn't breathe. I just stood there. I turned to look at Jonas, and he was clapping and trying hard to look humble and happy, but I could see the anger in his eyes. He wanted this for himself. He didn't want to share this applause or recognition with me. I found out after church that the pastors want to pass the church on to Jonas since they don't have any children of their own, and they felt that if I was going to be 1st lady someday, that I needed to function in that capacity. This way, they could take time to nurture, train and instruct me. They wanted to parent me spiritually. Wow! Okay, here we go.*

Rise and Shine

"Mildred," Jonas hollers from bottom of the stairs. "I'm going out. Don't wait up," he says as he goes out the door.

"Jonas?" I call out as the front door bangs shut. "That negro didn't even wait to make sure I heard him," I mumble under my breath. "Don't wait up." I got half a mind to follow him," I fuss as I walk downstairs to the kitchen. "This ain't even a church night." But then again, he usually just leaves without saying anything. An upgrade, maybe?

I go to the oven and check on the pot roast and vegetables I'm cooking for dinner. "Momma, can I get a snack?" asks Sammy, coming up behind me.

"Sammy, you know I'm fixing dinner. It'll be ready soon. Go over your homework and I'll call you when it's ready, okay?"

"Okay." He pouts as he leaves and goes into the den. I shake my head. "That boy is always ready to eat," I mutter to myself. The phone rings and I answer it. "Hello," I say, as I lean against the sink. "Oh, hey girl. Ain't nothing going on here. I'm just fixing dinner," I say to Trish.

"Is Jonas still acting strange about the announcement?" She asks.

"Compared to what?" I joke. "Anyway, he left."

"Where's he off to tonight?"

"I don't know, but he said not to wait up."

"Don't wait up? Girl, if it was me I would have followed him!"

"If these kids weren't here I would have followed him."

"Well, next time call me and I'll watch the kids for you," she offers. "You call me from wherever you end up and I'll come and get them."

"I may just take you up on that next time. Alright, I gotta go before these children pass out from lack of nourishment. Talk to you later. Bye."

"Come on, Samuel. Get up. You're gonna be late for school." I pull the covers back and drag my son out of bed. "Breakfast in twenty minutes," I tell him as he stumbles into the bathroom. Assistant co-Pastor or not, I still had to get these kids to school and get to work on time. Jonas is taking the day off, so he's still in bed with the covers over his head. Must be nice.

Downstairs, I gather my things together and sit them at the door. I pick up Mariah and carry her over to her walker. She smells so good. I just squeeze her and breathe in that sweet, milky scent all babies have. My heart just swells with love. I want to be strong for my girls. Show them how a woman should act, how a good woman should be treated, and how not to settle for less. I kiss Mariah and put her in the walker.

I go into the kitchen and get the eggs, butter, cheese and bacon from the refrigerator. As I prepare the food, I think back. Jonas was adamant that the kids have a hot meal before school—even though he never once fixed it for them. I gave them cereal one time because I was running late and he laid me out. Now I just get up extra early to make sure I don't run out of time. Besides, even though he could have said it a little nicer, I think that the kids do perform better with a good breakfast. Both Gabrielle and Sammy maintain A/B honor roll and they behave. I haven't had to go to school once for behavior issues.

I call them downstairs. When I hear their feet on the stairs, I put their plates on the table and give them time to eat before herding them out the house.

Once I get Mariah into her car seat, and see that Gabbi and Sammy are at the bus stop two houses down, I turn on the car and back out of the driveway. I take the interstate to get to the sitter's, so the trip is only seven minutes. Mariah is usually the first one there every morning and today is no different.

After making sure she's all set, I go on to work driving through some side streets to get back to the interstate. I notice there are a lot of houses for rent or for sale. "Must be getting bad out here," I say. I turn the radio up and sing along with my favorite gospel station until I get to work.

The rest of my week is uneventful with a couple of exceptions. I start researching colleges in my area where I can get a degree in religious studies or theology or something. Jonas is already ordained as an elder, but I want to at least have a degree. I have a certificate in religious studies that I got when I took classes at my dad's church. It took about two years to finish, but when I was done I was ordained as a deaconess. I just never functioned officially because I got married, moved away, became a mother and everything else. Plus, I kinda like working behind the scenes. I get more done that way. When Jonas sees my notebook, he just "humphs," and goes to his study. I just try to maintain my resolve, because I don't want to let the pastors down.

On Thursday a letter comes in the mail from the church office about a conference at Good Faith Baptist for couples and Jonas and I are listed as speakers for one of the sessions. "What?" I say, shocked. "I haven't been an assistant co-pastor a whole week, yet." I read on and realize that the conference is two weeks away. Our topic is 'What's love got to do with it'. "A whole lot," I say. I continue to read and see that we have to respond by tomorrow. I leave the letter on the desk for Jonas to see and go get my bible. "If I have to get before people and speak, I better know what I'm talking about."

The next week I get busy taking care of the house, kids, work, and church and still have to scramble to find time to study out our topic. I ask Jonas which direction he wants to go with our topic, and he tells me "Don't worry about it. You won't have to say nothing. I got this. I don't know why they invited you anyway; it's not like you know what you doing."

I just keep studying scriptures about love and try to tie it into what I feel God wants to relay about marriage. If Jonas does let me speak, I'll be ready.

Two days before the conference and I look a mess. "I think I'm gonna call my girl and get my hair done. What do y'all think?" I ask the girls at the office.

"Why not? You've been needing an extreme makeover for a while," Trudy says.

"Extreme? Thank you for letting a sister know!" I exclaim.

"Well, Mildred," starts Nora, "you could do better. I mean, you're beautiful, but you dress like you're older than you are. And you're hair is always pulled back. Some makeup wouldn't hurt. It would really bring out your eyes."

"You look like you gave up, girl," added Judy.

"Well, thank you all for letting me sit up in here every day thinking I was doing okay. Why didn't you say anything before now?" I ask.

"We didn't want to hurt your feelings," say Trudy and Judy.

"And they don't hurt now? Y'all better be glad I don't cuss, 'cause I would run up one side of y'all and down the other." I smile to let them know I'm joking.

"We got your back girl. Cut off some of that hair, get a new outfit and put some paint on and you might just look presentable for your conference," advises Judy.

"Yeah, I'll be glad to do your makeup for you," offers Nora.

"And we can take our lunch hour and go to that boutique up the street and get you some decent clothes," Trudy adds.

I smile at them, starting to get excited. "Okay." I agree, and pick up the phone to make a hair appointment for the next day.

I can hardly wait to see what my hair is going to look like. All morning I keep running my fingers through it, wondering how much shorter it's going to be. I didn't even tell Jonas about my appointment. He hates short hair. He told me about when his sister cut her hair; he didn't talk to her for two weeks. He also doesn't like braids or weave. He told me once that I better not ever get any of that in my hair. I stay so busy and usually run short of money, so I don't get my hair fixed regularly. I know it has to be cut because of all the split ends. I usually do my own perms and I trim it occasionally, but nothing replaces having it professionally done. Besides, I want to look presentable for this conference, so it's well worth the sacrifice. Jonas already told me don't make him look bad, that I had to represent. Well, here goes.

"Oh, my God!" I scream. I look good! "Is that really me?" I stare at myself, in disbelief. Willis bows and says, "Thank you, thank you. Yes, I am a magician. I have turned you into a silk purse." The other ladies in the shop just smile and nod. I can't stop looking at myself. My regular stylist couldn't get me in, so Willis agreed to take me and he earned his tip. My hair has so much body. He had to cut off a couple of inches because of the breakage and then he layered it to give it shape. "Wow." I smile at myself in the mirror. My hair comes just above my shoulders. *Jonas is going to hate it, but I love it.*

Willis gets his money and I go out the door floating--feeling like a princess. Nora did my makeup before my hair appointment and showed me how to apply it. The outfit we chose flatters me so well. I am so excited I drive home grinning and singing the whole way.

"What's that on your face? And where's the rest of your hair?" rants Jonas when he gets home. "We got this conference tomorrow and you do that?" He spits out. The kids are upstairs doing their homework, and I'm preparing dinner.

"Nora put some makeup on my face to even out my skin tone. I don't think it looks that bad." I explain, pulling out pots and pans. "My hair was damaged so he had to trim it."

"You're really trying to make me look bad at this meeting. I hope you at least dress like you got some sense." He storms off to his study and just like that, I feel like a sow's ear. He used to press me all the time about wearing makeup, but I was raised to not overly adorn yourself. My parents were strict Pentecostals. No pants, makeup, earrings, movies, skating, etc.... If it looked fun, sounded fun or felt fun, we couldn't do it. Period. Now that I have it on, he doesn't like it. "I think I look good," I mutter under my breath. "You just mad cause I went a did something for myself and it wasn't your idea." I look down the hall towards Jonas' study, making sure he didn't hear me. "Girl, go finish dinner," I tell myself, and I turn and go back into the kitchen.

In the morning, things get hectic. I get up early because Mariah wakes me up, so I wake the kids and get them breakfast. Once they're done with that everyone gets dressed and I drop them off at my sister-in-law's. She's watching the kids while Jonas and I are at the conference. Since it's for couples, children aren't allowed in the sessions. Besides, we're supposed to be working.

Back at home, I go in the bathroom and take my time applying the makeup the way Nora showed me and fixing my hair. I pull my dress over my head and go back into my bedroom to get my shoes on. The dress is black and purple. It has a scooped neck and it flairs out at the bottom. It flatters my shape beautifully.

Jonas is wearing a dark purple suit with a lavender shirt and a purple and lavender tie. He has purple gator shoes on his feet. *When did he get those?* He didn't see the dress I was wearing until last night when I set it out with my jewelry and shoes. Maybe I need to go through the closet and see what other surprises are in there.

We go downstairs and get in the car. I have my folder with my notes from my studying the past week. Jonas looks down at the folder on my lap and says, "I hope you remember that I'm doing the talking. You've never had to minister to people and I don't want you telling people wrong."

"Well, I just wanted to be prepared in case I was asked a question or something. We really don't know how they are going to do it. It may not be like Sunday sermons. It may be lecture style with a question and answer period," I tell him.

"Just sit back, watch, and learn. Okay?" He says impatiently.

"Alright, Jonas." We drive the rest of the way in silence. As we arrive at Good Faith, there are two ministers waiting for us. They show Jonas where to park and they lead us into the church, introducing themselves. The taller of the two, Minister Simpson, has us follow him down the hallway to a room with a desk and a small couch. It also has a small bathroom.

"You can take a minute to put your things away," said the other man, Minister Braxton. "I'll be outside waiting to escort you into the sanctuary when you're ready."

"Thank you, Brother," said Jonas. He has his 'holy face' on. I noticed a while back that he puts on this 'face' whenever he was around church folk, especially men of the cloth. So, I started referring to that look as his 'holy face'. It sure looks better than the one he shows me all the time. I guess he figures if people see the face, they'll miss the heart. That's what should show on your face—your heart. If you have to fake it, or cover it up, then something's wrong.

Jonas goes into the bathroom, and I take that opportunity to say a quick prayer. "Lord, let you will be done. Allow us to speak from Your heart concerning love. Whatever Your people need, allow us the honor of serving the banquet of Your word as meat to their souls. Bless this conference and allow Your Spirit free reign in us. Lord, we decrease so that You may increase and get the glory. In Jesus' name, amen." I gather my purse, bible and folder and wait for Jonas to come out of the bathroom.

He comes out and picks up his bible and notes and shoves them at me. He opens the door and proceeds to go out, not waiting for me. Brother Braxton leads us to a side door that takes us to the stairs of the pulpit. The other speakers are already sitting in their places. We are told that there will be a general opening of prayer, scripture, a welcome and brief overview of the conference, and then everyone will split up. Jonas and I don't have to move because our session is remaining in the sanctuary since more people are attending it.

We go take our respective seats and smile and nod at the other presenters. An usher hands us programs and I scan over mine while we wait. There is a session 'What Women Want' that's for the men. I remember that movie with Mel Gibson. He could hear women's thoughts. I hope Jonas can't hear some of the thoughts I have. I would really hear his mouth then. But it would be nice if he knew me and what I wanted--and even better if he gave it to me. The session for the women is called 'Women and M. E. N.'—men's emotional needs. It is about how to recognize and nurture men's emotions. They also have a session called 'Pleasure Principle'. I would love to go to that. It's about how to get your physical and spiritual needs met in intimacy.

It seems like a good conference in the making. I hope they record the sessions because I would like to purchase them and listen to them later.

A stout, stoic lady walks up to the lectern and says, "Please stand for the opening prayer." There's rustling and noise as everyone stands. I place my program in my chair and bow my head as she prays. "Father God, we come before you today giving you praise and honor. Lord, we don't take it lightly the burden of teaching and reaching Your people. Allow each minister to bring us Your directives straight from Your throne to govern our lives. Bless them. Use them. We will forever give Your name glory and honor. Amen."

"Amen," we repeat. She returns to her seat and Minister Simpson comes forward with his bible.

"I'm reading in your hearing today from Genesis 2:20-25. 'So Adam gave names to all cattle, to the birds of the air, and to every beast of the field. But for Adam there was not found a helper comparable to him. And the Lord caused a deep sleep to fall on Adam, and he slept; and He took one of his ribs, and closed up the flesh in its place. Then the rib which the Lord God had taken from man He made into a woman, and He brought her to the man. And Adam said: 'This is now bone of my bones and flesh of my flesh; She shall be called Woman, because she was taken out of Man.' Therefore a man shall leave his father and mother and be joined to his wife, and they shall become one flesh. And they were both naked, the man and his wife, and were not ashamed'. May the Lord add a blessing to the reading and hearing of His word."

The welcome and brief overview follows the scripture. The speakers who have sessions in other rooms leave the pulpit and some audience members file out, while those remaining move up, filling in the vacated seats. I look around at the sanctuary. It is fairly large with burgundy carpet and chairs. The musicians' pit is off to the side and the choir loft stretches across the entire pulpit behind where we're sitting. My eyes linger on the Hammond organ as I try to calm down my nerves. Even though Jonas is going to do most, if not all, of the talking, I'm still a little nervous about standing before so many people. It's not like being at my home church. Everyone there knows me, and I'm used to them.

Jonas grabs his things from me and puts them on the lectern. Someone put two chairs out for us to sit on and I go sit in the one on the left side of Jonas. The Pastor of Good Faith, Pastor Washington, walks up to Jonas and me and says, "Thank you both for coming out today. I've only heard good things about you Jonas Wilson," he shakes Jonas' hand, "and your lovely wife." He turns to me and takes my hand. "God bless you daughter. Your pastors have given me such a glowing report about you. I look forward to hearing from you today. We'll be having a women's conference later on in the year and I hope you'll consider teaching one of those sessions as well. Be blessed." He then signals for quiet so that the session can start.

Jonas goes into his hellos, we're honoreds… and my mind is reeling. I haven't said a word and already I've been invited back to speak. *Lord, what are you doing?* Jonas winds down and I get myself together so that I can focus on what he's saying. I have to be the attentive wife so that I can jump in if he needs me—or better yet, if he lets me.

When I started thinking about this topic, I wrote everything that I wanted to discuss in an outline. I defined the 'it' in our topic as marriage and relationships and wrote out what God said about marriage. I then went into what love is. I ended with how love applied can enhance the marriage and help to overcome the situations that come up in relationships. I also jotted down some related scriptures and my thoughts about what they meant. Just in case. I was taught to 'be ye also ready'.

Jonas has everyone to turn to Ephesians 5:22-24. "Wives, submit to your own husbands, as to the Lord. For the husband is head of the wife, as also Christ is head of the church; and He is the Savior of the body. Therefore, just as the church is subject to Christ, so let the wives be to their own husbands in everything." He looks up from his bible and says, "What's love got to do with what I just read is this. Christ is love. The relationship between a husband and wife is set up like the kingdom of God. There is a head, the husband, and a body, the wife and family. God placed man as head to look after the affairs of the body. And if, like Christ, he loves the body, then he will take care of it and make sure it flourishes." Several amens ring out among the congregation. I see that everyone is listening attentively. Jonas goes on.

"Love is the motivating factor when things get done or the missing element when things don't get done. So love plays a vital part in the relationship between husbands and wives." I sit there taking in what Jonas is saying and wondering where all this insight is coming from and how come I don't get the benefit of this "love" at home. I guess it's easier said than done.

A lady in the middle of the sanctuary raises her hand, and Jonas falters, thrown off that someone would be interrupting, but he acknowledges her and she asks, "Brother Jonas, you said that love is the reason things get done or not. Does that mean when things are bad that it's because the husband is not showing love to his wife, since he's supposed to be like Christ and Christ is love?"

Jonas clears his throat, and I look up at him seeing that he isn't prepared for this line of questioning. "Sister, the bible says that wives should submit to their husbands in everything. And when there are issues, it's usually because the vision that the husband has is being challenged. Now, I understand that it's hard to go from making your own decisions to relying on a husband to take care of you. Today's women are very independent. They have their own houses, jobs, cars, and many are raising children by themselves; but this is how God designed it for your protection. If Adam had properly understood his role, Eve never would have eaten the fruit. Man would never have lost his dominion."

Several men call out "Amen." The young lady nods and sits back down, but an older woman stands up and says, "Sister Wilson, as a wife, what can you tell me about our role in marriage." I look at her, surprise on my face. I turn to look at Jonas and he clearly doesn't like the direction this is going, but I swallow and address the woman.

"Well, what Elder Wilson is saying is true. God does things decently and in order. The order is God, husbands, wives, and children. When a man knows the order and is following God, the wife, if she has her own relationship, can safely trust in her husband because God will give her peace about each decision he makes that affects the family if it's the right one and direction on what to do if it's not. So what Elder Wilson said about women submitting in everything is true, that is, assuming he is doing his part." I start warming up, and then I continue. "Now, when a man is not demonstrating love towards his wife, he is in direct disobedience of the word. If we read further in Ephesians 5, verse 28 says that husbands should love their own wives like their own bodies. So when a man makes a decision with disregard to his wife, her well-being, or is being selfish and God's not in it, a wife should not feel obligated to submit to that. But she should submit only to the will of God. As a helpmate for our husbands, our role is prayer warrior for those times when they may stray or maybe not hear clearly what God's will is."

"Alright, Sister?" Jonas interrupts. "Okay, let's move on." He flips the pages in his bible and several more hands go up. He sighs inaudibly and recognizes a gentleman up front.

"So, Sister, you're saying that when a husband makes a decision that is supposed to help the family, if it makes the woman unhappy, she can oppose him?"

"Not necessarily. When a husband is outside of the will of God, a woman is not obligated to submit herself. That doesn't mean she goes around disrespecting him or arguing with him or even leaving him. It means that she should pray for him that God will bring him back around. Now if the man has a true relationship with God, he'll know when he is out of order. She should continue to love him and do the things she was always doing. I Peter 3:1-2 says, 'Wives, likewise, be submissive to your own husbands, that even if some do not obey the word, they, without a word, may be won by the conduct of their wives, when they observe your chaste conduct accompanied by fear.'" I quote. "So, as a wife, you continue to live by the word and God will change your situation for you. Now if you read farther down in I Peter it says that husbands should dwell with their wives with understanding so your prayers won't be hindered," I paraphrase. "If this is not happening, it's vital that the wife prays for her husband, because his prayers are bound by his disobedience on earth and are therefore bound in heaven. That affects everything. You can't move forward. You stagnate. That's why a lot of relationships turn sour. When milk spoils, can you unspoil it?" I ask, looking around at the people.

"That's good, right there." I hear the pastor saying behind me.

Jonas is sitting in his chair looking at me, and I continue addressing the people. "Love is the most vital component to making sure all this works. If a man maintains his relationship with God, God can then instruct that man how to love his wife. The wife, knowing she is loved, safely trusts in her husband. And ladies, you know if your husband is loving on you, there's nothing you wouldn't do for them. Everyone benefits. But love is the motivating factor, like Brother Jonas said. When things go right, love is there. When there's strife, love's not there. That's because God, who is love, can't dwell in confusion. He is a God of order. Now, I'm not saying there won't be disagreements. But you can disagree without being disagreeable. God's will is for us to be unified. To agree. So, to agree to disagree is still agreement, especially if each person's viewpoint is given validity. That comes from love and mutual respect for one another."

Another hand goes up in the back and two more down front and it's on.

"Sister Wilson," a fairly young woman stands up. "What if you husband doesn't respect you? Then what?"

I look at her and so many thoughts run through my head. *Act like it doesn't hurt. Pretend he really does care about you. Cry. Pray. Get angry. Blame yourself. Blame him. Blame his mama. Ignore it.* But what I say is different.

"Sweetheart, don't let his negative opinion of you become what you think of yourself. The bible says in Proverbs 23 and 7 'as he thinks in his heart so is he.' But what people fail to do is take that verse in its entirety. Open your bibles to Proverbs 23." I open my bible and find the scripture and read "'Do not eat the bread of a miser, nor desire his delicacies; For as he thinks in his heart, so is he. 'Eat and drink' he says to you, But his heart is not with you. The morsel you have eaten, you will vomit up, and waste your pleasant words.'" I look up at everyone and see they are waiting attentively.

"In this scripture, the 'he' is referring to the miser. We often use this scripture to refer to ourselves to be positive, but in this context, it's a negative statement. Most people assume misers are people who are tightwads. They are, but take it a little further. Miserable comes from the word miser. Miserable means wretched, causing shame. In this passage of scripture, this miser is attempting to cause this person shame by feeding him something unpleasant. We are being warned not to eat this bread. Most people know that 'bread' and 'word' are interchangeable in a lot of cases. From that stand point we are not to eat the 'words' of a miser-- Or a miserable person who is wretched and causing shame-- because his heart is not to build you up. Now in your case, do what the word says. Don't eat that bread. You need to find scriptures that affirm who you are in God. Take in those good words. Eat that bread. Understand that God's heart is with you and for you. And you pray about that situation. Ask God to help you to forgive him and to direct your prayers so you know how to effectively pray for your husband." With that said, my heart is burning within me. I feel like I am preaching to myself.

At this point, Jonas stands up and he acknowledges the next person. "Brother Jonas, where you been hiding this dynamic woman God done blessed you with?" a heavyset gentleman asks. Everyone within earshot laughs and I blush. I actually blush. But it feels good to get a compliment.

Jonas laughs with everyone else and says, "Alright, next question. Young man in the back, what's your question?"

A young man in his mid-twenties stands up and asks, "So, Brother Jonas, how do you get your wife to treat you like the head?"

"Well, young brother, you do what the word says. You do your part being the head of the house. Take care of your responsibilities. And your wife will treat you like the king of the castle. That's the way God meant for it to be. We're just modeling His kingdom. If we seek first His kingdom, He'll add everything else. You'll get the respect you want and your wife will get the love she needs. Amen."

I just look at Jonas. He's speaking with such wisdom. I just don't understand why our relationship is so far off from what we are giving these people. I heard a pastor once say that when he ministers the word it's for him first and everyone else next. There's something to that. I don't want to be a "do as I say not as I do" minister—or first lady or person for that matter. I need to start working on me. Heaven help me.

We take more questions that range from in-laws moving in to what's permissible in bed to disciplining the children. Overall, we give good advice because it's all from the word and a little personal experience thrown in. But I almost feel like a hypocrite because I'm giving counsel that isn't being followed in my own home. I know it's God speaking through us, but for me He's telling me exactly what I should be doing and I know I'm not. I'm hearing Him. He's saying, 'Mildred, change!'

After the conference, Jonas and I are greeting everyone and shaking hands. I feel like a celebrity. People actually want us to sign their bulletins. I had to laugh when someone asked if Jonas and I counseled couples. What is that all about? We finally make our way back to the car and I'm feeling pretty good about the whole day. I don't even notice that Jonas is not smiling. I get in the car and pull my seatbelt on.

"This was a one-time deal," he says.

"What?" I ask, a little confused.

"You heard me. That's the last time I'm doing a conference with you. I told Pastor Washington that you wouldn't be able to do the women's conference either," Jonas says.

"Well, why not? How can you just tell him that without discussing it with me?" I argue.

"Look, you need to remember all that stuff you were just telling those people in there and let me be the head. This family doesn't need two heads," he answers and drives the car out of the parking lot.

I don't know what's gotten into me, but I feel like arguing my case.

"Jonas, I don't think the pastors are going to agree to me not taking engagements. That's what they want me to do. I thought everything went really well," I complain.

"You let me do the thinking. And if I hear that you went back to Pastor Gilliam with this you'll regret it." I roll my eyes and stare out the window. One tear rolls down the side of my face, but I just let it. *This isn't over.*

When we get home, I go change into a pair of sweats and a t-shirt. Look out dirt. When I get really angry and upset, I clean. Dirt has no hiding place. I imagine every piece of dust has Jonas' face on it and has to be eradicated. When I'm in one of those moods, he leaves me alone. This time is no different. I put on some music and get to scrubbing. My mind is just whirling with thoughts. I mean, who does he thinks he is? Better still, who does he think I am? Who do I think I am? I'm a grown woman. Why am I letting him control me like this? What's wrong with me? I have a college degree, I'm over 21, and I have children. Why does this one person have so much influence over me? Why do I let him control me like that? He is not my daddy! So when am I going to tell him how I really feel? I'm gonna have to ponder that for a while.

I go upstairs into my children's rooms. Since it's Saturday, I set out their clothes for church. I usually do it before I go to bed, but now is as good a time as any. Plus, I still have some drive left in me. While going through Gabbi's drawer looking for her tights, my hand hits something hard. I pull out a journal. I remember giving that to her several Christmases ago for her poems and stories. She used to make me read them or she would read them to me all the time. I didn't realize I missed that until now. I flip open the book and turn several pages. I see a page with just a paragraph on it and I stop, thinking it's a poem.

It says:

> I'm never going to get married. I don't want to end up like my mom. I wish she would just stand up to my dad. Why does she let him treat her that way? I love them both, but I wish she would leave him. She used to be my hero, but not now. She lost her powers. I guess my family's no different than anyone else's.

My heart drops. I feel as if the floor fell away from under my feet. My own child has lost respect for me. I put the journal back in her drawer the way I found it and I walk back downstairs. I go through the kitchen to the side door and out onto the porch. Tears are streaming quietly down my face as I sit down wondering how I failed my daughter. All of our attempts to shield them from our issues were in vain. I want her to be strong and independent. I want her to make good choices and lead a happy and fulfilled life. Disillusionment was the last thing I wanted for her. Now what? I can't let her know that I read her journal. Those are her private thoughts and I would hate to lose any more respect in her eyes. Plus, I don't want her to feel I can't be trusted if she does need to confide in me. But somehow, I have to make things right. I have to be a better example of a woman, mother and wife. "Lord, help me," I pray.

February 22

A letter came in the mail today. It was from Good Hope Baptist asking me to be a speaker at their women's conference in May. I decided to do it. I sent them a letter letting them know that I would definitely do it. I'm kinda nervous about what Jonas'll do when he finds out, but too much is at stake here if I don't take a stand. I have my children to think about. I want my daughters to be strong and secure in themselves. So I guess I'm gonna have to get stronger and more secure in myself. Baby steps.

Every Sunday morning since the announcement, I get up early and get to church so that Pastor Evelyn and I can talk. The kids hate it, but as long as they get McDonald's, they're fine. She and I talk while she prepares herself for service. I enjoy our talks. She's basically walks me through her Sundays and tells me about her week. She's such a dynamic woman. I wish I could be just a little bit like her. I so admire her poise and her sense of self. She carries herself well, speaks well, and is admired by everyone. She represents Pastor Gilliam well, and she honors him. I wonder how I can represent Jonas like that. I also wonder if it's even worth it. Nothing he's shown me over the last few years makes me even want to, but I know it's not about him. It's about Jesus, but it does involve me, too.

"Pastor Evelyn," I ask her one Sunday, "how did you get to be such a godly woman? I mean, it seems you don't do anything wrong. Pastor Gilliam loves you and tells the world every week how blessed he is to have you. How does a woman get that?"

"Mildred, I love God. Everything I do is to please Him," she says, pointing upwards. "If serving my husband pleases God, then that's what I do. If praying every morning pleases Him, then I'm crawling out of my bed and lying on my face. If He tells me to do something, then I do it. It's that simple. Now I'm not saying my flesh doesn't fight me, but knowing what to do is always the easy part. Making up your mind to do it is where your battle really is. Pastor and I have had our share of challenges over the years. No one goes through this life without some struggle. But we made a vow 'until death do us part' and we decided we would enjoy life and each other in the meantime. We are committed to making our relationship work. We have rules that we use to deal with issues that come up and everything works out. Now, you and Jonas will be fine. I have faith that God will help you to have the kind of relationship that you desire." She reaches across her desk and pats my hand. "Sometimes God allows us to figure out for ourselves that the areas we think we need Him to work in are just secondary. It's always some other area that we actually need him to deliver us in, and when that gets fixed, the other problems work themselves out, too. But, you know, you learn those things from living."

I just sit there, drinking in her wisdom. My mind tries to find my hidden areas. I probably have too many to count.

"Mildred," she continues, "get in prayer. That's where you'll find your answers. Stay in the word and keep your heart pure and God will show you how to live. And what a life you will have." She smiles and stands so that we can go into the service. I gather her bible and portfolio and follow her into the sanctuary. We sit in the pulpit as the choir finishes up a song of praise. I mull over the things that Pastor shared with me, and I decide I'm going to step up my Christ walk. It couldn't hurt, could it? I get the sense that God is orchestrating and rearranging things in my life for a purpose. I feel that He is trying to renew my thinking. I try to stay positive and bold and spiritual, but then when things at home get bad, I slip back into my old habits. The only thing I can do is pray that God will help me when I'm weak. I want to do right. I want to be a good wife and mother, but those are just parts of who I am. I want the whole me to succeed in whatever it is I'm called to do. If it's being a good wife, then the whole me shouldn't have a problem with that. If it's being a good mother, then the whole me should pass with flying colors. I guess if I was whole before, then I would be a whole lot better off now.

It's funny how the journeys we take seem so important and we rush into them thinking we're prepared, but it's only after you pull onto the highway that you remember you left something behind and now you're too far away to go back. For some of us we can find a replacement or make do, but for some of us the thing we left behind can't be replaced, and we spend the entire journey looking out the back window wishing we'd never left it in the first place. Can I get a witness?

When It Rains, It Pours

Monday morning I get up early. If I'm going to work on becoming a better, godlier woman, then there's no time like the present. I yawn and stretch my way downstairs. I go into the den and turn on some worship music. I get my notebook off the end table and open it to my confessions. While *Shekinah Glory* is quietly filling the air I begin to say my confessions aloud. I start with a faith confession. I ask God to increase my faith in Him to fix those areas of my life that are broken, and I thank Him for doing just that. After the faith confession, I say my financial and my healing confessions. I take out my bible and begin reading Psalms 1-3. I start to pray to God to open up my understanding of the word. I pray that He will begin to show me the areas of my life that need work. As I pray, I feel His presence come over me. I start to cry and praise Him. I feel Him speaking to my spirit. It's like a warm blanket over my heart. I just want to stay in that place, but I hear footsteps above me. Jonas is up and getting ready for work.

I stand up and turn off the music and put my notebook away. "Lord, just stay with me all day today," I pray. I go into the kitchen, get a paper towel and wet it to wipe my face. I don't want Jonas asking what's wrong with me. He wouldn't understand. I feel like a door just opened up down the hall, and I'm walking down this hallway towards a bright light. And if I can make it through the door, I'll win this great prize. Such a feeling of anticipation! I used to want to share things with him, but he made me feel like I wasn't on his level. I've been in church all my life. I've been around great preachers, teachers, bishops, evangelists, prophets. Titles don't really impress me. How you act and treat people impresses me, and with Jonas, I am not impressed. I pray and I know God hears me, but he always acts like only his prayers work.

When we were going through a dry period financially, I prayed that God would intervene. I told him how much money we needed and I prayed that Jonas' salary would be enough to cover what we needed. The next week he told me that he had gotten an increase at work. But he explained what happened like God had nothing to do with it. Now, I'm not saying he didn't thank God, but it was like he got the increase because he was so good. I was truly flabbergasted that he even told me about it, honestly. I have no idea how much money he makes, but I know that he has several bank accounts and he has to have money stashed away somewhere to keep buying all these suits and shoes and things. Where is all this when the baby needs pampers or baby wipes or something? I don't think he bought diapers but once since Mariah was born. But I have to work on not dwelling on the past; it's really killing my spiritual buzz.

At work I settle in at my desk but my mind is drawn back to Gabrielle's journal. I know I should talk to her, but I can't let her know that I read her private thoughts. She's a teenager dealing with teenage things. She shouldn't have to deal with her feelings about me and her father, too. I have to be a better model before her. I just hope I'm not too late.

"Mildred, you okay?" Judy asks. "You look like you just lost your best friend, but I'm right here," she grins.

"Girl, I'm okay. I just have a lot on my mind."

"Well, you can tell us," says Trudy.

"Yeah, that's what friends are for," chimes in Nora. "You've been quiet all morning. Now share. What's going on with you?"

"I found Gabbi's journal and she wrote some things in there that have me wondering where I messed up. That's all. I'm just trying to figure out how to talk to her about it without letting on that I read it."

"What did she write? Is she sleeping around? Is she on drugs or something?" Judy stands up, walks around her desk and sits on the edge of my desk. The other ladies follow her, their eyes never leaving my face. Outside of Trish and my family, no one else knows about Jonas and me having problems—at least, not from me. I really don't think this is the time to share. Plus, I don't want them thinking I'm one of those weak women who let their men treat them any kind of way and say, "but I love him"—you know the ones. So I say, "It's nothing like that at all. She just sees me differently than I thought, that's all."

"Oh, girl, that's par for the course with teenagers," says Trudy. "Our brother has four and they are all tripping right now. I guess Bill Cosby was right when he said kids are 'brain-damaged'." She laughs and goes back to her computer.

"Yeah, I thought it was something serious, Mildred. Don't let that get to you. Children change their minds and moods more that women do--and not just once a month." Trudy pats my hand and stands up. "You are too sensitive sometimes. Just try to remember how you were at that age. You seem to have turned out alright," she jokes.

"Ha, ha," I reply.

"I'm so glad I have you girls," Nora gushes. "When Craig and I have kids, I'll know just who to go to for advice."

"Well, I don't know how much help we'll be," I say, "but we'll definitely be there for you."

I go back to my work, wondering if I should mention something to Jonas since our daughter is affected by our dysfunctional relationship, but

I decide that wouldn't be a good idea. He'd just find a way to blame it on me.

When I get home that evening, Jonas is dressed in a gray pin-striped suit with gray Stacy Adams on his feet. He looks good and smells good. I recognize the cologne is one I just bought him for his birthday.

"Where are you off to in a hurry," I ask.

"I'm going out," he answers.

"To church?"

"Yes," he answers reaching for his coat and bible.

"Is it our church or what?" I ask. I didn't remember an announcement about a special service.

"Why do you want to know? Why are you clocking me?" He snaps.

"I'm not clocking you. I just was thinking maybe I would like to go, that's all." Inside I'm starting to boil. *Why can't he just answer a question? He just has to be so secretive. He's probably sneaking around.*

"Well, I'm leaving right now and I don't have time to wait for you to get ready," he responds.

"Are you going to be home late?"

"Why? Didn't I just tell you don't be clocking me? I'll get home when I get home!" With that, he storms out of the door.

"God! Why do I put up with that?" I throw myself into the first chair I come to. "How dare he tell me not to 'clock him' and he's always up in my business when I want to go somewhere or do something." The walls don't answer. I just sit and stare at them waiting for a response. When I start to shake, I move from the chair to the CD player, put on some worship music and pace the floor. I notice that lately when I get upset, my hands start shaking. At first I thought I was having some kind of attack, but I think my mind is imagining my hands around Jonas' neck. He makes me that angry. I just can't express it, though. I feel like if I start to let loose on him, I'll go up one side and down the other before it's all said and done. Plus, God don't like ugly, and I don't look good in prison orange. And I would miss my kids too much.

I wonder how those old mothers could come into church praising God like they didn't have a care in the world and all the while they were living with the devil. Just because we are Christian women, does that mean we have to put up with all this abuse from our husbands? I can't imagine God wanting me to be unhappy. That's what I am. I'm not happy. I want out. If this is the best my marriage can be, then I don't want it. Sure, he doesn't hit me. I don't think he's cheating on me, but I'm starting to wonder about that now. I guess the kids love him, he is their daddy. But I was expecting something more—something better-- especially from a man of God. It didn't used to be like this. He used to open doors for me and talk to me all night and tell me his dreams. What could I have done to change all that? What was so bad that now I only deserve scorn? How can you say you believe in God, preach His word, and live your life by His precepts and treat your wife like a doormat or some cheap accessory? I don't understand it. What have I done to make him hate me? And why am I beginning to care less what he thinks about me and more about why I'm letting him treat me like that? I deserve better. I'm not perfect, but I haven't done anything that would warrant being treated like old garbage. The whole thing just stinks. It's time to start cleaning house.

March 2

What is going on! It seems like things are going from bad to worse. My mom and Jonas just had a big fight and now they both blame me for it. He thinks I should have backed him up and she thinks I should have stood up for her. My parents just wanted to spend time with the kids and since I've been so busy, I thought it would be great to have a break. Jonas acts like they are going to turn the kids against him or something. I think he has thoroughly convinced himself that he is perfect and everyone should love him without exception, but I wonder what we get in return. Now he's saying that the kids can't go visit my parents anymore. This is crazy! I hate being in the middle having to choose between two people I love. My mother thinks that Jonas is controlling me. He thinks I do whatever my family says. I'm trying to please everybody, but somebody always ends up mad cause they didn't get what they want. My mom thinks that Jonas is trying to alienate me from my family. When we got married, we moved 3 hours away from my home and everything I knew. I did go home often in the beginning. Now he thinks that I run home too much to see them and that I neglect him. That's just not true. I used to go home twice a month, but that changed when the kids came. He started complaining about how far away it was and gas was high, so I cut down my trips to maybe 4 or 5 times a year. I would love to see them all the time, but I know that is not realistic. It does bother me that we see his family all the time. If I decide not to go or want to cut the visit short, then he tells me that it's because I think I'm better than they are. Puh-leese. Give me a break! Then they sit and talk about me after I leave, like I don't know. Family shouldn't be yours and mine, but ours. Now he told me don't ever ask him to do anything with my family again. What kind of crap is that? I know the scripture about a man leaving his family and cleaving to his wife. But it shouldn't be me leaving my family who I know loves me and cleaving to him with questionable affection. I gave him my heart and he's mistreating it. So far I'm on the losing side of this deal. It seems like he wants his way, and if I get anything that makes me happy, then he has a problem with it. God, how can I keep going on like this? I thought I was Your daughter. I thought You wanted me to be happy. I need You so bad right now. I need to know if I should go. My dad said he would support me whatever I did and that You would make sure I was okay. He said to trust You. I do trust You, but help me to trust You with my marriage. Why is it that I know I'm going to heaven when I die, but I don't know if my marriage will last another year? Aren't you the same God that can do anything, fix anything, and heal anything? Help me, God. Just help me. I still love him, but I don't know if he loves me. I don't want to hold on if he's let go.

Morning's here and all is quiet. Jonas hasn't spoken to me for a week. He just comes and goes. I fix dinner, but he doesn't eat it. So why waste the effort, right? My only refuge is church and work. I hurry the kids out to the school bus, so that I can have some semblance of normalcy in my life.

My car ride is somber. I usually sing along with the radio, but my heart is so heavy. I'm surprised when I pull into the parking lot at work, because I don't remember how I got here.

"Okay, girl," I tell myself, "get it together." I open the car door and slide out. I take out my keys and open the office door. The phone is already ringing as I put my purse down on my desk. I grab it thinking one of the girls may be calling out.

"Good morning, New Ventures."

"Hey, girl. I was hoping you would answer," says Trish.

"What's up?" I ask, smiling.

"I was hoping we could go to lunch today—my treat."

"Okay, I haven't been taking my lunch all week, anyway. Plus, I have got to fill you in on everything."

"I know you do. You've been on my mind real heavy lately. Let's meet at our favorite spot about one o'clock."

"Okay, Trish. I'll be there. See you later." I hang up in a much better mood. This day is going to drag by. I wonder what she meant about me being on her mind lately. Well, I guess I'll find out at lunch.

Since I know I'm going out, I only have my one cup of coffee for the day. I notice that my pants are a little loose in the waist. Whenever I stand up I have to pull them up. That's a good sign. Maybe all this stress with Jonas will help me lose some weight. It's already started taking my hair out. I had almost as much hair in my brush as I had on my head this morning.

Judy and Trudy arrive this morning before Nora. "Hello, ladies," I greet them.

"Good morning," they chorus. "You're looking chipper today." Judy notices.

"I'm meeting Trish for lunch today. That girl is always making me laugh. Plus we are going to our 'spot'," I answer.

"Just don't overdo it like last time," teases Trudy.

"Yeah, girl, we had to throw stuff at you to wake you up the rest of the afternoon," laughs Judy. "And you snore!"

"I do not snore!" I protest.

"Yes, you do. And loudly," agrees Judy.

We all laugh and I suddenly don't feel so glum. I think God knew what he was doing when he placed me in this job. I go turn on the radio, start swaying to Kool and the Gang's 'Celebration' and I feel like celebrating. Judy and Trudy start dancing around with me and we are having a good time. The bell on the door chimes and we all look expecting Nora, but it's not her. We immediately stop as we recognize the boss standing there.

"G-g-good morning, Mr. Hughes," I stammer. "We were just getting ourselves warmed up for work, sir."

"Good morning, Mildred, Judy, Trudy," he smiles. "Don't mind me. I just came to get the last month's reports from my office computer. My home computer caught a virus, so I had to get it wiped. Carry on, girls." He walks down the hall to his office and closes the door.

"Wow, that was awkward," I say.

"Shhh!" Trudy waves at me. "I think I hear him laughing."

The sound of laughter comes floating down the hallway. We call off our dance party and get back to work. We used to have another girl, Shantae, who worked with us, but somehow she managed to get on the boss's wrong side. He said she wasn't serious about the job and he let her go. Mr. Hughes leaves about fifteen minutes later and we all relax. Nora calls out, but we figure she couldn't leave Craig—young love. I send the work orders to the maintenance crew so that the clients can get their repairs done and clear my desk of work until lunch time.

"Girls, you don't have to worry about keeping me up this afternoon. I will see you bright and early tomorrow." I get my purse and jacket and go out to my car. I feel energized. I guess it's because I know I'll get to unload some of this mess I'm carrying around. Plus, I get to have Chinese food. Trish and I found this little out of the way place after one of our shopping sprees. They have the best shrimp fried rice! Since then, when we want to splurge, we meet there. The ambience isn't the greatest, but the service is impeccable and the food is heavenly.

I take the back streets and get there about ten minutes early. Trish is already there. I go inside and slide into the booth across from her.

"Hey, girl," I say.

"Hi, Mill," she smiles. "I already ordered our drinks."

"Sweet tea?" I ask.

"You know it."

I pick up the menu trying to decide if I want the shrimp with lobster sauce or the pepper steak. Everything they make is so good. While I'm looking, the server brings our tea.

"I'm going to have the beef with broccoli," Trish tells her. "What about you, Mill? Get something we can share," she suggests.

"Um, give me the shrimp with lobster sauce," I decide. The portions are so big, we always have leftovers. While we wait I ask Trish about her family.

"Everybody's good. We just had a big get together at my grandmother's house. It was wall to wall people. I didn't know I had so many good looking cousins, girl. That's why family reunions are so important. You could trip up on some dude only to find out he's fam." We laugh and Trish says, "I didn't come here to talk about me, though, I'm worried about you, Mill. Is everything okay?"

I give her the 'Are you really asking me that question when you know I tell you everything and everything is not okay' look.

"Girl, you know what I mean. Is there something you haven't told me? I just had a conversation with someone and I didn't know if you just didn't want to tell me or if you were clueless. I take it you're clueless," she says as I stare at her.

I just look at Trish wondering what in the world she's talking about. "You know something. Just tell me. What is it?" I ask, not sure if I want to know or not.

"Well," she hesitates. "I have a friend who goes to that church over on Brookstone. Jonas was there about a few weeks ago, remember?"

I did remember he went to a service, but I didn't know where. "Yeah, I remember a service. What about it?"

"They served dinner afterwards and my friend said that Jonas was talking with a young lady and told her he and you were separated. She said he asked for her number to maybe call her after the divorce was final."

"Divorce? We are not getting divorced!" I say incredulously. I open my mouth to protest, but the server is bringing our food over. I am seething inside. I wait until we are alone before I say anything else. "Are you sure that's what he said?" I challenge her.

"Yes, she told me all about him and I pretended I didn't really know who she was talking about. She described him and the girl to me. But girl, Jonas is out there acting like he's available." She looks at my face and says, "I'm so sorry. I just couldn't not tell you. You are like my sister. I thought you should know."

"Thank you. I know most people wouldn't have said anything. I know you have my back. I just can't understand why he would do that." I think back to the times he didn't want me to go with him to some of his speaking engagements. "I can't believe I trusted him. You must think I'm a gullible fool."

"Mildred, girl, you know I would never think that! I do wonder sometimes what you see in him, especially since few other people see it.

But I don't think you are a fool. He can't be all bad. Look at those three beautiful kids you have. I just wish he treated you the way you deserve to be treated. As much as you do and put up with from him, he should be treating you like a queen. I just don't want to see you sacrifice yourself on the altar of his selfishness. There should be balance and I don't see it. You do so much! You work, you clean house, you take care of the kids, you cook, and you serve at church. I don't want to see you kill yourself and then a month later someone else is raising your kids. 'Cause sure as I'm sitting here, Jonas won't stay single for long. He's probably getting all these numbers so he can be ready, just in case."

I just sit there, pushing the food around my plate. My appetite is gone. I feel just sick listening, but I know she's right.

"Mill, you have to do something, 'cause if you die early behind his foolishness, I'm going to be so mad at you."

"What do I do? I can't change him. It's not like he's the worst person in the world," I say defensively. "There are women who put up with more than this."

"Yeah, but a lot of those women still reach a point when they say enough is enough. When is it going to be enough for you? When are you going to stop putting up with this emotional abuse? You may not have scars that show up, but you are bruised and battered, Mildred. I just sat here and told you your husband is trying to pick up other women and you are sitting here defending him. Wrong is wrong and he is dead wrong. It doesn't matter if you are saved or not. In my opinion, it's worse when you hide behind religion. I feel for you. It can't be easy. I just wish you didn't have to suffer behind his selfishness." Trish stops fussing and reaches for her tea.

"So, do you think I should confront him?" I ask. "I just don't like confrontation."

"You don't have to like it, but at some point you have to let loose on him. You're carrying around too much junk. You have to let it out."

"Girl, if I start I may not be able to stop."

"Good! It's probably what he needs. And what you need, too. You have allowed him to dictate this relationship. There's no compromise. You told me so yourself. You keep giving and he keeps taking. What are you going to do when you have nothing left to give?"

As I drive to pick up the kids, Trish's last statement is ringing in my ears. What do I give when I have nothing left? I feel so empty now. I feel like my spirit is dry heaving. I still have my children to think about. If Jonas takes the best of me, what's left for them? And what about me? Can I ever be happy married to a man who's not married to me?

Cruise Control

At home, it's business as usual. My focus is on homework, dinner, baths and bed, but it seems I have less energy to get everything done. The laundry's starting to pile up. I haven't dusted or vacuumed this week. Truthfully, I just don't feel like it. The kids have chores, but I haven't been after them to get them done. I feel punch drunk. My world is off kilter and spinning out of control. Maybe by next week I can get it together.

Plus, so much is going through my mind. It's like they say, hindsight is 20/20. I'm starting to understand Jonas' past actions and arguments. I thought it was something I did, but it was something he wanted to do that was the reason why he would storm out the house. I wonder if he really is cheating on me. There were nights that he didn't come home until four in the morning. He told me he was counseling someone who wanted to commit suicide or at the hospital with the family of someone in hospice. Now I don't believe him. How can I trust him when so much of his life is unknown to me? I'll always wonder. I don't want to live like that. Maybe that's why God decided to have us minister together.

I go upstairs to make sure that the kids are asleep and then I go to my quiet place to read and meditate. While I'm reading the book of Matthew, I get this strong impression to go to I John 4. My eyes are drawn to verse 18 that says 'there is no fear in love; but perfect love casteth out fear'. I just sit and drink in that scripture. I love Jonas, but I have so much fear that he will leave me, or be disappointed in me, or mad or whatever. But why don't I have that fear with God? I guess it's because I know He loves me. He doesn't make me wonder whether I'm good enough, or pretty enough, or if my hair is long enough, or if my waist is small enough. He loves me just the way I am. With all my flaws, he still loves me and would die again just for me. Tears rolls quietly down my face as I realize that's the difference in my relationship between Jonas and me and God and me. I know what unconditional love from God is and I expect that same love from somebody who only loves conditionally.

March 15

Jonas is still not talking to me except about the kids; and then only if I speak first. Just as well. I have so much frustration coursing through me; I probably wouldn't be able to hold my tongue. There was one moment when I was cleaning our bathroom and Jonas just stood in the door watching me. I thought he was going to end the tension between us, but he had the nerve to tell me to make sure I cleaned around the bottom of the toilet. What? This man doesn't even help me clean up and he has the nerve to tell me how it should be done. I was livid! I just rolled my eyes and pretended like he didn't say anything. Trish told me I should have told him to clean it himself if he wanted it done right. That would have gone over well. I just decided to clean common areas and leave all his things the way they were. I know I shouldn't be so petty, but he acts like I don't matter--like I add absolutely nothing to this family. I remember once when he hid the charger to the cell phone because he was mad at me because I accidentally threw away a box of his. He said it had something important in it, but it was empty. I checked it twice. I couldn't find the phone charger for a whole week, so I couldn't charge my phone. My family and friends couldn't reach me on my cell. They thought something had happened to me, but they wouldn't call the house phone because they didn't want to take the chance he would answer. That man has some passive aggressive anger issues. Sometimes I feel like he has a violent core. I think if I push the wrong buttons by mistake, verbal abuse could become physical abuse.

Church is finally over. I feel like I am in overdrive. I go back to pastor's office to see her. "Come in and close the door, Mildred," she tells me as I poke my head around the corner. I pull a chair up to her desk as I have been doing for the past few weeks when we talk.

"I have an assignment for you," she says. "I hope you can find a way to get it done."

"What is it?" I ask.

"You know the cruise that Pastor and I take in April every year?"

"Yes, I remember," I answer.

"Well, it's a working cruise. We each do a seminar while on the ship, but this year we want to attend a leadership conference in Texas, instead. So I was hoping that you would consider going in my place. All expenses paid."

"Pastor, I would be honored," I gasp. "I would have to find arrangements for the kids, and see if I can get off work."

"Well, see what you can do and let me know. Pastor Gilliam has already spoken with Jonas and he said that he wouldn't be able to take off from work. With it being tax time for a CPA, he would be working overtime as it is. But he said he had no problem with you going without him."

This is the first I'm hearing about this. Jonas doesn't have a problem with me leaving him at home and going on a cruise? I know something's up now.

"Pastor, I will make arrangements at work and with the kids and update you in a few days," I tell her.

"Wonderful. I think you will enjoy it. It will definitely give you an experience you won't soon forget. I believe you will come back refreshed and uplifted in spirit."

I thank her again as I replace the chair and leave her office. Wow, a cruise. And it's already paid for! I was planning on taking one for my 40th birthday in a couple of years, so I had already purchased my passport. That was me putting my faith in action, showing that my future had to line up with my confession. Now here I am going ahead of my intended schedule. Look at God! With the cruise just a few weeks away, I had some packing and planning to do.

When I get home Jonas is in his study working on his computer. "Hi, Jonas," I say, poking my head in the door.

"Hunh." He doesn't take his eyes off his monitor.

"Pastor told me about the cruise. She said that you told them it was okay if I go."

"Yeah. So?" He looks up at me standing in the doorway. I was never comfortable in his study. He caught me in there one day looking on his desk for a pen and he laid me out. Since then, I just don't go in there, even when he's there.

"I just wanted to know what to do about the kids? I was thinking maybe asking your sister to keep them since they have school."

"Well, why are you asking me? I can't speak for her. And I have to work, so I can't be picking them up and cooking and all that. I'll be coming home late and going in early," he barks at me.

"Okay, Jonas. I'll take care of it."

"Good, now close the door on your way out. I'm working."

Well, that went about the way I expected. I roll my eyes and pull the door shut. I go call my sister-in-law and see if she's available. I tell her all about my plans, and she's excited for me. She knows how her brother is and tries to help me out as much as she can. I really appreciate her support. Once I get an affirmative from her, I start a list of everything they will need while I'm gone. It won't be easy. I've never gone anywhere without my kids. I'm sure I'll feel like a fish out of water, but I'm still excited about the trip. I spend a few hours making sure that everything they could possibly need is either in the house or on my list of things to buy. I don't make it to bed until late.

I'm so excited about my trip that falling asleep is next to impossible. When I finally do, I have this dream that I'm on a boat. It's not moving, but there is a waterspout coming towards me. The spout is clear and when it passes over me, I feel this electric shock and then everything is quiet. I wake up a little shaken up, because I still feel the effects of the shock. Falling back to sleep takes a little time, but I eventually nod back off.

When the alarm clock goes off, I still remember the dream vividly. I make up in my mind to ask one of the elders or maybe the pastor what the dream means. I hope to God it's not a bad omen about the cruise. I still want to go and if there's a storm, I'll just have to pray to God that the boat doesn't sink and that no one drowns. But I'm still going.

I go downstairs to start my morning ritual of prayer and meditation. I guess it's doing something. I don't really see any difference, but my thinking is different. I seem to be getting more frustrated and angry about things that contradict what's in the bible--especially where my marriage is concerned. And not just with Jonas' behavior, but with me as well. I see where I have some shortcomings and I want to change, I really do. It's just that I don't see how to, yet. Not only that, I haven't found the courage to change. That's where a lot of my frustration is coming from. It seems like everything is too big for me and too overwhelming. I know some things Jonas is going to have a problem with. I've allowed him to get away with too much. It's hard to give someone room to run all over you and then cage them up. Then they just bang their wings against the bars and squawk louder. Then it's hard to tell which situation was worse. I don't know. I just continue to pray and trust God to help me. I pray for more wisdom and boldness. I pray for backbone. I pray that God would show him that I matter and that I am important. I know Trish and my family think that I should be praying that God removes him from my life, but I don't want that legacy with my kids. I want God to fix whatever's wrong. I know that I just have to wait on God's timing. I want to have more patience with Jonas, but I don't pray for that out loud. It seems to me that when you pray for patience, you pay for it. That's God smiling at us as we struggle. All the while, he knows we are going to come through all right but we're fussing and nearly cussing our way through. But somehow, we make it and have a whole heap of patience to show for it. I'd better make room for it, 'cause something tells me that God heard my thoughts anyway.

I have a lot of laundry to catch up on, so at breakfast I decide it's in my best interest to get Gabrielle to help me. "Young lady," I say, "when you get home this evening, I would like for you to help wash the clothes so I can get your bags packed up."

She moans. "Why do I have to go? I'm fourteen. Can't I stay home and you send Sammy and Mariah with Aunt Gina?"

"No, you can't because you would be here alone at odd times. Your daddy's gonna be working crazy hours and someone has to make sure you get to school and get your homework done. Plus, I don't like the idea of you here alone at night by yourself."

"I'm not a baby, ma. I don't get scared of the dark. I bet Daddy would let me stay," she argues.

"This is not up for debate, young lady," I say firmly. "When you get home, laundry. Do you understand?"

"Yes," she mumbles, pushing the food around her plate.

I go upstairs and finish getting ready for work. I'm wondering if maybe I should let Gabbi stay home. Maybe it will teach her some responsibility, allow her to stand on her own two feet and rely on herself. Maybe then, she'll think I'm a great mom. And she'll tell all her friends and they'll convince her to invite them over. And they'll tell some guys. And maybe she'll let some boy in the house and he'll tell her she's pretty and that he really likes her and then he'll convince her to show him her room and he'll lie to her and tell her everybody will talk about her if they don't do something. And because she wants him to like her, she'll believe him. And that's if he doesn't slip her anything in her drink. And then she'll end up pregnant like her friend Shawna and make me a grandmother before my time. No, thank you. She'll just have to be mad at me. I can take the kids anger better than Jonas'. It comes with the territory.

I remember I used to get mad with my mom when I was younger, because I couldn't understand why she was so strict. I've had many a shoe hurled in my direction and more whippings than I can count. But times are so much worse now than they were then. Plus, now that I am a mother myself, I get it. I really get it. She did those things because she loved me and saw how bad the world was. She only wanted the best for her children. It made me focus on what was going on around me and my actions and reactions to what was going on around me. It kept me out of serious trouble. I feel like as bad as things are now, that I should be even tougher on my kids than she was on me, just to keep them safe, out of jail and alive.

I put my earrings in and vow to spend some quality mother/daughter time with Gabrielle. I want her to know she can talk to me about anything, absolutely anything, but that I'm still the mother and my decisions are to keep her protected and happy, even if she doesn't always understand. Ahhh, the joys of motherhood!

April 3

I leave for the cruise tomorrow. I should be asleep, but I'm too excited. I've checked my bags a dozen times already making sure I have my passport and ID and bank cards and jewelry and money. I'm a little nervous going by myself, but I feel liberated, too. It's strange, Jonas hasn't had much to say about me going, but I think he's jealous. He's been acting like it's no big deal, and that his job is more important, but I know he wishes he was going. I would say, going too, but come on; this is Jonas I'm talking about.

Mr. Hughes was just as excited for me to go as I was. He said I deserved some time off. That I was doing a great job, to forget about work and enjoy myself. I think I'll take his advice.

The pastors took up a special offering for me at church on Sunday. How cool is that! Now I have some spending money for souvenirs or whatever.

The ship is leaving from Miami tomorrow and I'm riding down on a chartered bus. Our church, Good Faith, New Hope and Blessed Alliance are sponsoring this event, so it's a mixture from all the churches riding the bus. Hopefully, I'll have a good seatmate, but just in case, I bought a new book for me to read. Plus, I have to make sure my session is tight, so I'm bringing my study materials, too. I have big shoes to fill. I want to do my pastors proud.

The focus of my topic is 'The Love Bud'. I laughed when Pastor Evelyn told me. I asked her why not call it 'The Love Bug' or 'The Love Boat'. She giggled, too and said that God put that impression in her heart, but he didn't give her anything else. She said she believed it was because He knew all along that I would be the one speaking on it and that it was something he was trying to teach me. That everything would fit together at the right time. She said I was being fast-tracked by God, that I have been sitting back too long when I had so much in me to birth. What she actually said was, "Mildred, when you gonna drop them babies? Stop holding them in and push!"

These past months getting to know her have been so wonderful. I feel fortunate. Not too many people get the opportunity to have an intimate relationship with their pastors.

While I sit staring out the window of the bus, a very attractive woman stands beside my row and asks me if anyone is sitting next to me.

"No." I smile up at her. "You're more than welcome to join me."

She smiles back and sits down. "Thank you. I'm Aniyah Carlson. I go to Good Faith."

"Oh, okay," I say.

"I was there when you and your husband did the conference. You all did such a great job."

"Thank you, Aniyah. I appreciate that. I have to admit, that was my first time doing a conference."

"Really?" she asks in amazement. "Girl, you seemed so poised and confident, like you'd done several conferences."

"No, but my husband has. He's used to that sort of thing."

"Yeah, I've heard him speak before. He's ministered at our church several times in the past, but I was more interested in hearing you. You know what they say, 'behind every strong man is a strong woman'."

I'm sitting there wondering who she saw standing behind Jonas. Whoever it was must favor me. "Thank you, I'm flattered."

"I hope you don't find me too forward or annoying, but I was hoping you could answer some questions that I couldn't ask then." She looks down at her hands folded in her lap, like she was embarrassed.

"I don't mind," I tell her, patting her on her arm. "We're going to be on this bus for a while; we might as well make good use of the time. Besides, you look like you have a lot on your mind."

"Yes, I do. I haven't had anyone I could really talk to. My family doesn't live around here and I don't have a lot of close friends," she admits.

As we talk, the bus is filling up. I watch as people get settled into their seats and wonder what Aniyah is hiding. I get the impression something is wrong. I hope it's not too deep. I have a hard enough time keeping up with myself. I would hate to lead someone else astray. I just pray to myself that God will guide me and give me the words to encourage her.

"So," I ask, "how long have you been at Good Faith?"

"I've been there about six years, but my husband has been there all his life. I joined when we got married," she shares. "I guess I felt I had to, you know? Families should worship together, but I wasn't raised Baptist."

"Me either. My parents were strict Pentecostals, but they've lightened up a lot over the years. My mom even wears pants sometimes," I joke. "So, tell me what you mean about feeling you had to join Good Faith."

"Well, I like the church and all. It wasn't that. It's just that I didn't feel like I was being fed. You know what I mean?"

I did know what she meant. It took Jonas and me a few years to find the Gilliams. It was the first time I had been to a 'word church', but I loved it. I learned so much and I was taught how to apply the word to my life. I wouldn't leave for anything now.

"Plus," she continues, "all his family is there. It's like I can't say anything about him or our marriage or the church without a full frontal attack."

"Wow, girl! So you have to deal with him and you can't because they take up for him?"

"Yes. It's crazy. I love him so much, but it frustrates me that he goes running back to his momma telling her things about me. And when I go visit, she acts like she's on my side, but then she tells him things I've told her in confidence. Some of those things she actually said about him herself and I just agreed with her. They make me out to be the bad guy and I just don't know what to do." Aniyah shakes her head and stares at the headrest in front of her.

"Mildred, what do I do?"

"Well, first thing we're going to do is pray. My pastor, Evelyn Gilliam, is teaching me to always go to God and pray for direction first when you are counseling someone or giving advice, because we want to make sure we acknowledge God and His word as sovereign." I explain, "it keeps you from giving your own opinion based on how you would feel and puts the burden on the word of God to work. It's hard sometimes in these situations not to express our feelings, but in the end, we have to abide by the Word of God. The bible says that God watches over His word to make sure it does what it's supposed to do. It can't fail."

"I understand that. That makes so much sense."

"Okay, well, let's pray." I take her hands in mine and we bow our heads. "Father, God, we come before You this evening giving You praise and honor as the Omniscient One. Lord, in the name of Your son, Jesus, we ask that You would allow the Holy Spirit to speak through me to uplift, encourage and edify Aniyah. Lord, we know You have all wisdom and You know our end before our beginning. Help us to follow the plans You have set for our lives. Breathe a fresh word of life into this marriage for You have said that what You have joined together, let no man put asunder. We come against the enemy who is now trying to bring division into this household. We rebuke you, Satan, and command you to be loosed from this family. We cover this couple in the blood of our Lord and Savior, Jesus Christ and we thank You, God, knowing that this is a finished work. We believe that we receive the answer to our prayer, in Jesus' name. Amen."

"Amen," she repeats. "Wow, I feel the power of that prayer already. You really are somebody special, Mildred," she squeezes my hand and then releases it.

I just reach for my bible and open it to Genesis chapter 2. I'm a little embarrassed because I don't feel all that special. "Let's look at Genesis," I tell her. "This is the beginning. The start of the institution we call marriage. When God puts Adam to sleep and takes his rib and makes woman, he shows us that marriage is in a very real sense a joining of two people--a connection on a whole other level. That's why in verse 24 it says, 'Therefore a man shall leave his father and mother and be joined to his wife, and they shall become one flesh'. Now, you and your husband are going to have to somehow sit down and figure out how to get your marriage back down to two—God and you."

"Yeah, that would be great. We don't have that. Everybody is in our business."

"The only one who should be in the middle of you and your husband is God." A thought struck me and I say, "You know when Jesus said if I be lifted up, I'll draw all men unto me?" I ask.

"Yeah, we sing that song during devotions," Aniyah tells me.

"Well, if you are lifting Him up in your own prayer and devotion time, and your husband—what's his name, by the way?" I interrupt myself.

"Richard," she answers.

"Okay, and Richard has his own prayer and devotion time where he's lifting up God, then He'll be drawing you both nearer to Himself, right?"

"Right."

"Stay with me," I tell her, "'this is gone bless you', like Madea says. If you're being drawn to God, and Richard is being drawn to God, and God is in the middle of your marriage, doesn't it mean that you and Richard should be drawn toward each other?" I pause there because that word is hitting home. I see some similarities between what Aniyah and Richard are dealing with and what Jonas and I are going through.

"Mildred, I have never looked at it like that before. You are truly opening my eyes up," says Aniyah, with amazement in her voice.

"Well, it's one thing to see it, but it takes constant prayer to have it manifest in your life. You know, women have an insight that men don't have. They see black and white, right and wrong, and up and down. We see nuances, shades and degrees. When the devil shows up full blown in a man's life, trust me, he was warned long before by a woman. It may have been something as small as telling him he should speak when he walks into a room of people or don't talk back. Before long, he has problems with authority or he's disrespecting his elders. But we saw the signs." Aniyah nods and shifts in her seat, turning more towards me.

"As wives, when things start going awry in our marriages and we try to point it out to our husbands, they think we're nagging them, but that's really not what we are trying to do. We're seeing spiritually that things are out of order and we are trying to get them back on track. When we back off because they keep telling us nothing is wrong and we're imagining it, we start believing it, but our spirit is at war with us telling us to do something. Most women just let things get worse and then when their husbands say they want out, they wonder how it happened all of a sudden. It was there all the time. You saw it, you addressed it, you might have even prayed about it at some point, but now things are out of hand. It seems like you're in the early stages where you know things aren't right and you're trying to address it. Am I right?" I ask.

"Yes, I've tried talking to him about our relationship, but he tells me I'm just looking for trouble."

"Well, you and your husband are going to have to talk about some serious issues between you. For one, if I'm hearing you right, you want to leave Good Faith?" I ask in a soft voice, because some of the members are on the bus.

"Yeah," she whispers back.

"You're going to have to talk to God first about that one, and then your husband. Ask God what you should do. Don't mention anything to Richard until you've heard from God, because you could open up a mess of something that you'll have to clean up later. What would have taken a napkin is now going to require a mop and bucket. That all goes back to how men are different from us," I tell her.

She grins and reaches for her backpack under the seat. "You want a drink. I brought some snacks in my bag for this trip."

"Sure, as long as you don't mind sharing my chips with me." I get out my cooler bag and we sit and munch for a while in silence, digesting both the food and the conversation. Most of the people on the bus are napping, since it's nearing midnight. I'm actually feeling energized and happy that Aniyah no longer looks distraught. I think I may have actually found a new friend. This trip is looking more and more like a godsend.

We talk a little more about our favorite music and television shows and a whole host of things before we eventually nod off. Like me, her husband had to work and told her it was ok if she still went. At one of our scheduled stops, we get out and answer nature's call and stretch our legs a while.

"So, Mildred, how are things going with you and your husband. Not trying to be nosy, I'm just wondering how you keep it all together," Aniyah inquires.

"It's certainly not easy. And it's really not all that together to be honest with you. Marriage is hard. Taking two different people, with different views, different experiences and getting them to come into agreement is a challenge." We stroll over to the side of the building and sit down on a bench. "You're going to have tough times and you're going to feel overwhelmed, like you can't make it, but those are the times you have to press into God more. He gets you through those moments. That's what I'm working on now, getting closer to God."

"I just wish I could tell Richard how I feel sometimes. I hate to admit it, but I'm afraid of him sometimes." Aniyah looks down at the ground like she's ashamed to face me.

"Has he ever hit you?" I ask.

"A couple times," she confesses, "but we were arguing and I got in his face. I shouldn't have provoked him."

"Wait a minute. Don't you dare defend him! He was wrong. There is never an excuse for a man to put his hand on a woman."

"But he lost his job and I was paying all the bills and I started complaining that he needed to do something. I shouldn't have pushed. I knew he was trying," she says, defending him.

"Sweetheart, stop making excuses for him. That's the first thing you should do. Does his family know he hit you?" I ask.

"No. He told me not to tell them because he was sorry and he wouldn't do it again."

"But you said he hit you a couple times, so obviously he did do it again, right?"

"Well, yeah, but that was a misunderstanding." Aniyah crosses her arms in front of her, in a defensive posture, but I keep probing.

"I guess he misunderstood his role as head and husband. His job is to protect you from harm not cause you any." I feel indignant, like he hit me. "Look, I can't begin to understand what it's like for you, but I do know that God didn't plan that for your life and you shouldn't accept anything less than His best."

"So, you think I should leave him?" She questions.

"I'm not saying that, but I think it must be on your mind to even ask me. Look, let's get back on this bus before they leave us. We'll talk some more about this." We stand and walk over to the bus. Nearly everyone was back in their seats. In a matter of minutes we were back on the highway.

I reach for my bible and then change my mind. "Let's just talk for a minute, Aniyah. What's going on with you? What's on your mind? What do you want out of your marriage?"

She sighs and says, "I don't know. Some days I want to work it out and some days I want to get as far away from him as I can. In the beginning, I used to cry whenever he was upset with me. He used to stop talking to me and shut me out if I did something to make him mad. I felt so lost. I would apologize, even if I didn't do anything wrong, just to keep the peace. I guess I felt dependent on him. I couldn't understand how someone like him would want to be with me—like I didn't deserve him."

"So, you have some self-esteem issues. You can't let him bring you down like that. You are a child of the Most High God. Somehow we are going to have to change how you see yourself. If we can change that, we can change how you allow Richard to treat you. Men are a lot like kids. They learn by rote. If you allow him to treat you a certain way in situations, anytime that situation comes around again, he's going to treat you that way again. You have to set the standards of what's acceptable and what's not. For one thing, hitting is not acceptable. The next time he raises his hand to you, you need to give him something to think about." I think I'm preaching to myself right here. I'm just as guilty as she is of letting Jonas get away with disrespecting me.

"How do I do that?" Aniyah asks.

"You pick up something and act like you gon' throw it," says a voice behind us. A gray head peeks over the top of the headrest and a smooth skinned elderly woman says, "I've been listening to you talk and this sister," she points at me, "is telling you right. I've been married for over forty years and my husband thought he was going to hit me early on. I picked up the heaviest thing I could find and slammed it into the wall by his head."

"Oh, my," gasps Aniyah.

"What did he do?" I ask her.

"He ran out the front door and stayed out there on the porch until he thought I was asleep. When he opened the front door, I was sitting in the dark right there in a chair facing the door. I told him if he ever tried to hit me again, no one would find him. Then I told him to come on in and eat. I had wrapped a plate for him and set it on the counter next to a box of rat poison. It took him a week before he would eat any of my cooking."

"Oohh," we giggle.

"I know I'm a church lady, but no one is gonna put their hands on me like that—not if you're supposed to love me. We never had that problem again. I'm Emma Lewis, by the way."

"Well, Emma, we are so honored to meet you. I'm Mildred and this is Aniyah." We shake hands.

"And I agree. It takes men a while to realize how much they love us and in the meantime they do dumb stuff that makes us wonder why we love them."

"You are telling the truth. To be so young, you got it together. How long have you been married?" Emma asks me.

"Fifteen years. And they haven't been easy ones," I answer.

"What about you, dear?"

"Six. And Mildred is right. They haven't been easy," admits Aniyah. "The thought of quitting crosses my mind so many times in a day, but in the end I just stay."

"Well, when you look at your options today, it just makes sense to fight through. Besides, there must have been something there for you to say "I do" to in the first place. It's still there, it's just up to us wives to dig it back out."

"You're right about that," I agree with Emma. "I imagine our marriages like a clean room, and our husbands go rifling through the closets for something in their past or childhoods they think they lost and they pull out all their old dirty laundry, baggage and skeletons and scatter them all over the room. And as usual, we wives have to clean up the mess. Wading through childhood issues that have nothing to do with us, but we're getting the fallout."

"Yeah, I can see that," agrees Aniyah. "So, when we're picking up different things, instead of throwing it somewhere else or pushing it under the bed, we need to put them in their proper places."

"Exactly. Some things get cleaned up, some get thrown out, some get fixed up, or whatever. I guess the hard part is in knowing how to deal with each thing we pick up."

"That's where prayer comes in, girls," chimes in Emma. "God shows us what to do and how to do it when we go to him in prayer. I had to go back to my husband and apologize for that little misunderstanding, even though he was at fault. That broke something in him…and me. Since then, we have been the best of friends and he's never tried to hit me again. He treats me like a queen and I respect him as my king. Only God could do that."

"Communication is the key," I say, "And not just with each other, but with God. I think sometimes, we hear what He's saying, but we don't want to give in. It makes us feel weak, like doormats." I'm thinking about all the times Jonas' laid into me and I just cried. I didn't even try to defend myself. I thought I was supposed to put up with it, to take it. I thought I was just being his wife. Apparently, I haven't been a very good one.

We talk some more until Emma and Aniyah fall asleep. I just stare out the window watching the scenery and wondering about my life and where it's going. I think about my kids and how they are affected even with my attempts to protect them. I think about Jonas and wonder if I still love him. I think about my marriage and what it will take for me to say enough and walk away.

At some point I fall asleep, too. Not much later, Aniyah shakes me awake and I see we are at the port. We get off the bus and collect our bags. I check my purse and make sure I have my passport and tickets and money. We get in the line behind another group and wait. My stomach is full of butterflies and I'm straining my neck to take in everything. I don't want to miss anything. The ship is huge. It takes us a while to get our ID's and tickets checked. We get our pictures taken and our room keys and Aniyah and I promise to meet up again for dinner. After the safety presentation, I try to find the meeting room for the seminar. I get turned around several times but I finally find it near the middle of the ship. It is beautiful. There are chandeliers, and a dance floor, a small stage with a podium, a bar and tables immaculately laid out. I go inside and walk over to the stage. I step up behind the podium and look out across the room. As I take in the elegance of the décor and the overall ambience, someone calls out to me.

"Hello. I thought I was the only one who liked to map his routes beforehand," says this tall, very attractive, brown-skinned man walking towards me.

"Hi. I just wanted to make sure I knew how to get here so I wouldn't be wandering around lost and miss the seminar," I blush. "I didn't realize anyone else was in here." I notice he has the prettiest smile and the straightest, whitest teeth I think I've ever seen. I tear my eyes away from his face when I realize that I am staring into his hazel colored eyes.

"Well," I stammer, "I guess I better get back to my room or cabin or whatever." I step down off the stage and start walking towards the door.

"Wait a minute," he reaches out and takes my hand, cutting off my grand escape. "What's your name?" He asks.

"Mildred," I answer.

"My name is Keith. It's a pleasure to meet you, Mildred."

Oh, my! Did my name just drip from his lips? I think to myself. *What in the world? Do you realize you haven't let his hand go? Come on, girl, get a grip on yourself!*

"I'm married," I blurt out. Keith chuckles and releases my hand.

"I'm sorry," he grins, "I didn't mean to make you uncomfortable. Besides, I don't want your husband to walk in and get the wrong impression. It was just nice to see a friendly face."

"Don't worry my husband's not here." *What?*

Keith just raises his eyebrows and it looks so sexy with that half smile.

"I mean he didn't come with me... couldn't come with me. Um...he had to work." By now I am blushing all over myself and I really need to get out of this man's presence.

"So you came alone or with friends?" He asks.

"Uh, alone."

"Well, maybe we'll run into each other, perhaps at one of the seminars this week?"

"Uh, okay," I say as he nods, turns and walks out the door. "My God, you have given me all things lovely to behold." I say. I take a deep breath and let it out slowly. I walk out the door, shaking my head and wondering where all my sense ran to when I needed it the most. You would think I had never seen a deliciously gorgeous, scrumptiously sexy--wait, girl! That's enough! I mentally shake myself and continue touring the ship, trying to put Mr. Keith--I'm-glad-you-didn't-tell-me-your-last-name-because-I-would-be-scribbling-it-all-over-my-notebook-like-I-was-still-in-middle-school--out of my mind.

When we finally get underway, I head back towards my cabin just in case I need to take a Dramamine for seasickness. I pass by one of the dining areas and decide to grab a quick bite, since I feel fine so far and it is so close to lunchtime. I grab a tray, silverware and a plate and proceed down the service line. I get smoked salmon, steamed vegetables, a roll and some fruit. With all the preparations for the cruise—packing, getting the kids clothes together, cleaning, and working on my seminar notes and still going to work every day—I didn't do a lot of the snacking and eating I normally do, so I lost a few pounds. I was so happy when I saw my clothes were loose. If I can, I want to drop a few more pounds. I take my tray and go find a spot where I can sit discreetly and look out towards the deck. There are already people taking advantage of the pool and deck chairs. I bow my head and say grace. Then I grab my fork and begin by sampling the salmon. I've never eaten it before, but Trish loves it and I thought I'd give it a try. "Ugghh," I say chewing slowly. This is not the treat I thought it would be.

"Hey," says a familiar voice.

"Hi," I reply, swallowing and nearly choking as I look up and see the very smile I was trying to forget.

"Do you mind if I join you?" Keith asks.

"No, I don't mind," I tell him, feeling my stomach start to do flips that I can't blame on motion sickness.

"Thanks," he says, "I hate eating alone."

"Did you come with anyone?" I ask him.

"Actually, no." He takes a minute and situates his plate, drink and silverware on the table. He takes a napkin and places it in his lap. I just sit there watching his every move like some dumbstruck teenager. Before he notices me staring at him, I look down and start eating some of my vegetables. I force myself to look around the dining room at the different groups of people scattered about while I chew. Keith says his grace then he begins eating.

"This is my first cruise alone," he tells me. "I usually come with my wife."

"Oh," I say, relaxing a little, "you're married. Did your wife have to work, too?"

"No," he pauses and takes of sip of his tea. "My wife passed away last year."

"I'm sorry," I say. I can't stop my hand from reaching across the table and taking his. "It must have been hard losing her."

"It's a little easier now. She was sick for a while, so we both knew her time was short. We just made the most of everyday we had left. We used to take a cruise every year before she got sick. It was one of those gospel cruises. She made me promise to still go. I told her I would, but I just couldn't, it would have been hard to see so many of the people we've become friends with over the years and have them ask about her."

"I can understand that."

"So, to keep in the spirit of my promise, I chose this one instead."

"Well, I'm glad you are honoring your wife's wishes. I'm sure she made you promise so that you would know it was okay to move on."

"Yeah, we had a lot of discussions about me meeting someone special who would understand my love for my wife and not be threatened by it."

"I'm sure that special lady will show up when the time is right."

"Mildred! I have been looking all over for you," Aniyah calls out. She's walking towards me and I feel my face burning.

"Hey, Aniyah," I say. "Um, this is Aniyah. Aniyah, Keith." I introduce them as she plops into a chair beside me. Looking slightly green, she smiles shyly at Keith. "Hi. Nice to meet you. I'm sorry to interrupt your lunch."

"No problem. I think we were just about finished with lunch."

"What's wrong? You look terrible," I tell her. The ship had been sailing only about a couple hours.

"That's why I was looking for you. I forgot my Dramamine. I wanted to borrow some and tell you that I couldn't meet you for dinner. I couldn't possibly eat feeling like this."

"Sure, you could borrow some. I don't blame you for not wanting to eat. Once you get settled and that medicine kicks in, you'll feel better. I think they serve food until midnight or so. In case you want something later." I stand up and start to clear my mess. "Keith, I guess I'll see you around. It was nice talking to you."

"Don't worry about the mess; I'll get it for you. You take care of your friend. Aniyah," he turns to her, "it was a pleasure meeting you. I hope you feel better."

"Bye," we say and I take her arm and drag her out of there.

"Wow! He sure is fine," she remarks.

"He's nice-looking," I admit as I lead her down the hallways to the elevator.

"You know him? Is he a friend of yours?" Aniyah asks. I pull her into the car and I push the button for my floor.

"No, I actually met him while I was touring the ship. We just happened to run into each other again in the dining room."

"Oh, y'all looked so serious when I walked up. I felt like I was getting in the middle of something." The elevator stops, and I steer her out and down the hall to my room.

"Look, nothing happened," I tell her, feeling guilty. "If it looked deep, it was because he was telling me about his wife dying."

"Oh, that's sad."

"Yeah, it is. I couldn't imagine going through that and having to move on." I get my room card out and open the door. I see that my attendant put my bags on the bed. I open my makeup bag and dig around until I find the Dramamine. I get a glass and pour water from the pitcher on the desk. "Here, take these." I hand the pills and glass to Aniyah and she swallows them. "It's may take a while for those pills to work. You should lie down for a while." I tell her. "You sure you want to miss dinner? We still have about five hours until then and you may feel like eating by then. Or I could meet you back in the cafeteria later tonight. It's up to you, but you don't want to go all day without putting something on your stomach."

"Okay, girl. I'm going back to my room and fall out across my bed. I'll meet you tonight at eleven." She walks over to the door and opens it.

"Okay, it's a date. Then we can make plans for breakfast in the morning. The ship has a gym and I want to work out a little before I eat."

"Alright. Bye." I shut the door behind her and survey my temporary home for the next five days. It's small, but it's mine. I turn on the TV and flip through the few channels there are and leave it on one that's playing music videos. I push my bags to the floor and flop down on the bed. I kick off my shoes and take a deep breath, relishing the peace and quiet. I just lie here with so many thoughts twirling through my head. I should be looking over my notes, I wonder how the kids are getting along without me, what Jonas is doing. I wish Trish could be here with me, what the girls at work are up to, and, of course, Keith. I try to stop those thoughts, but when I close my eyes, I see that beautiful smile.

"God, help me." I call out. There's a knock on the door. I jump. "Oh, Lord," I say. Did he come see about me? My heart is beating double-time. I go over to the door and open it.

"Hello, Sister Mildred. I'm Abigail Marshall, the coordinator. I know we only spoke on the phone briefly, but can I come in for a moment?" She asks.

"Sure, Sister Abigail, how are you doing?" I move so she can get past me and she sits on the lone chair in the room. I sit back down on the bed.

"Well, Sister Mildred, I have a bit of a situation," she starts off. I have a sinking feeling—pun intended—that this isn't going to go well. "You see, your pastor, Pastor Gilliam, was to be the MC this year and when he couldn't come, we secured Pastor Washington from Blessed Alliance."

"Okay," I say haltingly, knowing there's a hook in there somewhere.

"Well, he didn't make it to the ship before we embarked."

"What happened?" I ask her.

"Well, before we got too far from port, he called to say his grandson was hurt real bad in a car accident and that he was on his way to see about him at the hospital."

"Oh, my! I'm sorry to hear that."

"Yes, we were, too. But you see, now we need someone to officiate the seminars." UH-OH! I see where this is going. I don't think so.

"Well, you should be great at that since you coordinated everything so well," I tell her.

"Sister Mildred, I would really appreciate it if you would do this for me. You would have your seminar, the one Pastor Gilliam was to deliver and you would oversee the other ones. You know, open with prayer and scriptures, introduce the speakers and help with the Q and A."

"Sister Abigail, I don't know. I mean that's a lot of responsibility. Shouldn't you try to find someone more qualified than me?"

"Everyone I spoke to said they felt you would be the perfect choice. Plus, there is an honorarium that you would be entitled to receive if you agree."

"Really? Wow. I still don't know. I mean, I haven't done anything like this before."

"Sister Mildred, if you flow anything like you did at that conference you did with your husband, I know you'll do a wonderful job. I was there and you handled yourself well. I know you have a relationship with God. It comes across when you talk about the word."

"Well, then I guess the only thing I can do is my best."

"Oh, thank you, Sister Mildred," she smiles. Sister Abigail stands up and hugs me and gives me the folder she brought with her. "I just knew you would say yes. There's something special in you. Allow God to bring it to the light. This is the list of seminars and times and the presenters. I also have a description of what they will be speaking on, so you can familiarize yourself with that. You be blessed, Sister Mildred, and thank you, again." She walks over to the door and lets herself out. I just sit there on the bed staring at the folder in my hand. What is going on? It seems like my life is moving in fast forward. Now I'm officiating conferences? I didn't even ask her how much the honorarium was. Not that I'm motivated by money, but it could make this ordeal a little less aversive. Why wouldn't any of the other pastors and elders agree to step in? Am I being set up?

Since I have a few hours before dinner, I decide to make the best use of my time by going over the papers inside the folder. The whole focus of the Conference is 'Kingdom Life'. There are seminars on Building Kingdom Character, the Kingdom Agenda, Financing the Kingdom, Kingdom Fruits, Thy Kingdom Come and the Kingdom Family. I sit there feeling a little overwhelmed. It's like I have to come up with mini-sermon summaries on each of these topics. I brought my bible and concordance with me, but I didn't realize I would have to study so hard. I begin flipping through the books to find scriptures that are relevant to these topics. "Lord, please help me!" I cry out. "I don't know what I've gotten myself into, but I trust You to be with me."

For the next few hours, I tear through my bible and jot down notes and scriptures pertaining to each person's topic. I also begin working on the seminar Pastor Gilliam was supposed to give on Building Kingdom Character. It ties in with the one that I'm doing on the 'Love Bud', which is a subtext under Kingdom Fruits. I use some of the same scriptures, but bring out different points.

I check the time and see that it is after five. I picked the six o'clock dinner slot and I don't want to be late. I stand and stretch, trying to roll some of the kinks out of my neck. I quickly wash, change for dinner and vow to come back and finish up my work. Both the seminars I'm presenting are for the day after tomorrow. I know I'll have time to go over them again, but I want to make sure my information is together for the others.

I grab my clutch purse and room key and head out the door to the elevator. The dining area has a big ice sculpture in the middle next to a spiral staircase. It looks so elegant. There are hostesses and wait-staff galore, but everyone has a smile. I notice many of them speak with foreign accents. My hostess shows me to a small table near the window, off to the side. Perfect. I can sit, think and meditate on this whole trip thus far in relative peace. I tell my waiter, Saldor, my drink request, and sit back to begin my musing.

"Do you mind if I join you?" Keith asks, appearing out of my thoughts.

"Uh, no, sure. Be my guest." I stammer. Keith again. What are the chances? Is this man stalking me?

"Thank you, I saw you walk in just as I got off the elevator. I'm surprised you have such a secluded spot. They usually put you at a table with other people. You know, to get as many people in as possible."

"Actually, this is my first cruise, so I don't have a clue what to expect," I admit. "I thought everyone sitting together knew each other."

"Really," he looks at me questioningly. "I thought maybe you had just been on a different cruise, like me."

"No, this whole thing is new to me." I pick up my glass and take a sip.

"Well, I'm just going to have to show you how to get the most out of this whole experience," he says in this really sexy Billie D voice. And then I choke. I mean literally. My mind went somewhere it shouldn't have and I choke on my lemonade. Keith jumps up and pats me on my back, like I'm four—all concerned and helpful. I just soak it in. Jonas would probably have looked at me like I just grew fur with spots.

"I'm okay," I cough. "Really. Thank you." I pat my mouth with my linen napkin and place it back on my lap.

"You scared me there." Keith exhales.

"Sorry, I guess it went down the wrong pipe." I turn and look out the window to avoid looking into those beautiful eyes--and because I am still slightly embarrassed about where my mind was going. *Lord, forgive me*, I pray, hoping He hears my sincerity.

"So, what do you have planned for later?" He asks.

"Well, I have some studying to do."

"Studying? On a cruise? You brought work with you?" He looks at me dubiously and even that look is sexy. Wow!

"No, not that kind. I was asked to present one of the seminars for my first lady." I share with him.

"Oh, that's interesting."

"Well, right after lunch today, I was asked to do another seminar and to officiate the other seminars for my pastor. He couldn't be here and his back-up had a family emergency, so they asked me to fill in."

Keith just sits there looking at me with his eyebrows raised. "I am impressed," he says. "I saw the itinerary and was planning on going to a couple of the seminars myself—Kingdom Fruits and the Kingdom Agenda. You must really be good for them to put you in charge."

"Well, I don't know about all that," I say modestly. "They just needed someone to fill in and I have a hard time saying 'no'."

"Naw, it's gotta be more than that. They wouldn't have even asked you if you couldn't pull it off. You should stop selling yourself short," he admonishes.

"Well, I'm going to do my best, that's why I have to finish studying." I try to not dwell on the fact that Keith picked my seminar as one he would be interested in attending. I feel honored, like he did it on purpose, or something.

"I do hope you take a break for a little while. There's a casino on board. I can meet you there. My wife used to play the machine where the bar slides back and forth. And when you put your money in it pushes the money towards the edge and it drops out. She won quite a bit. She always knew when to drop her quarter in."

"I've never gambled before. I wouldn't feel right just wasting money like that."

"I tell you what. You let me pay for a few games so you can see how fun it can be. If you win, you can just pay me back from your winnings," Keith offers.

"But what if I don't win?" I ask him.

"Then you would have shown me gambling is wrong. Okay? Do we have a deal?"

"Okay," I agree, smiling and shaking his outstretched hand to seal the deal.

We eat our four courses. The food is delicious—salad, she crab soup, stuffed flounder with steamed vegetables and cheese cake. I feel like a stuffed turkey. We make small talk while our food digests and agree to meet around nine-thirty. As we are leaving, the eight-o'clock dinner crowd is starting to arrive. Keith goes left towards the elevator; I go right and take the stairs down. I don't want anyone to think we came together, since a lot of the people know Jonas and that I'm his wife. I would hate for something to get back to him before I did.

Back at my room, I pick up where I left off. I tend to get lost when I search through the scriptures. When I get stuck or can't seem to tie it all together, something I heard from an old sermon or a quote from a book will come back to me and bring it all home. I am basking in that sense of accomplishment right now.

"Oh, man! Keith!" I jump up, slide my shoes on, grab my purse and race out of my cabin. I remember which direction the casino is, but not which floor, since I didn't pay much attention to it when I toured the ship. I get turned around a couple of times before I ask for directions. When I get there, I'm more than a few minutes late. Keith is sitting at a slot machine, slowly pulling the handle down. I take a few moments to watch him. He really is a nice looking man. Maybe if things were different.... But I digress. I walk over to him and put my hand on his shoulder.

"Hey, win anything?" I ask. He turns and smiles at me. "I thought maybe you had changed you mind."

"Sorry, I kinda lost track of time," I apologize. "So, where's this amazing machine that will make me like gambling?" I glance around the room. There are a few blackjack tables, more slot machines and roulette tables. A cashier booth is in the corner and attendants are carrying trays with drinks and plastic cups to hold coins.

"Let's go over here," Keith points me to a quiet corner where there are two shiny machines side by side. They both are filled with quarters and bills balanced precariously on the edges. "Wow! That looks like it's about to fall!" I say, getting excited.

"Well, let's see if we can help it along." Keith hands me a cup full of quarters. "Just put one in the slot. You have to time it so it falls when the bar is at the back," he instructs me. I take out a quarter and hold it at the slot until the bar starts to swing towards the back, and then I let it go. It lands near the middle and the bar pushes it against the old coins. Several coins fall down and Keith cheers. "See? You won!" I reach inside and take out the quarters. I count out three dollars and fifty cents.

"That was great! I want to try that again." I put the winnings into the cup and another quarter in the slot. Again, letting it go when the bar swings towards the back. This time only three quarters fall, but I think I'm hooked.

Keith sits at the machine next to mine and plays. We spend the next couple hours winning some and losing some. I finally find out his last name is Robbins. I tell him mine and that I am named after my grandmother, and about my kids, my family, church and my job. I even tell him about my dreams for the future. Jonas doesn't even ask me anything about myself, but here is someone who seems genuinely interested in me as a person. I am loving this! God, why can't it be like this with me and Jonas?

"Oh, no! Look at the time!" I jump up and hand Keith the cup of coins. "I was supposed to meet Aniyah in the dining room. She's probably still waiting on me."

"Why don't I walk you down?" Keith offers.

"No, that's okay. I'll probably see you around this week. This was fun. Thanks."

I hurry out of there and race to the dining room. There are a few people here and there, but no Aniyah. I leave and run back to my room. Maybe she came looking for me. When I get to my room, I open the door and find a note on the floor.

"Man, I missed her." The note said she waited for me, but after twenty minutes, she figured I must have fallen asleep. She would meet me for breakfast in the morning.

"Well, it's probably for the best," I sigh. "I was having too much fun. And I have a busy day tomorrow." I spend the next few minutes getting ready for bed. I put away my clothes and stack my notes on the desk. I get into the bed and pull the covers up to my chin. "God, give me an unforgettable experience, this week," I pray. "Allow me to see and feel you like never before. Be with me during each seminar and allow me to speak only what you want heard. In Jesus' name, I pray. Amen."

I turn over on my side and stare at the wall. I think about my kids and wonder if they had trouble going to sleep. I miss them. I want to call them, but I don't have an international calling plan on my cell phone. "Lord, watch over my babies, while I'm gone." I turn over to my other side, facing the TV, which is still on. I stare at the screen waiting for sleep to come. It takes its own sweet time. Around two a.m., after much tossing and turning, I have to admit that I miss not having Jonas beside me. It's something about having a body next to you, even though we haven't been intimate for a while. As I lay there, I begin to explore this line of thought. What if anybody will do? Does it have to be Jonas? He acts like he can't stand to touch me anyway. He hasn't kissed me or tried to hold my hand in months. I held his hand once in church when we were in prayer and it felt like a dead fish. He didn't even try to hold mine back! Forget intimacy and cuddling. He's usually getting home late and he goes straight to bed. Sometimes he falls asleep before his head hits the pillow. I bet Keith would cuddle. He seems like he genuinely loved and cared for his wife. He told me that they both cried together when they learned she couldn't have any children. He told her he still loved her and that they could adopt if she wanted to, but in the end they decided not to.

"Come on, Mildred," I scold myself. "You need to quit thinking about that man and go to sleep. You got a big day ahead of you." I cover my head with the pillow and sleep finally takes a hold of me.

Less than five hours later, I am up, dressed and on my way to the gym. I decide to get in at least thirty minutes on the treadmill before I have to meet Aniyah. Hopefully, I'll feel energized after not getting much sleep. I tossed all night long. I even had some crazy dream with me and Keith in a park sitting on a swing set on top of a hill. What was that all about anyway?

There is only one treadmill machine open as I walk into the gym, and I hurry and grab it because there are people still coming in behind me. I guess something about being on a cruise ship inspires people to exercise like they should be doing at home. I know it does for me. I set the speed on the machine for a brisk walk, with no incline. I don't want to sweat my hair out too much; I still have the rest of the week to get through. I brought my mp3 player with me and listen as I walk. It makes the time go by so fast. Before I know it, my thirty minutes are up. I get off the machine and walk over to the mats to stretch. They are laid out in front of these big mirrors. As I bend and stretch out my legs, I notice Keith on a stationary bicycle. He is all sweaty, like he's been here for a while. I know he must have seen me, but I wonder why he didn't say hi. I decide to walk past like I didn't see him. I saunter over to the door, playing with my mp3 player to give him time to notice me, but I get to the door and still nothing. The only thing I could do was leave. I get out in the hallway and fume. All that time we spent together and he doesn't notice me? *Why is that such a big deal anyway? Girl, you are tripping! You are married. You can't have him! So stop flaunting yourself, trying to get his attention.* I have to meet Aniyah for breakfast anyway, so I head in that direction.

There are meeting rooms and small venues all over the ship, so I poke my head in when I come across one with an open door. I see that they are playing movies in one room. They have a list of the movies playing all day and I decide to come back after today's sessions and watch one or two before dinner, to unwind. It's so hard for me to watch movies at home because the kids talk through it, or I don't get to watch the whole thing because I have to finish cleaning or cooking or bathing somebody or I have to be at church or something. I vow that I am going to have some fun doing something just for me before I get off this boat.

In the dining room, almost every table is full. I see Aniyah waving at me when I get my tray and I wave back so she knows I saw her. They have everything you could want for breakfast—waffles, pancakes, fish, chicken strips, steak, fried potatoes, sausage links, grapefruit, and so on. I get some bacon, scrambled eggs, toast, fruit and juice and walk over to join Aniyah.

"Good morning, Mildred. You get my note?" She asks as I put my tray down on the table.

"Morning. Yes I did." I pull out my seat and sit down. "I'm so sorry I didn't meet you."

"It's okay; I know you were probably worn out from the trip down and everything. I almost slept through myself, but my stomach woke me up. That Dramamine is some good stuff. I was so hungry! And they had so much food! I didn't overdo it, though. I didn't want to make myself sick."

"Well, I'm glad you got some dinner. I wasn't sleep, though. I was at the casino," I admit.

"Casino? You?" She smiles at me skeptically. "I would have never pegged you for a gambler." She giggles.

"It wasn't my idea. I just went along." As soon as the words are out, I wish I could take them back.

"Whose idea was it, Mildred?"

"Umm, Keith's," I admit, haltingly.

"You ran into each other again?" She questions. Now I feel like I have to defend myself.

"I didn't go looking for him or anything. I was at dinner and he asked if he could join me. And since you weren't there I told him he could. So we talked about his wife and the conference and stuff. Then he invited me to the casino."

Aniyah just looks at me like I'm hiding something. "Really! That's all there is to it. We were playing some game his wife used to play and I lost track of time. When I realized how late it was I ran out of there hoping to catch you. I really am sorry."

"Well, you need to be careful, Mildred. I mean, what do you really know about this guy, anyway? He could be here looking for some unsuspecting female to replace his dead wife. Besides, if someone sees you eating and talking and hanging out with him, they may get the wrong impression."

"Well, if they don't have anything better to do than sit around and make mountains out of molehills, then they should have stayed home," I say indignantly. "I can have friends. My husband has several female friends and nothing is going on between them. I'm just being nice to somebody who happens to be male."

"And fine," she adds.

"Yes, and fine," I agree. "Let's not talk about Keith. There is absolutely nothing going on there. Besides, I didn't get a chance to tell you what happened after you left my cabin yesterday!" I say excitedly.

"Did you tell Keith?" Aniyah jokes.

"Girl, you are crazy!" I toss a napkin at her. "So what if I did? He just happened to be there. And it's not like I'm not about to tell you. They asked me to MC all the seminars." I tell her.

"What? Everybody's?" She leans forward in disbelief.

"Yeah, everybody's. Isn't that something? I'm here to stand in for my first lady and now I have to stand in for my pastor, too. His replacement had a family emergency and couldn't make it."

"Girl, look at God! Now I know you need to be careful."

"What do mean?" I look at her, playing with her food.

"Mildred, you're being elevated and everyone will be looking at you. If they see you around the ship with Keith, they are going to recognize you and wonder if something's going on."

"But I told you nothing's going on,"

"It doesn't matter. If they think it is, then it is." She has a point. The bible does say shun the very appearance of evil, but I haven't been seeking him out. We just ran into each other. I don't even know what room he's in; and I sure didn't tell him mine. I'm not that stupid--or that strong. If he were to come knocking on my door, I don't know if I would have the willpower not to open it. It's been a long time since someone has made me feel the way he does. And he's just being himself. I didn't get the impression that he was trying to impress me or come on to me.

"You know, let's not go there. I'm not trying to hook up with him, but I'm not going to be rude if we happen to bump into each other, either. Besides, you and I are probably going to be together most of the time, right?"

"Sure," she agrees.

"So if he shows up, it won't look so bad if we all three are hanging out or something."

"Okay, Mildred. Just remember that scripture about being sober and vigilant," Aniyah warns me.

"You just remember to meet me at the movie room after today's meetings, little Miss Prophet. I want to watch the comedies that are playing today. And I think they are showing *Independence Day* this evening. I may go back and watch that one. Will Smith was so good in that movie."

"Yeah, and he looked good, too."

"Girl, you are a mess!" I laugh, "Let's get out of here. I have to be presentable for my public." We get up and leave. When we get to the elevator, I get to my floor before she does. She's two levels below me. "See you in a few," I call out before the door closes.

I let myself into my cabin and go to the wardrobe. I brought along business casual attire that could be dressed up or down, depending on the situation. But since I was officiating, I thought maybe something a little more "churchy" was in order—at least for the first day. I pull out a blue retro-styled dress with some black sling back pumps. These are my favorite shoes because I can stand in them all day, run the fifty, double-dutch and my feet still won't hurt. Perfect. They were definitely worth the small fortune I paid for them. Jonas complained, but I think I got more than my money's worth out of them. I take a quick shower, fix my hair, get dressed and put on a little makeup. I check myself out in the mirror above the desk. Not too bad. I almost look like a first lady--on a dress down day, of course—but first lady, nonetheless. I gather my materials, my purse and head out the door. My plan is to be early, so that I can watch people as they come in and talk to each presenter beforehand. I don't know everyone, but I will try to get a flow for how they operate, so that each session can go smoothly.

I go straight to the Rendezvous Lounge and it strikes me as ironic that this is the room where Keith and I first met. It wasn't even like that. It was a chance meeting, very innocent. Why am I even thinking about him right now? I have to focus. "Kingdom, kingdom, kingdom," I repeat under my breath. Inside, the room has changed a little. There are chairs set up on the stage behind the lectern and the tables are bare. Sister Abigail is already there, showing every presenter to their seat and making sure everyone is attended to.

"Sister Mildred, good morning." She greets me as I walk over.

"Good morning, Sister Abigail. You look like you got everything under control," I tell her, looking at all the activity around me.

"Pretty much, but I'm sure glad to see you. We'll be getting started in a few moments. I'm going to introduce you and you go on from there. Just let the Lord use you. You know the basic order. Each session is forty-five minutes to an hour long, depending on the Q and A. And there is a thirty minute window before the next session starts. Now, I'm just going to sit in for a few minutes, and then you got it. Okay?"

"Okay," I see that chairs are filling up and my stomach starts to flip. I turn towards my seat and put my things down. "Lord, just be with me. I want to make you proud, but you have to help me. Give me a word for your people," I whisper a prayer.

I feel someone tap my shoulder, and I turn around to see Aniyah standing behind me. "You made it."

"Yeah. I just wanted you to know that we'll be sitting over there," she points to a table near the front, close to the door. Keith is sitting down, with his Bible and notepad under his elbow.

"Be sober and vigilant," I tease her, and we both laugh.

"You know it ain't like that. I saw him in the hallway, and he asked if we could sit together."

"Um hunh. And you talking about me being careful," I shake my head, smiling.

"He really is a sweetheart. I hope you don't mind, but I told him we were going to watch movies later and he asked if he could come. I told him he could," she admits.

"That's cool. I'll talk to y'all when this is over. Take good notes. We can talk and you can tell me what I need to do better next time."

"Mildred, you are going to be fine. I'll talk to you after it's over." Aniyah turns and walks back to her seat. It's just about time to start, so Sister Abigail goes up to the podium and tests the microphone.

"Good morning, everyone. If you could please take your seats, we are about to get started." She pauses to wait for a few more people to come in and fill the tables in the back. There is some quiet rustling and then the room is silent. "For those of you who don't know," she continues, "Pastor Scott, wasn't able to make the trip because of a family emergency. His grandson was in a car accident, but when we last heard, he was stable and will make a full recovery." There is clapping and shouts of "thank God" and "Hallelujah".

"Yes, God is good." She pauses until the praises fade. "We are very fortunate that God sent a 'ram in the bush'. Sister Mildred Wilson from Word of Truth will be serving as the Mistress of Ceremony this week. Come on and give God praise for that." There is applause and cheers from the audience and I feel so humble and nervous. "Some of y'all remember how God used her to speak into couples' lives at Good Faith. I can't wait to hear her insight and revelation on Kingdom Life. I believe we will hear God's heart through His servants this week. So without further ado, welcome Sister Mildred Wilson." Sister Abigail turns and hugs me and steps down off the stage and I walk up to the microphone.

"Isn't God good?" I ask.

"Yes, He is!" They respond.

"Before we get started I want to take the opportunity to thank Sister Abigail and her committee for the privilege to stand before you. I believe that we are going to have a glorious time this week learning about God's Kingdom. He is calling us to a higher standard of living, but we have to renew our minds in some areas." I hear some 'amens' from the group. "We are living in the last and evil days, but God is still on the throne."

"Hallelujah," someone shouts from the back.

"Amen, sister. We have to realize that we are not citizens of this world and are therefore not subject to the pitfalls of this world's systems. We are called to a higher dimension. That's why these seminars this week are so timely. We are being taught Kingdom principles so that we can establish God's Kingdom on earth as it is in Heaven. See," I say warming up, "it's not just a cute little prayer you teach children-'Thy kingdom come, Thy will be done on earth as it is in heaven'. We have to take it to heart. We call Matthew 6:9-13 the 'Lord's Prayer', but that was our prayer. Jesus gave us a model of how to approach God. We just have to look beyond the simplicity of it and get to the meaning of it. Every element has purpose. And when you follow it from the beginning to the end that is how God's Kingdom gets established in this realm." I notice that everyone is watching me, enraptured. "Now, I'll be going into details about that tomorrow, so you are going to have to come back for that." I hear several groans of impatience. I notice that Sister Abigail is still sitting in her chair, so I hurry and get the opening prayer and scripture done. I want to make sure that I uphold my duties. The first topic is Kingdom Life and Pastor Lucas of New Hope Baptist is presenting, so I introduce him and sit back down.

He is coming from the perspective that God's original intent in Genesis was for us to live on Earth ruling and reigning as kings. He reads from Philippians 3:20 that our 'citizenship is in heaven' and we are ambassadors here in the earth. He brings out interesting points that we have to be 'heavenly minded to do earthly good'. And he explains how sometimes people get that wrong.

"Those of us who know God's purpose and plan need to share that with others. Instead, we go around acting so holy and forgetting that we should be serving our brothers and sisters and showing them God's love and revealing to them their true rights and authority in the earth. We allow them to live defeated lives, because it makes us look like we must really be saved since we appear to be so blessed compared to them. And instead of them wanting to be like Christ, they want to be like us and that makes our egos swell up, but God doesn't get the glory."

"Amen," I say.

"We have to love God and love one another. We show God's love by serving one another. We maintain our relationship with God and stay unified with our brethren. We follow God's precepts and keep the devil subdued. And we when do that, God blesses. We establish a pattern that can be duplicated through our children and our children's children. Always keeping heaven as our goal, but doing good while we're here," he teaches. "We want a heavenly atmosphere on earth. So let's stay heavenly minded and do some earthly good."

He takes his seat and I go back to the lectern. There is scattered applause around the room.

"Come on," I encourage, "you can do better than that." The applause picks up. I take a moment and survey the room while the clapping dies down. I see that some of the attendees look like they wandered in to see what was going on in here.

"God wants us all to enjoy the good life," I tell them. "When you are part of an earthly kingdom, it's the king's responsibility to take care of you—to protect you, to feed you, and to shelter you. And in turn, you give your loyalty and honor to that good king. That is how God's kingdom works. He takes care of your every need. The only thing He wants in return is your loyalty—your faithfulness. But you can't reap the benefits of the kingdom if you are outside the walls." I feel the Holy Spirit welling up in me. "Now we can't assume that everyone in here is a part of that kingdom, but we can give you the opportunity to come inside the walls." I hear some 'amens' and 'yes, Lords' and I continue.

"Brothers and sisters, we're not here to put you on the spot, but we are here to show you that we love you and God loves you and to give you the opportunity to give your life to Him. It doesn't take a whole lot of drama and whooping and hollering. It's just a matter of you confessing with your mouth and believing in your heart that Jesus is the son of God and He rose from the dead. Now, if you're here and you would like to belong to the Kingdom of God, make your way up front and we'll lead you in the confession of salvation." I pause and give people an opportunity to come up. I've never done an alter call on this level before, but I feel God leading me strongly to do it. I look around and no one is moving, but I know God wants this time, so I wait.

Before long, a gentleman in the back stands up. He starts walking towards the stage and the people around him start clapping and praising God. Then a young lady in her twenties stands and comes forward. Next thing I know, people are popping up and walking towards the stage. I lift my hands to God and praise Him for the souls that are coming.

"Come on, everybody. The heavens are rejoicing at the souls coming in," I exhort. "Give God praise in this place."

There are fourteen people lined up across the front. Some are crying, some are clapping and praising God.

"Bless God. Now lift your hands towards heaven and repeat after me. Father God," I lead.

"Father God," they respond.

"I am a sinner in need of a Savior."

"I am a sinner in need of a Savior."

"I confess that You sent Your son to die for my sins."

"I confess that You sent Your son to die for my sins."

"And I believe that He rose on the third day."

"And I believe that He rose on the third day."

"Father, I repent now of all my sins."

"Father, I repent now of all my sins."

"Wash me now in the precious blood of Your Son, Jesus."

"Wash me now in the precious blood of Your Son, Jesus."

"Satan, I now renounce you."

"Satan, I now renounce you."

"I am forgiven, redeemed and made whole by Christ Jesus, who is now Lord of my life."

"I am forgiven, redeemed and made whole by Christ Jesus, who is now Lord of my life."

"Now come on and celebrate with your new sisters and brothers in Christ."

Some of the people at the front tables get up and start hugging and rejoicing with the new converts.

"Now we are going to be having seminars today and tomorrow, so please come back. Now that you are in the Kingdom of God, come and learn how to conduct yourselves as citizens and learn what your rights are. Amen."

I get a few 'amens' in return.

"Now I would like for those who gave their lives to Christ today to stick around and pray with these fine pastors on the stage. I am sure they can give you some information about how to start studying the Word and getting to know more about God, Jesus and the Holy Spirit. So let's take an intermission and come back in thirty minutes. God bless you." I step away from the microphone, while people begin to file out of the room. Some are standing around talking, and some stay in their seats. I notice that Sister Abigail is making her way towards me. The pastors and some ministers come up and start talking to the converts.

"Sister Mildred, that was right on time. Since we've been having this conference, we've only had maybe seven or eight people get converted during the week. Today, fourteen souls were won for the kingdom of God. I knew we were making the right choice to have you officiate."

"I only did what the Spirit led me to do. I'm just glad they followed the prompting in their own hearts."

"Well, sister, you better believe your pastors are going to hear about this. You are representing them well. And I know God is well pleased with you. Keep on doing what you are doing." She hugs me and then turns to leave.

"Sister Mildred," a voice calls. I see Sister Emma waving at me and working her way through the crowd towards the stage.

"Hey, Sister Emma. How are you?" I ask reaching out to take her hand.

"I am blessed. Girl, you keep letting the Lord use you like that! That was awesome! I feel so fortunate to be here to see God move through you."

"Oh, it was definitely all Him. He gets all the glory." I'm starting to feel uncomfortable with all the compliments. The last thing I want is to get a big head. I know a lot of preachers who think God moves in their names. I definitely don't want to exalt myself and have Him humble me.

"I look forward to the rest of the workshops. Be blessed, dear." She kisses my cheek and goes back to her table.

I see Aniyah and Keith still sitting down and they wave at me. I make my way over to their table, shaking hands and hugging folks as I go. When I sit down they both tell me how wonderful a job I had done.

"I can't believe you've never done this before," says Keith.

"Yeah, you are so natural and at ease," Aniyah agrees. "She was the same way at the conference she did with her husband, too," she tells Keith. "And so much insight and wisdom! It was amazing."

"Okay, stop, before you make my head swell. I'm just doing what God wants me to do. I give Him all the credit. I open my mouth; He fills it with His words. That's all there is to it."

"Well, I am truly impressed with you, Mildred Wilson. I hope your husband sees what a gifted woman you are," remarks Keith.

That makes two of us. Aniyah just gives me a look. I pretend that I didn't catch it. I'm sure Keith didn't mean anything by that. Right? Besides, we are here in a Christian atmosphere for a Godly purpose. I already promised to 'shun the appearance of evil'. I'm just glad someone appreciates something about me. If Jonas were here, I probably wouldn't have been given this opportunity. Maybe it's a blessing in disguise. Or maybe God has something up His sleeve. Whatever the case, I just have to trust Him. I'm sure everything will work out for the good.

Thy Keith-dom Come

April 4

I can't sleep. The conferences went so well today. Everyone was so pleased and the Lord showed up. Over thirty souls gave their lives to Christ! But I'm so confused. After the conferences, I went back to my room to change and went to meet Aniyah. She didn't show up, but Keith did. He told me that Aniyah said she was going to take some Dramamine, because the boat was rocking more than usual and it was upsetting her stomach. I guess she decided to lie down. So that left me and Keith alone in a dark room. There wasn't anyone else there. Convenient, right? We watched Tyler Perry's 'Diary of a Mad Black Woman'. We laughed and really had a good time. Before the movie was over, Keith told me he was glad to have met me and he said it was all in God's will. He told me how wonderful I was and how impressed he was with me--a genuine compliment! Then he kissed me! Okay, so it was on the cheek. But the problem now is I wonder what would have happened if he kissed me for real. I am actually sitting here wondering what his lips would have felt like or tasted like. I must say I have been repenting every half hour for my thoughts and as hard as I try, they keep coming back to that kiss. God, help me! I haven't felt like this for a while. I wish things between Jonas and me were solid, then I could have pushed Keith away or even slapped him. Instead, I'm lying here wondering where his room is and if he's awake, too. Why is it that the devil always shows up when God shows out? After the time we had today, he should be ashamed to show his face. I know I'll probably have a hard time looking Keith in the eye. All I know is Aniyah better not stand me up anymore. I don't trust myself alone with Keith. My spirit is willing, but my flesh sure is weak!

I wake up, grudgingly--not having had much sleep—and I get dressed to work out. I hope it helps to energize me, since I have my own seminar to deliver. I get to the exercise room and peek in, hoping Keith's not there.

I put my towel across the handle of the treadmill, punch in my program and push start. I don't have my music with me, so I think about the seminar I'm presenting and try to keep thoughts of Keith at bay. By the time my walk is done, I feel better, like I can handle myself. Besides, I see several of the church members in here and it wouldn't do for me to be tripping over myself where he's concerned. I gather my things and head out the door to meet Aniyah.

When I get to the dining area, she is waiting for me with a cup of coffee and a piece of toast. "I'm afraid to eat anything more," she tells me.

"Girl, I am so sorry for you. Maybe you should take the Dramamine every day until we get back," I suggest. "That way you can enjoy yourself. And stop leaving me alone with Keith," I whisper the last part.

"Why, what happened?" She leans forward.

"I'm going to get myself some nourishment first. You'll just have to wait to hear the juicy details." I get up and grab a tray. Since I'm not that hungry, I opt for fruit, a bowl of cereal and juice. I carry my tray back to the table and Aniyah is giving me a mean look.

"What?" I ask innocently.

"Girl, you know what! Spill it!"

"Can I at least eat first?" I joke. She picks up a napkin, balls it up slowly and throws it at my head. I laugh because I think of how many times my co-workers have done that very same thing.

"Okay, okay," I give in. I place my spoon down and lean in towards her.

"You know how we were planning to watch movies?" I start, lowering my voice.

"Yeah, I'm sorry by the way, for not coming, but I felt bad. I told Keith to tell you. Did he?"

"He did. But it left me in a bad position. Remember how you warned me to be careful?"

"Yes," she says, tentatively.

"Well, there was nobody else in that movie room--just him and me alone in the dark!"

"Why didn't you leave?" She asks, her eyes as wide as saucers.

"I didn't want to be rude. And I didn't want him to get the impression that I was avoiding him or that maybe being alone with him makes me uncomfortable."

"But you are and it does, right?" She questions me.

"Yeah, but he can't know that."

"Why not?" Aniyah asks, bewildered.

"Cause, then he'll get ideas. It'll start his mind wandering into places it wasn't thinking of going before. And then I'll really have to be careful," I explain.

"Mildred, I don't get it. You're going to have to break it down 'short yellow bus' style for me."

"Men are hunters by nature. But they only hunt for things they have a hard time catching. If I all of a sudden start avoiding him or acting shy and nervous around him, then he's going to think he has to work harder. It'll only make him step up his game," I elaborate.

"But why would he think he stands a chance? You're married."

"Because that's what men love—a challenge. The bigger the challenge, the more virulent they feel. If you throw yourself at a guy, he'll take you, for sure, because men are dogs. But the woman he has to move heaven and earth to impress, the one that doesn't come easily, but does eventually, that's the one that validates his male hood. It makes them feel like they did something no other man could do."

"I think I get it now," she nods. "That explains a whole lot of things I went through when my husband and I were dating. Mildred, where were you when I needed you? You could have saved me a whole lot of heartache, girl."

"Yeah, well, if I knew then what I know now, my life would be a whole lot different, too. But that's not the worst of it," I continue. "He kissed me!"

"What? Are you serious?" Aniyah gasps. "Mildred, what did you do? I know you slapped him right?"

"No, but trust me that won't happen again. Besides, it was just on the cheek," I explain. "Let's just say grace was extended...this time."

We clear our mess and head back to my room. Aniyah's already dressed so she helps me pick out my clothes—a plum colored pant suit with a sleeveless ivory shell and matching pumps.

"Girl, you have some nice things," she compliments.

"I borrowed some of those clothes from my girlfriend. She has way more style than me," I admit.

"Well, they look real nice on you, like they were tailor-made for you."

I catch a glimpse of myself in the mirror and have to admit to myself that she was right. I look pretty good. I put my earrings on and get my materials and purse. "Let's go, I want to be there ready and waiting." I open the door.

"Ready for and waiting on who? Or is it whom?" Aniyah jokes.

"Girl, get out this door." I push her out into the hallway and close the door behind me.

When we get to the Rendezvous Room, there is a sign on the door saying the conference was moved.

"Why didn't someone come tell me," I complain. "Now we have to go to the auditorium. That's on the other side of the ship. Come on," I say, half-running half-walking down the hall.

"Slow down, Mildred," Aniyah pants. "We have a whole thirty minutes before it starts."

"I know. I just don't like to be late, especially when there is no real excuse for it."

We hurry down hallways and stairs until we come to a line outside the auditorium. "Why is there a line?" I ask a brother waiting to get in.

"They just opened the doors a few minutes ago. I heard that the other room was too small for the people that showed up, so they had to rush and get this place ready."

"Oh, my God!" Aniyah exclaims. "Mildred, did you hear that? That's awesome."

"It is, isn't it? So many people want to hear about God and His Kingdom. That is excellent! Let's hurry and get in here. I have to get to my seat."

Aniyah and I excuse ourselves all the way down to the front. I see Sister Abigail waving at me. "Find yourself a seat. I need to go up on the stage," I tell Aniyah.

"Sister Mildred I'm so glad you're here. Do you see this? We've never had to move our venue before. This is so blessed!" Sister Abigail practically squeals.

"God is good. I just hope we deliver. I want so much for people to leave here better than they came."

"That's why I do this every year. It's good to see people growing in God. I'm going to get to my seat so we can get started on time. You will be sitting over there." She points to a chair on the other side of the stage. There is a piano behind it and one of the ministers is playing softly while people are filing their way inside. I walk over and sit down and pray quietly to myself, my sleeplessness from last night all but forgotten. It's time to go to work. I take several deep breaths to calm my nerves and quiet my spirit. I can tell some of the attendees are here just to see what the excitement is all about. But some are here to learn something. They have this expectancy about them. When Sister Abigail signals me, I walk up to the lectern.

"Good morning, everyone," I begin. "I would like to thank you for coming out to day two of our Kingdom Life seminars. Yesterday was blessed and we praise God for showing up in such a mighty way." There is applause and some people lift their hands in praise. I say a prayer and read Matthew 6:9-13 for the opening scripture.

"Yesterday, I spoke briefly about this passage of scripture that is referred to as the 'Lord's prayer'. I know sometimes when you're taught something, you teach someone else that same thing and that someone teaches someone else until everyone accepts it as true. In the body of Christ, we have to study for ourselves and 'rightly divide the word of truth'. Now, I don't want to presume that I know everything, or that I have more knowledge than these great pastors on this stage with me, but I do know that God wants us to get it right. This passage wasn't the Lord's Prayer. This prayer is really a model given to the disciples by Jesus of how they should approach the Father. If we use this as an example then we should approach Him reverently, with praise. We should ask His will to be done here, because in the heavenly realm it's already done. Then we ask for the desires of our hearts. But," I emphasize, "we end with His will and His Kingdom and more reverence. Now what does this all have to do with Kingdom Living?" "Everything," I answer. "It has everything to do with it. In order to have a successful kingdom, the inhabitants must love, respect and honor their King. Without that there is rebellion and mutiny. Just look at Lucifer. No kingdom can stand if someone is constantly challenging the

King and corrupting the citizens. God must be exalted above all else—
'Hallowed be Thy Name.' And His will is paramount to your wishes.
'Thy Kingdom come, Thy will be done.' Now, you can't have a
successful kingdom if your basic needs are not being met, either. You'll
be distracted thinking about whatever it is you lack—money, food,
clothes, etc. All those things fall under the responsibility of the King.
"Give us this day our daily bread'. It's His responsibility to make sure you
are taken care of and protected. And because God is such a loving and
wonderful God, you can ask for what you need and He will give you 'the
desires of your heart'. Now what's left is your relationship with others
inside and outside of the Kingdom. You have to dwell with your
brothers in peace, forgiving them their debts as God forgives you of your
trespasses; and you should love them with the God kind of love. This
brings me to my topic, The Love Bud. The only thing that makes all of
this work flawlessly is love." I pause right there because I'm starting to
see where this is going. I can hear my first lady telling me that God
would reveal to me the purpose of this topic.

"Love is so important. It's the motivating purpose behind everything
we do. Well, let me amend that. It should be the motivating purpose
behind everything we do. It is a deep down root permeating through
every part of our earthly experience. Love is so powerful, that it
overcomes every obstacle and challenge we face. Love keeps the
Kingdom running smoothly. I did a marriage conference with my
husband and we talked about how love can make marriage work. If love
is there, there is no strife or enmity because God can't dwell in
confusion; and that works for any relationship, not just marriage. What
God wants is for people to agree, to walk in unity. He wants us to love
one another with just as much intensity as He loves us, regardless of our
differences in race, nationality, gender, or whatever. To be a part of this
kingdom means love, peace, and joy. It doesn't mean you won't have
problems. It just means that your problems won't have you. You'll take

joy in knowing that the King loves you and will get you through whatever you're going through because He loves you. That, in turn, should cause you to recruit everyone you can into this Kingdom. When you show them the same love, care and consideration, they should want to know your King and your God. You should want them to know Him. You should want them to experience God's love for themselves." I pause here so everything could sink in. Some of my struggles start to make sense to me. "Everyone wants to be loved," I say. "Most of the things we do are an attempt to gain someone's love and affection. And if they show us just a small sign of love—a love bud-- it makes the biggest difference in our lives, our attitudes and our feeling about ourselves." I think about how much better I feel when Jonas does something for me, like bring home some candy that I like or a movie that I want to see. At those times I feel like everything is going to be okay. But I don't want scattered showers here and there, I want a steady downpour. I get that from God, but I'm trying to get that from someone who doesn't even love himself.

"The problem is," I continue, "we should be trying to get to God. We already have His love, but outside of the Kingdom—and sometimes inside the Kingdom--so much is going on that we fail to recognize it. There are too many distractions and cares. But if we 'seek first the kingdom of God and His righteousness' He'll add all that other stuff. Whatever you stand in need of, He'll give it to you. You'll recognize His hand on your life and you'll feel His love for you. When you are confident in the love God has for you, you should want to share that love with everyone you come in contact with. That kind of love causes you to forgive your brother, love on your wife, and go the extra mile for your friends. The bible says that 'For God so loved the world that He gave His only begotten Son, that whoever believes in Him should not perish but have everlasting life.' John 3:16. God's love was so strong He was willing to let His Son die so that we could live forever. That was His plan--for us to rule and reign forever. Kingdom life is eternal life. All you have to do is believe on Him and you are born again into the Kingdom of God with all its rights and privileges, power and authority." I step from behind the podium and signal for the minister on the piano and he begins playing.

"He gives us power to overcome the obstacles in our lives, to overcome sickness and disease, to obtain wealth and to call forth the things we want with our words. Who wouldn't serve a God like that? A God who gives us all things richly to enjoy? Just because He loves us. And that perfect love casts out all fear. You never have to suffer the fear of rejection or abandonment. If there is one who is looking for unconditional, pure love, who wants to know this loving King, will you please come forward?" The pastors stand and line up down at the foot of the stage. I begin to sing along with the pianist as people come streaming down the aisles.

"Just love on them men of God. Just show them God's love. Come on and worship in here. Rejoice for the souls coming forth." I usher the congregation into worship. When they settle down, I lead the converts into a confession of salvation and the pastors pray for them before they return to their seats.

The spirit is so high in the place that most people praise, pray and cry through the intermission. The next couple of seminars go pretty much the same. Information is given out, but the people just want to praise and worship. As worship leader, I let the spirit have his way. When it's all over, I leave several people still praising as I make my way back to my room. I am so exhausted; I don't even notice Keith following me. I open my door, toss my keys and notes in the chair and fall across the bed. I should be getting ready for dinner, but I just can't move. It's like this unnatural weight is pulling me down into the mattress. I sigh and decide to take a nap and eat later.

Someone knocks on the door. "Ugghh," I moan. "Yes?" I squawk.

"Sister Mildred, it's me Abigail. Are you alright?" She asks.

"Oh, yes, I'm coming." I drag myself off the bed and over to the door. When I open it, she comes on in and helps me back over to the bed.

"Sister Mildred, that was so blessed today! I know you're tired, but you need to eat something."

"I will, I just wanted to take a quick nap first," I tell her.

"You'll get a nap, all right, but it won't be quick," she chuckles. "You need to eat first, and then lie down. When you minister like you did today, you need to build yourself back up. Get some nourishment in you. Come on let me help you. Your friend Keith sent me in here because he was worried about you. I ran into him in the hallway. My room is only a few doors down. He said he followed you to make sure you made it back. I told him and Aniyah--I think that was her name--I would bring you to dinner at six o'clock, so we need to get moving.

Sister Abigail and I walk into the dining room at 5:59. Aniyah and Keith are already seated and they wave us over.

"Mildred, you look better," she says, smiling. "Girl, I thought you were going to pass out. Didn't you hear us calling you?"

"No. All I could do was get to my room," I tell her, sitting down in the chair that Keith pulled out for me.

"You all enjoy your dinner, and Mildred I will see you tomorrow, okay?"

"Okay, Sister Abigail. Thank you." She walks across the room and joins a table of ladies who are on the conference committee.

"We saw you leaving the auditorium in a daze. It was kind of scary," admits Aniyah. "I told Keith to run after you, but with all the people filing out, he got hung up. By the time he caught up to you, you were going into your room. It's good we ran into Sister Abigail. Wasn't it Keith?"

"Yes, it was fortunate. I didn't even get a chance to knock," says Keith. "I asked her if she would check up on you, but she just looked at me strange. I think she might have gotten the wrong impression. That's when Aniyah caught up and explained that you didn't look right and didn't hear us calling you. She said she would take care of you and get you to dinner. So here we are," Keith explains.

"Yes, here we are. And I can only imagine what she's telling her friends over there about me."

"Don't worry about it, Mildred. I'm sure once she took a look at you she knew we were only concerned about you. She's probably just enjoying her soup. So stop stressing and let's enjoy our soup, too." We laugh and make small talk while the servers bring out our meal. I start feeling better as I eat. Even though I'm still tired, it's not as overwhelming as it was before.

While we are waiting on dessert, Keith asks if we are planning on leaving the ship tomorrow when we get to the Grand Cayman Islands.

"I don't know. I'm just getting used to being on the water. If I get off I might not want to get back on," Aniyah says. "What about you, Mildred?"

"I would love to see the Cayman Islands. This whole trip has been wonderful for me. Plus, I want to get some souvenirs for my kids. Come on, Aniyah. It'll be fun. We can get off for a couple hours and walk around and if you take the Dramamine, you shouldn't have any problems," I urge her.

"Well, if you think so. Okay, count me in."

"Great. My wife and I have been here several times. There are some great shops I could show you," Keith says, excitedly.

"We could leave right after the last seminar. That should give us a few hours to explore. So is everybody good with that?" I ask.

"Yes, let's meet on the deck by the pool," offers Aniyah.

"That's fine with me," agrees Keith. "Twelve-fifteen. That should give us time to change and get back."

"Okay," I yawn. "Sorry, I'm going to call it a night. I want to be able to get up in the morning. See you tomorrow." I stand up and walk towards the elevator. People who were at the conference smile and wave at me as I walk past. I smile and wave back. When I reach my room, I get undressed in record time and fall into bed. I fall asleep as soon as my head touches the pillow.

When I wake up, the room is pitch black. I don't remember turning off the lights. I roll over and turn on the lamp, but someone is lying there beside me. "Mildred, you're awake," Keith says sleepily. "Come here."

He pulls me towards him and holds me close. My mind is racing. When did he get here? How did he get in my room? What have I done? Why haven't I pushed him away? This must be a dream. I would never cheat on Jonas, would I? Would I?

"You are one amazing lady, Mildred. Your husband must be blind if he can't see that. Well, it's his loss. I thank God I ran into you. You are the answer to my prayers." Keith leans over me and smiles. He lowers his head and just as his lips touch mine, someone knocks on the door.

I sit up. Keith isn't there. It was just a dream. "Oh, Lord, what was that?"

"Mildred." Aniyah knocks again. "Are you up?"

"Hold on, I'm coming." I glance at my watch and it's after seven. I should have been up.

"Come on in, girl," I pull the door open and she steps inside. "You look terrible! Do you feel okay?" She asks, closing the door.

"Thank you so much for the compliment," I go and start pulling clothes from my drawer. "I feel fine. I just overslept that's all. Let me get in the shower and I'll be right as rain."

Aniyah watches TV until I get dressed; then we go to breakfast. I decide to skip the gym after the exhaustion from the previous day. While we are eating breakfast, I tell her about my dream.

"What do you think it means?" I ask.

"I think maybe you have feelings for him and your subconscious just ran away with it. It's probably because he's been around so much, you know? And you were exhausted yesterday."

"But I know better! I would never cheat on my husband. Not because he's so perfect, but because I know it would disappoint God. I couldn't do it. I don't think I could do that. I couldn't live knowing I broke my wedding vows."

"Mildred, let me be honest with you. You never know what you could do until you are put in that position. I never thought I could either," Aniyah admits.

"What are you saying? Did you cheat on your husband?" I ask, incredulously.

"I didn't intend to. It just happened. And I know it sounds cliché, but it just happened."

"I know it's probably none of my business, but how did you get yourself in that position?" I probe.

"It was after he hit me the first time. I was feeling vulnerable and scared. I went out wandering around the mall and I ran into a co-worker of mine. We talked at work, you know, and he seemed like a nice guy. So when he asked me if I wanted to get something to eat, I said okay. It was all innocent. I just wanted to forget what just happened and do something normal. We ate at the food court and talked. That was it." She stops and plays with her food.

"What happened after that?" I ask.

"Well, we started talking at work more--just innocent stuff at first. Then I started talking to him about my marriage and my fears. He told me if I needed a safe place I could always come to his house and we could figure out how to get help for me if I needed it—that his door was always open for me. So when Richard hit me again, that's where I went. I felt betrayed and hurt because he said he wouldn't hit me again. I was afraid and so I ran to my friend. When he opened the door, I just fell into his arms. He held me while I cried. He didn't push me or tell me what to do. He just held me. The next thing I know we were in his bed. It all happened so fast." Tears were rolling down Aniyah's face. "I never told Richard. I was afraid he would leave me. I never dreamed that I would be unfaithful." She reaches for a napkin and blots her face. "I got out of there as soon as he fell asleep. I couldn't face him. I put in for a transfer to a different building at my job. Richard didn't understand why, but he left me alone about it. I've never told anyone this. You don't hate me, do you?"

"No, of course not! I'm just at guilty as you are. If the truth be told, I cheated on my husband, too—just in my mind, but Jesus says it's the same thing," I tell her. "I think we should just repent, ask for forgiveness, and move on."

"Do you think I should tell Richard?"

"The bible says to confess your sins one to another. You've done that. He didn't say you had to confess to Richard. If he knows something and confronts you about it, then you should tell him the truth, but my grandmother used to say 'don't go borrowing trouble' and in your case I agree. He's already hit you before. You don't know what that kind of confession would make him do." I stare at Aniyah and pieces of the puzzle start to come together.

"That's why you stay with him. You feel like it's your penance for cheating. But what you don't realize is that if you've asked God to forgive you, He has. You just need to forgive yourself and know that it's under the blood. You don't have to live 'entangled in that bondage'. That's a trick of the enemy to keep you from fulfilling your destiny. You short circuit your own dreams because you feel you don't deserve them.

I'm not saying that you should leave him, but you deserve better treatment. You deserve the type of covenant God had in mind for marriage. If you want, when we get back, you and I could come together sometimes, maybe once a week and pray concerning our marriages. We can be spiritual partners and maybe study the word for scriptures and confessions we can stand on—and find out what our purpose and roles are as wives."

"That would be great, Mildred. I'm so glad we met. I can finally say I have a true friend here. Thank you—and thank you for not judging me."

"Girl, I am fresh out of rocks. Besides, only Jesus can throw stones, but He'd rather throw mercy our way. And I thank Him for it."

"Me, too."

We leave the dining room to finish out the conferences for the morning. When we get to the auditorium, there are a lot of people inside. I go up to my place on the pulpit and sit down. Aniyah finds a seat up front and makes small talk with the ladies around her. I look around and try to imprint this moment in my memory. This has been the best time I've had in a long time. I do miss my kids, but I feel fulfilled. I feel useful and needed and liked and respected. I know I have people who care for me, but with family it's not the same. These people don't know me and they have given me such a high level of trust, that I am humbled. Pastors are shaking my hand and calling me by name. I kind of got used to being 'Brother Jonas' wife'. That's how some ministers would address me. Now that I sit here reminiscing, I haven't heard too many of these great men mention Jonas since the first conference. Hunh, well that's something to think about at another time.

I stand and make my way to the podium. I open with prayer for the new converts and the seasoned believers to live kingdom lives. I pray for the safety of everyone on the ship and our return home and I close with praise and adoration to God for such a blessed conference. There is a swell of applause in agreement with that. "Alright, everyone, we are about to learn about Kingdom finances. Just like any government, you need money to operate. Pastor Scott will be presenting today. Y'all come on show him some love as he comes forward." I clap and step away from the microphone as Pastor Scott comes up. He's a stout man with a big voice. When he speaks, everyone listens. He tells us that God doesn't need our money, but we need to give it to Him so that he can give it back to us in a 'good measure, pressed down and shaken together'. He also talked about the economy of God working seemingly backwards. The bible said to receive you have to give, to live you must die to yourself, and to lead you must serve. There are a lot of 'amens' on that. I know of some pastors who expect their congregation to give tithes and offerings, but they don't pay tithes themselves. One incident involved them having their lights cut off at home and the pastor saying he expected the congregation to take care of them instead of him getting a job and taking care of his household. I know the bible says something about being faithful over that which is another man's, but it also says in 1 Timothy 3:5 if a man can't take of his own house, how is he going to take care of God's house? I truly believe that when we as a body get a hold of God's take on finances, we will start to see true prosperity. I know I struggle more than I should; and it's not all because of how I was raised. Jonas and I keep our accounts separate. He doesn't help me with any of the bills that I have to pay, but he always asks me for half of whatever he's paying. On top if that, I buy all the detergent, toothpaste, soap, lunch items, or whatever is needed for the house and kids. I guess somehow it's my fault for continuing to do it. I should be asking him for half, but then I feel like he should just do it. Crazy, huh? Don't forget the Proverbs 31 woman. That's a standard that is so hard to live up to when you take it at face value. The only thing the man does is sit at the gate watching his wife take care of everything and he just says, "Wow, look at her go!" When I get to heaven, God is going to have to explain that one to me.

Pastor Scott opens the floor for questions and a few hands go up. He answers them quickly and since everyone seems satisfied, I dismiss. I meet up with Aniyah in the hallway and we talk about our upcoming jaunt on the island. I'm excited. I get to step foot on foreign land. I hurry back to my cabin and change clothes. I grab my purse, room key and passport. I open my door just as Sister Abigail raises her hand to knock.

"Oh, Sister Abigail, I was just on my way out." I catch myself from running into her.

"Sister Mildred, don't let me hold you up, I just wanted to give you your honorarium. You left before I had a chance to give you the envelope." She hands a business sized envelope to me.

"Thank you so much," I hug her. "I enjoyed this more than I thought I would. It was great."

"Well, we sure appreciate you filling in; and you did a wonderful job. Don't be surprised if you hear from us again soon." She turns to leave and I call out, "Thanks again, bye." I put the envelope on the bed and as excited as I am to know what's inside, I'm more excited about getting off this ship, so I again open the door and rush out. I get to the deck and I'm the first one there. I sit on one of the deck chairs and watch several people swimming and enjoying the pool. The weather is so beautiful and there are no clouds in sight. I check my watch and see that I have almost fifteen minutes to wait, so I lie back on the chair and put my feet up. This is the life--no worrying, no strife, no frustrations, just the gentle swaying of the ship and the sounds of splashing and laughter. I fall asleep. I dream that I own my own company and I decide to go on holiday. I didn't even have to check my bank account first or save up. I just decided I wanted to go and I went. I was shopping and eating at all the finest restaurants. People knew me and wanted my autograph. My children were so well-behaved and dressed in the latest fashions. Even Jonas was there, treating me like a queen. He stood by ready to fulfill my every whim--and was happy to do it! I must be dreaming. Then Keith shows up. Everything gets quiet. The color fades. Everyone turns and looks at him when he says my name, "Mildred! Mildred!" Everything starts shaking and then I wake up.

"Mildred, wake up," Keith says.

"Good, Lord! I didn't mean to fall asleep," I say, embarrassed.

"Girl, you were sleeping deep!" Aniyah cracks, "I told him to toss you into the pool. That would have woken you up!"

"I'm so glad you didn't or trust me you would have been in there with me. Y'all ready to go?" I stand and stretch then we head down to disembark. There are people in front of us waiting to board a small chartered boat that will take us to the port. We get in line behind them.

"Aniyah, it'll be okay," I soothe her when I notice she looks more than a little nervous.

"The whole trip won't take but a few minutes," Keith tells her.

"I don't know, y'all. Look how that boat is just bouncing in the water like that!" She points to another small boat coming towards us to retrieve all of us wanting to disembark.

"You can hold my hand the whole time, I promise. It won't be as bad as it looks." I say. "I know it's scary, but you can do it." I convince her. Or at least I try to. The look she gives me isn't very convinced but when our time comes to step out of the ship, she handles it well. Me, I nearly fall, but Keith is right there to catch me—my hero. On the ride over, he stays real close to me, asking me several times if I'm okay. I just smile and nod and squeeze Aniyah's hand to reassure myself she is still there. I know I can't be alone with this man for one minute. He has just been so many things that I wish I had in Jonas; and it seems to be genuine.

When we get to the pier, everyone streams off the boat. I can't say I blame them. I was ready to get off myself, post haste. I look over the side and see tropical fish darting around in the water.

"Wow, look," I point, "real tropical fish! I haven't seen any outside a fish tank before."

We walk up the pier and there is a photographer who takes our picture. We all stand together, Keith in the center and Aniyah and I on either side. At the last minute, he puts his arms around our shoulders, but I notice he pulls me closer. After the flash I pull away, pretending to be too excited to stand still. That really wasn't too far from the truth, but I did say I didn't trust myself with this man. We start following the crowd of people going towards the shops. There are so many places to choose from, but they are pretty much like shops we have at home and I'm a little disappointed. I think I was expecting some 'island flavor'. Keith tells us a little about the area and some of his favorite places to shop. We go to this little shop off the main street and find some really good deals on jewelry. I am amazed at the prices. I find a cute bracelet and necklace for Gabrielle. I even buy myself a pair of earrings. Aniyah buys herself an ankle bracelet and then we walk back outside. Keith takes us a few more blocks away from the crowds and tells us about this restaurant he and his wife found. It is quaint with that 'island flavor' I was expecting to see. There are bright colors everywhere, but the lighting is low. The hostess is barefoot and her hair is in braids that hang down her back. She seats us and brings us a drink that Keith says we'll love. It tastes like soda, but sweeter and fruity.

"My wife and I took a wrong turn and came in here to ask for directions." Keith explains when Aniyah asks how he knew this place was here.

"The owner is actually a Christian. She told my wife and me some things about ourselves that no one knew. She was pretty amazing."

"Are you sure she's not into voodoo? You can never tell on these islands. I hear so much stuff about other gods and religions," says Aniyah.

"I'm sure. Marla actually quoted scriptures and told us about the church she started here. We don't have time to actually go there, but I didn't get the impression she was lying."

"Well, the devil can quote scriptures, too," I say agreeing with Aniyah. "You still have to be mindful of where we are and the influences around us."

"Well, let me just say you were warned. Here she comes." He looks towards the back of the room where a small statured woman is pushing aside a bead curtain and walking towards us. Her clothes are a mixture of colors and patterns, seemingly unrelated, but surprisingly fitting. She wore beads in her hair and her necklace and bracelet had beads hanging from them.

"Hi, my brother," she greets Keith with a hug and kisses him on his cheek. "You have come back to visit Marla while your lady rests."

"You know I couldn't come this close and not see you," Keith smiles and offers her his chair. She sits down and he grabs a chair from another table, pulls it over and sits down.

"These are your friends, Brother Keith?" She asks, looking Aniyah and me over pretty thoroughly.

"Yes, this is Mildred and Aniyah. We met on our trip down," he introduces us.

"It's nice to meet you. You have a nice little place here," I say.

"Yes and this drink is delicious," Aniyah offers.

"You are a spirited lady, you are," she tells me.

"Excuse me?"

"You are very strong in the spirit," she says. "I felt you when you walked in. I came out to see who you were."

I just look at her dumbfounded. "I have something for you. God wants you to know that you will live and not die. He has purpose for you. You wonder about the storm in your dream, but you were not moved. It washed over you, but you and the foundation you were on was sure. Remember that. You will weather the storm. You'll come out fine."

I sit there with my mouth open. I didn't tell anyone about that dream. I got busy and forgot. How would she know that?! And I never realized that in my dream the only thing that moved was the storm. Wow! Who is this woman? I have to know if she is for real or not.

"Yes, I confess Jesus Christ. He rose from the dead and is now my Lord and Savior," she smirks. "I know you want to test the spirit in me. I would, too, if I was you. God is real to me. He tells me things and I tell you. No one who comes here does by accident. I have this gift from a child. My family thought I was a seer, but I was always different. I try to help and uplift all people. My family wanted to make money with my gift, but I refused. When a missionary came here, she told me about God and my life made sense. That's when I started the church. There are hundreds of us now, all serving God. It's good."

"That's wonderful," smiles Aniyah.

"You'll be okay, too. There's strength in you untapped. Find your purpose and you'll find your courage. He forgives you. You can move forward into your future without looking over your shoulder. All's forgotten," Marla tells Aniyah.

She starts crying. I feel tears well up in my eyes, too. I am so overwhelmed by this woman. "There is still more for you to discover, Mildred. You have only tasted a bite of what God has for you. And when you go up, a new man will go with you. You be blessed." With that she hugs us all and goes back into the room behind the curtain. I look at my watch and stand up. "We need to start getting back. We don't want to miss the boat."

Aniyah wipes her eyes and gathers her things. I see that Keith is watching me. Yeah, I heard what she said about a new man, but that doesn't mean it's Keith, does it? We hurry out and start walking back towards the pier. I dart into a store on the main street and get presents for Samuel and Mariah. I don't have a clue what to get for Jonas, so I decide to get him something off the ship. We make it back to the dock and climb on before the boat pulls off. Our trip back is only slightly less bumpy, but we make it safely and get back onto our ship. We scan our keys, show our passports and then head back up to our rooms. We say goodbye as Aniyah gets off the elevator first. After the door closes, Keith turns to me and says, "What did you think of Marla?"

"She was very interesting. Nice." I offer. I know where this is going, but I am trying to steer away from it.

"She certainly said some positive things about you. I guess, now you'll believe me when I tell you someone's 'amazing'."

"Well, you were right. She was 'amazing'."

"And you are, too, Mildred." He reaches out and turns my face towards his. "You are so amazing." How many of you know God to be a prayer answering God? I do. The elevator stops and the doors open. I hurry out of there and holler, "Bye" over my shoulder. My room key is already in my hand, so I swipe it quick and dart into my cabin, shutting the door behind me. "Thank you, Lord for making a way of escape." There is a knock on my door. "Uh-oh".

I turn around and grab the doorknob. I turn it and, of course, Keith is standing there. "Are you trying to run from me?" He jokes.

Not you, just fleeing fornication. "Of course not," I say aloud. "We just have to hurry so we can get to dinner on time, that's all." Keith pushes the door open wider and steps towards me. I back up. Stupid, stupid, stupid! Now he's in my room. He shuts the door. "Mildred, can I talk to you about something? Just you and me without Aniyah?" He asks.

"I guess. W-what's up?" I stammer, trying to look nonchalant, while this sexy fine man is permeating my room with his manliness.

"Please, sit down," he gestures towards the bed. *Oh no! Uh-uhn! You are so not going to hem me up like that!* I think, while my body betrays me and sits down. He comes over and sits down next to me. Yeah, you heard me. And I'm still sitting on the bed, too, like this can end well. "Mildred, I know you are married. I respect you and your commitment to your husband. I just can't help what I've been feeling since I met you. I believe it's fate that brought us together. I came on this cruise to say goodbye to my wife and found you. I can't believe that's just coincidence." He reaches for my hand and takes it in his.

"Keith, I think you must feel what you feel, but you have to know that this can't happen. I'm married. I won't break my vows. I can't." I pull my hand away.

"I'm just asking you to listen to your heart. Can you honestly tell me you don't feel anything for me?"

"Honestly, no. But it's not enough to make me do something I might regret," I admit.

"But you heard Marla. She's never wrong. She said you were going to have a 'new man'," he counters.

"But she didn't say that 'new man' was you. Look Keith, I don't want to make this any harder than it is, but we have to part ways. I can't continue spending time with you knowing how you feel about me. Plus, I can't keep exposing myself to temptation. There is a scripture in James chapter 1 that says we're tempted when we're drawn away by our own desires, then sin, then death. I just can't do this." I move to stand and he stops me.

"Mildred, are you sure? I will wait for you if I have to," he pleads.

"Don't wait. I'm sure." I stand and walk to the door.

"Mildred, please. I need you." Keith hangs his head and starts to cry. Oh, Lord! No one ever cried for me! Jonas never cried for me, pleaded, begged or anything. Help me, Holy Ghost! I feel my heart melting and I want so bad to comfort him, but I know I have to be strong. This is for all the women who ever faced Mr. Sure Seems like the Right One to me and if Not Won't It be Fun Trying. Like Sophia said in *Color Purple*, 'He ain't worth it. He ain't worth it'.

"Goodbye, Keith." And with that I open the door. He stands up and slowly walks out. I push the door closed and the lock clicks. It almost sounds like the key turning in the chains that have me bound to a man that acts like I'm his enemy. I hope I didn't let a good thing get away only to settle for what has already left.

April 5,

Dinner was crazy. I had to explain to Aniyah what happened when Keith didn't show up for dinner. She told me I did the right thing. But that's not the crazy part. Crazy was Sister Abigail asking me to step outside while we were waiting for our entrees. She said she saw Keith leaving my room. Uh-oh! She grilled me like a four star general! I explained to her that nothing happened. I told her that he wanted to talk to me and kind of pushed his way into my room. I couldn't be rude, could I? 'Yes!' She said, emphatically. 'You certainly can be rude. Especially when it comes to matters of impropriety.' I told her he felt some designs, but that I quickly squashed his male ego and gave him the boot and sent him packing with his tail between his legs— not in those exact words, of course—but she told me she was glad I handled it and if she hadn't seen him crying with her own eyes, she would have confronted both of us, especially after finding him outside of my room for a second time. And, well, that the real reason she wanted to talk to me was because her committee took a vote and decided to double my honorarium. She handed me another envelope and explained that the MC usually receives more than the presenters, and they felt that I deserved double for stepping up and presenting two workshops, as well as being MC. Shut up! I opened that envelope and let's just say I felt really blessed! Hallelujah! Of course, I will definitely pay tithes. It's only fitting. Whoo-hoo! I must have passed the test. Thank You, Lord! Bless God and goodnight.

When *Endeavor* docks, I am a little deflated and excited at the same time. I miss my kids, so I really want to see them, but I'm not all that sure about Jonas and how he might act. I sort of hope he acts like he missed me, even a little. I bought him a leather briefcase and portfolio with a "W" for Wilson engraved on it, for when he goes to minister. I even recognize that I did it out of guilt after what happened with Keith and also to try to ease things between us. I shouldn't have to go through this, but I'm working on it. Besides, I still have the bus ride home to work some things out in my head. This trip has shown me so many things about myself, both the good and the bad. I haven't seen Keith anymore since I told him goodbye. It's for the best, I guess. That night I sat up wondering what would have happened if I gave in. Who really would have known? And trust me; God gave me 'what for'. I felt like He laid me across His lap and spanked me. So many scriptures came at me and when I said, "But, God…" He just flooded me with compassion and love and that just ended that. How can you argue with God's love? He made me see that to sin pales in comparison to wanting to please Him.

I hand my suitcase and garment bag to the driver to put in the luggage compartment under the bus. I keep the leather bag with me. It cost too much to trust that someone won't 'accidentally' take it. Aniyah is already on the bus in the very row we rode down on; I squeeze past her and reclaim my seat next to the window. I glance out at the port at all the people darting around and do a double-take when I see Keith. I look again and he's not there. Maybe I just imagined it. I turn away from the window, because Lot's wife comes to mind. I don't want to look back regretting what could never be. I've been trying to cut back on salt in my life anyway; my blood pressure is raising enough with the stress I'm under.

The conversation on the ride back is about how this was the best conference ever. I only respond when spoken to directly because I don't want to toot my own horn. Truth be told, it's God's horn. I'm still thinking about what Jonas is going to say when I get home. I'm sure someone's told him already. I can't imagine the way these women like to talk, that no one's called him or my pastors. I bet the ones with international calling plans spread the word days ago. Anyway, I know this was a great thing for me. If nothing else, I have a new friend, some extra money and I got to get some practice on the church stage without a safety net.

Our ride home seems much shorter than the ride down, and before I know it, we are pulling into the church parking lot. I left my car here, because I really didn't expect Jonas to pick me up. He's usually too busy or something. I get my bags, put them in the trunk, hug Aniyah and promise to call her in a couple days and I drive off. I already made arrangements for the kids to stay with my sister in law until tomorrow, and even though I miss them, I head for home. I just need to unwind from my trip and get my focus back on my home life.

I pull up in the driveway and Jonas' car isn't there. He knew I was coming back today; and I called him and told him the time I would be getting in. I don't know what I was thinking. I guess I expected him to at least be home. And it's late! He should be here. I'm sure I'll get some plausible sounding excuse as to why he wasn't at home--if I get one at all. He'll make is sound so important and reasonable and I should believe it and not question him. I get my bags out of the trunk and drag them up to the door. I unlock the door and push it open, flipping on lights as I go upstairs. I put my suitcase into the closet, vowing to empty it tomorrow and I start pulling off my clothes. I am just overwhelmed with exhaustion. It's like the air is filled with heaviness. I flop down on the bed face forward and grab a pillow and pull it up under my head. The thought of turning on the television crosses my mind, but I can't make myself move. I feel oppressed. It's like a weight pinning me to the bed. I know it's a spirit. And I know what you're supposed to do with spirits—cast them out. I push myself up off the bed. I keep a bottle of anointing oil in my dresser drawer. I get it and start anointing the door posts over all the bedrooms. I also anoint the beds. I start praying aloud and binding and rebuking spirits and demons and praising God for cleaning out my house. After I go downstairs and anoint the rooms down there, I come back upstairs and anoint Jonas' pillow, pajamas, slippers and anything else of his laying out. I put the oil away and climb back into bed. I can feel a big difference in the atmosphere. "Now this is how my house should feel—peaceful," I tell the room. I get the remote off the nightstand and turn on the TV. I flip through a few channels until I come to TBN. Joel Osteen is on, so I leave it there and lay back. This is a treat for me because when Jonas and I are in the room together, he usually watches what he wants, and we like different things. I like sci-fi, some comedies, old movies and religious programs. Jonas likes real life dramas and murder mysteries. I usually wait until he falls asleep and change the channel.

I watch TV until my eyes get too heavy and then the TV watches me as I sleep. At some point, Jonas comes home. I roll over and he's lying there. I wonder briefly when he got in and where he was and then sleep overtakes me again. I sleep so peacefully that I actually sleep past eight. When I sit up, Jonas is already gone. I peek out the window and see that his car is gone. "Where in the world he got to go this early on a Saturday morning?" I get up and start getting myself together before I go get the kids. I pull my bags out of the closet and empty them. I put the dirty clothes in the hamper and stack the suitcase back in the closet. I go downstairs and get some coffee and start the washer. I sit down and enjoy the quiet, reflecting on the past week and even the past few years of my life. They haven't always been happy, where my marriage is concerned, but I've enjoyed my children, my job, my friends and church life. That seems like enough good going on to give God glory. It could be worse. I haven't had it as bad as some people living with abusers, whether it's domestic or alcohol or drugs, so I can thank God for that. I feel like I can get through even this dry spell. I just have to keep everything in perspective. I know what I want out of my life—to please God and fulfill my purpose; to raise God-fearing, God-loving, saved children who are successful; and to have a wonderful, loving marriage with a man who adores me and whom I adore. Honestly, I have a long way to go on that one, but it's not impossible. "God, I want Jonas to consider me before himself. Is that too much to ask?" I pray. "I believe in salvation, I believe I'll be with you in heaven when I die, but I need help believing my husband loves me or even cares anything about me. Can you please help us! We have to get it right. God, don't let my kids be affected by our mishandling and mismanagement of our relationship."

After some time of devotion and bible reading, I put my clothes in the dryer and get dressed. I eat a boiled egg, since there isn't any food in the house. Jonas usually doesn't buy groceries and since he was home alone, there was no need. So I choose to go to the store before I pick up the kids. It's less hectic when I go by myself. And since I have some extra cash, I decide to stock up on everything—paper products, soap, toothpaste, diapers, wipes, cereal, canned food, vegetables, meat and snacks. Of course I made sure it was on sale, but it felt good to be able to buy things and not worry about the bill. I wish I could live like that all the time. I've come to realize that it's the little things that make me happy—seeing my children well-taken care of, getting things for myself every once in a while, having my husband smile and laugh with me or even kiss me. It doesn't take much. I've never needed fancy clothes or jewelry. I valued the poems Jonas used to write me more than the earrings and watches he bought. I guess my lack of enthusiasm for gold trinkets is why he stopped buying them. I had a hard time keeping up with them. I've lost a bracelet and a necklace, so far--accidentally, of course—but to him that meant I didn't want or like it, even though they fell off because the clasps broke.

Well, I've come to acknowledge that if I want my marriage to get better, I will have to do better. I know God can help me with me, but it will take both of us to get this relationship back in order. I know I'm all in, but after what Trish told me, I wonder how committed he is to me. I'll just have to trust God. Maybe I need a sign that I'm on the right track. I know a lot of women wouldn't put up with a man coming and going the way he does. You can't put your confidence and faith in that. You never know if they're being faithful or what they're doing. It's hard to build trust that way. But the second you call them on it, then they want to start tripping.

I go over to check the mail that came since I've been gone. We keep it on a small table in the front hallway. I pick it up and see that it's mostly junk mail, thankfully, and I toss it in the small trash can under the table. A piece of paper catches my eye and I pull it out. It's a letter and a flyer inviting me to speak at a conference in a month. I didn't put it there, so Jonas must have opened it and threw it away when he saw it was for me. I can't believe he would do that. No, that's not true. That is something he would do, for sure. I read the letter and see that it's a women's conference being held at the city's convention center. There is a contact person and a number to call. I go into the kitchen and pick up the phone and call. When the answering machine picks up, I leave my name and my cell phone number and that I would be honored to be a part of the conference. Now, let him try and stop me. I know I'm livid, but God said I could be angry if I didn't sin. I put the letter into my purse and go out the door to pick up my kids. I hope the drive is long enough for me to calm down. I would hate for them to pick up on my mood and think I'm upset with them.

The church is packed this Sunday morning. There are more visitors than usual and I am on time. Praise God! After I picked up the kids, I bought Chinese takeout and went home. We ate, watched TV together, they took baths and I laid out their clothes to wear. So when we got up late this morning, getting dressed didn't take as long. Now, I've been laying clothes out the night before for a long time to no avail, but it just worked out this time. I hope we can keep the trend going. I have a few minutes to talk to Pastor and First Lady before service and they tell me they want me to share highlights about the cruise. I tell them that would be fine and I go to my seat.

Praise and worship is so blessed. It seems like God is in every nook and cranny of this sanctuary. Even Jonas is getting into the praise. It's amazing to me that while I'm giving God His due that my mind can still take in everything around me and process what I'm seeing. I see Trish waving her hands, but her eyes are on this lady I've never seen before. She's tall and slender with long straight hair and a form fitting skirt and a stylish ruffled shirt and shrug. I figure Trish must be hating on how nice she looks, and I go back to praising. But then I see how much more animated Jonas is and I catch him looking at the same young lady and my "spidey-senses" start tingling. I hope he's not putting on a show for this lady. "Lord, bring this back to me later so that I can deal with it," I pray under my breath. I got a feeling that whether I remember on my own or God brings it back to me, I will be dealing with this again—and sooner rather than later.

As everyone settles down and start taking their seats, Pastor Gilliam gets up and tells us that we are entering a new phase of ministry and that we are moving into another dimension. "This ministry is taking the world by storm, church," he says. "We are being spoken well of all over town and abroad. We just need to be ready for the harvest," he pauses, and looks around the room. "I've been speaking with many pastors of late and they have been reporting that Word of Truth is making waves in the spirit." The congregation claps and shouts out praises. When it quiets down again, he says, "Sister Mildred, come on over here." He holds out his hand and I walk over and take it. Pastor Evelyn comes up behind me and puts her arm around my waist. I knew he was going to call me up, but now I'm just as nervous as a country mouse in a room full of rocking chairs, especially once I make eye contact with Jonas. We haven't talked about the cruise at all. I figured if he wanted to know how it was, he would ask me. Plus, I still feel a little guilty about Keith. Jonas could ask what the temperature was and I would probably spill my guts and tell him everything, even though nothing happened—really. Anyway, I turn my attention back to my pastor and he's telling everyone about how wonderful a job I did representing them. He hands me the mike and tells me to take my time.

"Good morning, church," I say. There is enthusiastic reply, and I continue, "God is good!"

"Yes He is!" The congregation replies.

"Well, it's hard to describe how great everything was. The whole thing pales when compared to God and how He moved on that ship. I really wish everyone could have gone and experienced what I experienced. Souls were saved and lives were changed—and for the better. I appreciate the honor that was placed upon me by my pastors, allowing me to represent them. And I thank God for using me to introduce His Son to so many. And not everyone who accepted Christ was with our group. There were many different other groups who wanted to see what was going on and tripped up on salvation." The people laugh and holler out "amens". "God is so good. He showed me through this experience that we should take every opportunity to tell others about Jesus. There are so many hungry and thirsty souls who can only be satisfied by the Bread of Life and the Living Water. It's not about us, Church. We need to get out of self, get in God and go do what we were created to do." At this point, I'm feeling it.

"Some of us are so hung up on titles, prestige and what others think, and none of that matters to those lost souls. They could care less what you want to be called or how many degrees you have or even what church you go to. They just want someone to care enough about them, to love on them and to feed them. They don't want fake or phony. You have to truly have a heart for God's people. If you're just trying to heap up praise to yourself, you might as well quit. It won't last. You're not doing anybody any good, and you're not doing God any favors. He can get it done without you. He wants the glory. He deserves the glory. And that's what I give Him. Every success and blessing and good report from this cruise, all the praise and glory go to God. Come on and bless the Lord in this place." I step back from the podium and throw up my hands and praise God. I see Jonas looking at me, but I can't react to it because the spirit is all over me.

"Amen, that's why we have been getting such glowing reports. Pastor Evelyn, I know we were hearing from God to elevate this young lady. You can't fabricate that kind of anointing. Either you have it or you don't. And Sister Mildred, you have it. Praise God."

After church, Jonas and I stand with the pastors as members of the congregation come up to greet us. I stand on the left side of Pastor Evelyn and Jonas stands to the right of Pastor Gilliam. It looks orchestrated, but I get the sense that he's trying to distance himself from me. Oh, well. I think I've had about enough of being "aren't you Jonas Wilson's wife?" anyway. Now I can be who I am without hiding behind someone else. It's very liberating. Going on that cruise opened something up inside of me and I don't want to close that door. I think there is more there and I'm excited to see what comes out next.

Awakening

On Monday morning, I come into work excited and ready to start my day. Instead of my usual cup of coffee, I get hot tea. So far, I've lost about ten pounds and I want to keep the momentum going. Plus, I feel much better and my clothes fit better. And I think I look better. The most amazing thing is that I don't care if Jonas notices or not. I like feeling good about myself. I feel like I can take on the world--and Jonas, too.

I go through my in-box and prioritize my work. I have to go over the budget so paychecks can go out to the maintenance staff and us, too.

The door opens and Judy and Trudy walk in. I say, "Hey, girls."

"Well, look at what the waves washed up," smiles Trudy.

"You look great, Mildred. You are positively glowing! Are you sure Jonas didn't get on the ship with you?" jokes Judy.

"Girl, don't even play. How was everything last week?" I ask.

As they settle in, they get somber expressions and I start wondering what's wrong. "Girls, what's going on?" I ask, with concern in my voice.

"Well, you remember how Nora didn't come in before you left?" Judy whispers.

"Yeah, I just figured she was taking a personal day. Is she okay?"

"That was the day she found out she was pregnant. She was waiting until she was further along before she told us, but she had a miscarriage, Mildred," reveals Trudy.

"Oh, no! That's terrible! How is she doing?" I ask.

"Not good. She's taking it pretty hard. Craig has been calling us and keeping us informed," Trudy tells me.

"She won't get out of the bed. He's afraid for her. She's not eating, just crying all day."

"I'm so sorry to hear that. Have you tried to see her or talk to her?"

"She won't talk to us on the phone and when we tried to visit, she told Craig not to let us in. He's so worried; he just does what she asks to keep her from getting even more upset than she already is." Judy shakes her head and sighs. "We sent a card and we signed for you, but I can't say she even read it."

"Well, I'm going over there and talk to her. She can't just lie up there all day making herself sick with grief."

"She won't see you, Mildred. We tried," says Trudy.

"Well, I'm not leaving until I talk to her face to face. Even if all I can do is hug her and let her cry, she's going to know she's not by herself."

When lunch time comes around, I get in my car and drive over to Craig and Nora's house. I was last here after her bridal shower. I helped bring her gifts home. I pull into the driveway and get out. I walk up to the front door and knock. After a few moments, I hear Craig's voice asking, "Who is it?"

"It's me, Mildred," I answer.

He opens the door and greets me. "I don't think she'll want to see you," he tells me. "She's not crying as much today, but she's just lying in the bed and staring at the wall. I don't know what to do. She won't talk to me. I asked her if she wanted to talk to a therapist, but she just yelled at me to get out because I didn't understand what she was going through." Craig runs his fingers through his hair in frustration.

"Why don't you go get yourself some air. Go for a drive and I'll talk to her." He nods and grabs his keys. "Call me if you need to. I won't be too far."

"It'll be okay, Craig. Don't worry." I walk down the hall as he opens the front door and lets himself out. I poke my head into the last room on the left and see Nora lying on her back, eyes open, gazing up at the ceiling. Quiet tears are rolling down her face into her hair.

"Hello, Nora," I call out softly. She starts and turns her face from me and wipes the tears.

"What are you doing here? Where's Craig? I told him I didn't want to see anyone!"

"I know. He told me, but I'm your friend, Nora. I can't sit by and let you tear yourself up inside over something you had no control over."

"What do you know? You don't know what I'm going through! Just go and leave me alone!" She yells.

"I can't leave you alone. I know you're hurting, that's why I'm here." I walk towards the bed and sit on the edge of it.

"Mildred, please just go. I want to be alone," she begs.

"No, you don't need to be alone. You need a friend and a shoulder. That's why I'm here."

"You can't know what I'm going through, you have kids!"

"Yes, I have three beautiful children and I thank God for them, but if all things were equal, it would have been five," I admit.

"Five? So you lost two?" She asks.

"Yes, I lost two. The first one was devastating to me. I thought I had done something wrong. I blamed myself. I tried to go back and track everything I had done to find where I messed up. And Jonas just wasn't there for me. He probably felt some remorse, too, but he didn't share it with me. So, I felt by myself. I tried to go on and accept it and keep moving, but I just broke down. I was so torn up inside," I reveal to her.

"What did you do?" She asked me sitting up.

"I went to see a therapist to help me put everything in perspective, but the most important thing I did was pray. I cried out to God and shared my pain and hurt with Him, and it was like He cried with me. I felt His love and His presence so strong. But He spoke to me and told me that He allowed it because I couldn't handle it at the time. I was having so many issues with my marriage, my money and my kids. I was a mess. To add a baby to that would have probably broke me. I was on the verge of a nervous breakdown, and God knew I didn't need any more on me. The bible says that He won't 'put more on you than you can bear.'

"But what kind of God would kill an innocent baby? Why would He do that to me?" She cries.

"God is a giver of life. He doesn't take life, but He will receive it unto Himself. The adversary, the devil, is the one who likes to take life. The bible says he comes to 'steal, kill, and destroy.' See, Christ came so that you could have an abundant life. I know I never talked much to you before about my faith in God, but let me tell you, it's what got me through some difficult times in my life. The love God has for me has more than made up for what I thought I lost. When I had the second miscarriage, I didn't even tell Jonas about it, because he didn't give me the support I needed the first time. Right or wrong, I made that choice. I can't take it back now, but I know God didn't abandon me. He didn't throw it in my face or make me feel like I wasn't a real woman or that I was weak. He just wanted me to give Him my burdens. He wanted me to draw closer to Him and that's what I did. I prayed more, read my bible and developed a deeper relationship with Him. Once I got stronger in Him, and I saw situations in my life change, Mariah came. The other times were not in the timing of God, but that little girl is a blessing to me. I thank God every day for her. I didn't have any complications or issues—everything went smoothly. Now if I had had those other two, who knows what could have gone wrong. I could have lost them or myself in childbirth or they could have had birth defects that would have drained me even more. I just believe and trust God's judgment when it comes to my life. He loves me and He loves you, too."

"I don't know, Mildred. It still hurts me."

"I don't expect you to just get over it. It's going to take some time, and it's going to take you giving God your pain. He can handle it. Even if you get a little upset with Him, He can take it. He'll love you through it."

"I'm not a Christian like you, why would He love me?"

"Because He knew you before the foundations of the world. He's always loved you. You just didn't know it. But I'm telling you, if you give your heart to Him, you'll open yourself up to that love. If you need proof that He loves you, look at Craig. That man has stayed by your side this whole time. He's a good man. Even when you pushed him away, he stayed. He's hurting too, but he's also hurting because he can't help you and he wants to. You give your life to Christ today, and He will help the two of you through this. I know your relationship will be even stronger. What do you say?" I ask her.

"I just don't want to hurt like this anymore. Make it stop," she cries.

I hug her and I pray to God to comfort her heart and bring her peace. After her crying subsides, I lead her in a prayer of salvation. When we finish, Craig walks in and she stands up and hugs him. They both cry together and I pray quietly for God to be with them both and show Himself mighty in their lives. I also lead Craig to Christ, and I instruct them both to spend time praying and reading the bible together, starting in the book of John. They thank me as I get up to leave and walk me to the door. I give them both a great big hug, get in my car and drive back to work. When I pull into the parking lot, the presence of God falls on me so heavy I can't get out of the car. I just sit and bawl. I can't do anything but sit there and cry. I cry for the loss of life, for restoration of hope, for the years Jonas and I wasted being selfish, for my kids, for myself, for everyone who doesn't know Christ, for not putting God first. After my tears dry up, I feel so free. It's like I got a new lease on life. The heaviness lifts and I feel so refreshed. I have a sense of urgency in me. I feel purpose driven, like I matter. Like I have a job to do and God needs me to get it done, but I don't feel like I'm alone in it. It's like I've awakened from a bad dream, but instead of being anxious and scared, I feel rested and ready. "Okay, God. Here we go."

The next few weeks fly by so fast. It seems like every time I blink, Jonas and I are at somebody's church service. And the funny thing is, even though he would rather go without me, I make him look so good that he walks a little taller. We get so many compliments. I just say 'thank you' and keep moving. At home it's a little different. He's not really saying much, but more than he was before the cruise. Instead of getting all upset and bent out of shape about it, I just go about my business like nothing's wrong. I caught Gabbi staring at me one day when I was fixing dinner. I was humming to myself and I looked up and she had this puzzled look on her face. I smiled and went back to my humming. She just shook her head and walked out of the kitchen. I prayed for her that God would keep her protected and keep her in His will. I gave her to Him. I actually did that. It was always hard to do before. I would give my problems to God only to find out that I took them back, but something changed down inside of me. I have a peace I really can't explain. I don't think that means that everything is perfect and that I won't have any more problems, but I don't have to face them alone. God has my back, my front and all my sides. It's a good thing too because after dinner Jonas tells me we have a service to go to the same day as the women's conference at the convention center.

"I can't go," I tell him.

"What do you mean you can't go? What you got to do that's more important?" He asks.

"I have to speak at a women's conference—the one at the convention center."

He looks at me with this stupid look, because he knows he threw that paper away. I'm just waiting to hear what excuse he comes up with. "We already have an engagement. You just gonna have to call and cancel. This was confirmed long before that conference. Besides, you can't be speaking at conferences all the time. You need to be in churches speaking. The Gilliams are expecting both of us to be there."

"Well, I'll call and tell them I'm committed elsewhere." I get up to pick up the phone and Jonas reaches over and snatches it from me. "You need to stop smelling yourself and do what I told you to do." He sneers.

"Jonas, the conference is in two days and you're just now telling me about this church service. If it was that important for me to be there, then you should have said something sooner. I'm speaking at the conference. You speak at the service." I get up to leave the room and he jumps up and blocks me.

"I don't know what's gotten into you, but I'm the head of this house, and my wife isn't going to disrespect me and do whatever she wants to do."

"But it's okay for you to disrespect me? You do whatever you want to do, whenever you want to, with whomever you want to and you have a problem with me?" I was indignant. "Jonas, I never do anything you don't know about, I'm never anywhere you can't find me and you know everyone I talk to, but I can't say the same for you. So much of your life is a secret to me. I hear things, but I don't throw it in your face. I don't follow you or call over town looking for you. But you say I'm disrespecting you." I stand up a little taller, with my chest out and my shoulders back. "It's not about you or me, but it's about God and about those kids up there. I have work to do that is not subject to your approval, but to God's."

"Don't be trying to act all high and mighty now. I've been doing this longer than you. I know what's going on. You're getting power struck. If you think you're going to go around talking to me like that then you better think again."

"The only power that matters is the power of God, and since I know where my help comes from, I can keep it all in perspective. But what about you? How many phone numbers have you gotten from women caught up on your position? How many women run up to you after church to shake hands with 'the preacher'? Do you push them away? Do you discourage them? Do you tell them about me or do you enjoy it?" I ask, getting angry. "The only person who's been acting 'high and mighty' around here is you and since I refuse to let you walk all over me anymore, now you have a problem with me. Then I tell you what you do, pray about it! Give me to God. He knows how to treat me better than you do, anyway!" I walk out of the room, down the hallway, through the kitchen and out the back door to sit on the porch.

While I sit there fuming, I hear the front door slam shut. I cradle my head in my hands, and I realize for the first time that I'm angry, but I'm not blubbering. I stood up for myself. Good or bad, I realize that I drew a line in the sand. Jonas is not allowed to disrespect me like that anymore. I don't have any idea what's going to happen after this, but I know I'm not backing down and cowering like some weakling. To do that would be to undermine everything that God is doing in me. He's making me bolder and more confident in who He is and therefore defining who I am in Him. I have a little project that I've been working on since the cruise, and I can't be some weak little girl who's scared of her husband. My pastor gave me permission to start a women's group in my home. I've invited my coworkers and some of the women I met on the cruise and opened it up to whoever they wanted to bring with them. I have to maintain my focus. There are a lot of women who need someone to talk to and help them through some of the situations we face by taking them to the word.

I feel like my encounter with Nora allowed this to be birthed. It was always there, but it incubated and took shape after I saw her. "God, if I'm wrong, allow me the opportunity to fix it," I say aloud, "but please bless this women's group and the conference and even the service on Saturday. Please help Jonas and me to work together as one instead of against each other. You know my heart. I don't want this confusion. I put my marriage in Your capable hands. In Jesus' name, amen."

"Momma, why do you stay?" Gabbi says, stepping through the door and sitting down beside me.

"I guess you heard me and your daddy. Baby, I'm sorry you have to see our flaws. I wanted so much to protect you from our issues. Your father isn't perfect and neither am I. We mess up."

"But he talks to you like a dog and you just let him! Are you scared of him?"

"I've spent a lot of years trying to figure out just what it is I'm really afraid of. I thought it was him leaving me. I was afraid no one else would want me. I was afraid that I would fail you guys; that I wouldn't know who I was supposed to be--so many things. But God is showing me there is more to me than meets the eye. I'm stronger than I realized, because He's on the inside of me. Gabbi, I don't want you to stop loving your father. You only get one, and I know he loves you. You respect him, because God commands it, but when you see something you don't like or understand, pray about it; and you can always talk to me. I love you all. I guess I just wanted to insulate you from all the bad stuff, but life isn't perfect, and you need to see how to cope and overcome." I hug her tight and we just sit there holding each other.

"I'm glad you stood up to him instead of crying this time." I kiss her forehead and stand up. "Yeah, me too." I reply.

"You need to get in bed. You have school in the morning, and I have work. Come on." We go back into the house, and I turn the lights off on my way upstairs. Gabbi hugs me again and goes into her room. I smile as I walk into my room. I undress and get in bed. I fall asleep so quickly and peacefully, I don't even hear what time Jonas comes in or feel him standing there watching me sleep.

J.U.S.T.

The conference went great and I got to promote my women's group 'Just Us Sistahs Talking' or J.U.S.T. for short. I had so many promises to attend that I decided to move it from my house to the church. It was probably for the best anyway, with everything going on with me and Jonas. He probably would have sabotaged it or something, anyway. Aniyah, Trish, Sister Emma, Sister Abigail, Nora, Judy, Trudy and their guests all show up at the church. I chose Thursday night because that's the one night the church is free. We set up chairs in the social hall to make it more informal and cozy. A lot of other women I don't recognize show up. They are wearing the name tags that I set out by the door so that we could call each other by name. Another lady shows up that I do recognize. Trish comes over to me and tells me that was the woman that Jonas told we were divorcing and the same one he was eyeballing during service. "She's pretty," I say. Trish just rolls her eyes and sucks her teeth.

"Tell me how pretty she is when your kids are calling her 'momma'," she fusses.

"Girl, you're crazy. Behave! Let's have a good time and not dwell on that. She's here and maybe we can deal with that issue discreetly without calling her out."

"Okay, it's your party, but you know how I feel. I say cut the fool loose. You are wasting too much of your energy and life on him, anyway. You deserve better. Maybe I can hunt Keith down for you," she teases. "He sounds like he knows your value."

"Girl, hush. That is a dead issue. Let's go get the hors d'oeuvres so you can stuff something in your mouth before you slip up and let the wrong person hear you."

"You're getting right bossy and mouthy lately," she wrinkles her nose up at me. "About time!" She laughs. "I think I like this new you."

"Yeah, I'm starting to like her, too. Now come on!" We go into the kitchen and get the food. We have mostly finger foods—ham biscuits, wing dings, fruit and veggie trays, cookies, and punch. I didn't want to go overboard with the food, but I did want to entice people to come. I have Gabbi and Trish's niece watching a couple of the women's kids in the nursery. They would only do it if we promised to take them to get manicures and pedicures. Why not? I think we got off cheap.

We bring the food out and place it on the table. Once everything is ready, we instruct the ladies to go ahead and get something to eat. I go over to my chair and pick up my agenda. I had typed up the order on my lunch break at work and just wanted to refresh my mind so that we stayed on course. Hopefully we can have a good time and still get out at a decent hour. I pray everyone enjoys themselves. I realize I have the same fluttery feeling in my stomach I had when I did the first conference. I thought I would be more comfortable since the setting was so informal. Oh, well. It's too late to back out now. I put my paper down and stand to go introduce myself to the ladies that I don't know.

The chairs are set up in a circle, and I plan to have the ladies pair up with someone they don't know or didn't come with as the first order of business. As the women finish up their food and it looks like everyone who is coming is there, I call the women to attention.

"Hello, ladies. I'm so glad you all decided to come out tonight. I really feel that it is God-ordained that we come together like this. I call this 'Bible study meets support group'." A few chuckles erupt around the room. "I know as women we are naturally sociable beings, but I found out that we are and can be as non-communicative as men in certain situations. So, let's open in prayer and then go over a few things before the fun can begin. Father God, we come to You tonight with praise and honor for Your goodness to each and every one of us. Lord, we thank You for keeping us, blessing us, sustaining us and allowing us the opportunity to assemble together to collectively strengthen our relationships with You and each other. Bless this time and bind the enemy and his attempts to pervert what You have blessed and ordained. Allow there to be no misunderstandings, miscommunications, or mishandling of Your word. Allow each of us to be ministered to in our individual areas of need. We give You praise glory and honor in the Name of Your most precious Son, Jesus, amen."

Several 'amens' reverberate around the room. All eyes look up at me expectantly. "Well, the first order of business is for me to explain a little more about 'J.U.S.T.' Some of you already know that the acronym stands for "Just Us Sistahs Talking." I wanted to have a forum where we as women can express our concerns with our 'sistahs' and get some support and solutions. This is not a pity party where misery loves company, but it's an opportunity for us to share our issues and get real help. When we kick it with our girls at work, we are just gossiping. Most of the time, we leave that conversation the same way. Nothing has changed. But 'JUST' is our opportunity to come up with solutions in the Word to things that concern us, to really communicate our hearts and get some practical help from one another, especially if you've gone through the same thing and made it out on the other side. Also, what is discussed here is confidential. I want to stress that the things shared here are someone's personal issues. They should only be discussed here or with someone you choose to be your prayer partner who will help you and support you when we are not together. Our goal is not to tear down one another, but to uplift and encourage each other in our walk. Any questions so far?" I wait, but no hands go up.

"Okay, now back to communication. I need for everyone who came together to stand up." I wait as nearly everyone on my left stands up. "Okay, now go find someone over on my right that you do not know and sit with that person." I give the women time to pick up and then to move their belongings. I signal to Trish to start handing out the pens and pieces of paper to everyone. Since its more people who came together than those who came alone, I tell the remaining ladies to pair with someone they don't know well.

"Now I'm going to give you about five minutes and I want you to introduce yourself to your partner and write down some information about them, like their name, marital status, if they have children or siblings, church they attend or what they expect to get out of this meeting. If you find out something else interesting about them, you can write that down as well." I go get myself something to eat while they talk and Trish and I munch while we wait.

When it looks like everyone is about ready, I stand up and put my plate in the trash. "Is everyone just about done?" I ask. When I get almost everyone's affirmative, I point to Sister Emma, who is sitting next to the pretty lady Jonas was staring at. "We'll start with you, Emma. Stand and introduce your partner to the group and she'll introduce you and then the next person and so on until everyone has had a turn."

"Okay, this is Cherise Johnson. She's single and an only child. She sings and teaches dance. She's thirty-two and she came out today to meet some ladies who have the same struggles she does as a single woman."

"Um, this is Emma Lewis and she's been married for forty years. She has two sons and a daughter and four granddaughters and two grandsons, so far. She likes to travel and hopes to go to Hawaii someday." Cherise and Emma sit back down and the next two people stand up. It's time consuming letting everyone stand up and speak, but it helps to loosen everyone up. Once everyone has been introduced to the group, I tell them why I had them do this.

"I know this took a bit of time, but I wanted everyone to tell others about someone else. As 'sistahs' we are going to have times when we have to pray for one another. You have to go to God for that person. You have to share what that person's needs and desires are and without prejudice, especially if you expect God to answer. We, as women, sometimes communicate without words, shunning someone because of how they dress or talk or carry themselves, but for this to work we have to be accepting and supportive of one another. It's easier when you know something personal or have a relationship with someone to want the best for them. I want everyone to be on the same footing—level ground. Now, I know that some of us have more experience in some areas than others. For example, Sister Emma has forty years of marriage experience and Nora is a newlywed. There could be some things, Nora that Sister Emma can share with you. That's what this format is designed for. Now that we know a little more about each other, I would like suggestions on topics that we can deal with or address within the group. And we can get a tentative outline or schedule together with those topics. Ladies?" Trish gets the dry erase easel and grabs a pen. I point to Nora, who stands and says "How to cope with losing a child, and when is the right time to try again."

Trish writes it down, and I acknowledge Trudy. "I think Cherise and I have the same interest. How do you deal with being single today without settling or getting hurt?"

"That's a good one. Aniyah?"

"Domestic abuse. How do you forgive, and should you stay married?"

"Okay, that's good, too. Judy, you have a topic?" I ask.

"Yeah, how do you manage finances as a single woman when you don't get the same pay as a man?" Several women call out in agreement with that one.

"All right, Judy, looks like you brought a good one to the table. And the topics like finance and domestic abuse that may need a professional opinion will be addressed. I will find a person who is qualified in those areas to come in and give us sound advice. I don't presume to know everything. I need help myself in the finance department, so I'm sure we could appreciate sound information in that area.

"Anybody else?" Several hands go up and I acknowledge them. Trish writes them down--dealing with children on drugs or in gangs, teenage pregnancy, choosing the right church, finding Mr. Right, losing weight and eating right, dealing with aging parents, trusting God through unemployment, increasing self-esteem, women in ministry and a lot of other topics. Trish ran out of room on the board and had to start writing them down on the notebook that I brought with me.

"Okay, ladies. Thank you for that. I know that everyone's issue is important, but we will definitely seek God on which ones to delve into first. The topics that don't really need a professional we can get started on, but the financial one and the domestic violence and even dealing with children in gangs or aging parents, there is a host of information out there that I would need time to assemble so that we have some practical information to go along with the spiritual. But tonight, let's just have a free session where we just talk about ourselves and our journey as women. Some of the things we've experienced--good or bad--that made an impression or shaped the way we are today. We'll start with Sister Emma and then anyone else can chime in. If it gets confusing then we'll go to raising our hands if we want to speak. So Sister Emma, you can begin." I sit down and yield the floor.

"Well, I've been around for a while. I've seen a lot of things in my lifetime, but we never had anything like this. When I was growing up whatever went on in the family, stayed in the family. Nowadays, it seems like nobody values privacy. There's so much craziness on TV, people airing their dirty laundry, showing too much skin, talking dirty and disrespectful. Children in my day were seen and not heard."

"But that seems so demoralizing to me," interrupts a young mother named Ciara. "I want my kids to know that what they feels matters."

"We never felt we didn't matter, we just knew to stay out of grown peoples' business. See, today we allow our children to grow up too fast and deal with adult issues at an age where they are not mature enough to handle it properly. It's no wonder there are so many people with mental issues and migraines today. You have so many children today being diagnosed with ADD and ADHD and all adults are attempting to do is get the children back to the state where they are seen and not heard by doping them up," Sister Emma expounds.

"So true," Aniyah agrees.

"I think good discipline takes the place of most kinds of medicine. And it starts at home. If you allow a child to have their way and their say, it gets out of hand quickly. Then you have them throwing tantrums in the grocery store when they can't get what they want. When I see that, I want to smack the parent," Trish says.

"Girl, that's so true. I know not everyone agrees with that, but when you look at the long term effects, those children usually have behavior problems all throughout their formative years. We, as mothers, aunts, grandparents or whatever, should be able to allow that child to grow, develop and mature without sacrificing their individual gifts and talents; and to be children for as long as they can," I tell them, "but with boundaries and limitations on unacceptable behavior. They just cannot be allowed to grow up like weeds overrunning our authority. They must be shaped and groomed to become productive people. We have to realize we are not raising children, but adults. They have to be well prepared to take care of themselves, stay out of trouble, bless their families and add something to this world, but not before they are ready. It does us no good to push a child out of the nest too soon only to have them dashed to pieces on the hardness of a society that only accepts certain qualities or status."

"I want so much to be a good mom, but my own parents didn't pay much attention to me because they were working so hard. I can see what you mean about growing up like a weed. That was me," Cherise admits. "I got into all kinds of things as a young girl, but there were no consequences."

"There are always consequences, you just didn't see them immediately," Judy tells her.

"Yeah, you're right," agrees Cherise. "They showed up later and now I have to live with the guilt and regret of my past."

"You can choose to live with it or let it go," I say. "That's what this is all about. I don't know everything you've experienced in life, but I do know that God forgives. The hardest thing, though, is forgiving yourself for your mistakes."

"Amen, sister. The best thing I ever did was repent, ask God for forgiveness and then forgive myself. Now I'm starting to move forward. You don't want to wallow in self-pity. It keeps you from advancing and reaching your full potential," adds Aniyah.

Sister Abigail says, "We have a lot of work to do that most of us would naturally be doing, but when we get hung up on our pasts, then we start spinning our wheels. We feel like we don't deserve to succeed or be blessed. Depending on what our hang-ups are, the devil can capitalize on that and really shut us down—send the wrong person, the wrong job, temptations."

"You know the bible says that 'all have sinned and come short of the glory of God', but what I love is that we don't have to stay there. There is no condemnation in God. He loves us and is 'willing that no man should perish'. His mercies and grace are new every morning and is extended to each of us. His love covers a multitude of sins. There is nothing that He can't love us through. We just have to accept it. Nobody really deserves His forgiveness, but He freely gave His Son to redeem us back to Himself. It would be a travesty not to accept His sacrifice. And I truly believe that when we choose to live in defeat, we are throwing His Son's sacrifice back in His face."

A few 'my Gods' and 'forgive us, Lords' ring out. I look around at everyone and see that the group is absorbing this revelation. I am too, honestly. I think back on all the times I've gone to God complaining about my life and what I've been going through, instead of thanking Him that it wasn't as bad as it could be and then giving it to Him. I've been living like I was less than Jonas. I know he sometimes said and did things to make me feel like I wasn't as important as he was, but I think it's because I forgot who I was. I am a child of God! He died just for me. He always hears me when I pray, and He loves me unconditionally. I matter to Him! So why wouldn't he give me the desires of my heart? The only thing I can figure is that I don't know what the desires of my heart are. I want my marriage to be better, but then I wish I could get out. I want my finances in order, but then I don't budget. I want to lose weight, but I love peanut M&M's. Sometimes I treat God like my issues are too big even for Him or too trifling to bother Him with. But I cry out to Him because I'm not happy. If God wasn't infinitely more intelligent than us and if he didn't already know our end, He would probably be confused by our wishy-washy, vacillating faith. I have so much work to do on myself. The funny thing is I think this is the point Pastor Evelyn was trying to get me to see in her office. I thought God needed to help me be bolder or stronger, but he just needs me to be certain, sure and steady. If I pray about something, I should stand on that until it manifests, instead of praying the opposite thing the next time

I go to Him because He didn't answer like I thought or as fast as I wanted. I've tried it my way so many times. It can't hurt to try it His way, can it?

The rest of the group discussion goes really well. I take a vote from the ladies as to how often we should meet. The majority agrees to twice a month, although a lot of them want to meet every week. I think bi-monthly is better for now. We have the ladies fill out a sign in sheet with their names, addresses, e-mail and phone numbers so we can reach them if we have to cancel. I put Aniyah in charge of calling everyone and sending out information as needed. We dismiss, and she, Trish and I begin cleaning up the room. I get the food and trays and carry them back to the kitchen, while they put the chairs back. While I'm in the kitchen washing the serving utensils, Cherise comes in and asks to talk to me.

"Do you mind?" She questions.

"No, I don't mind. How can I help you?"

"Well, I wanted to talk to you since that Sunday I came to your church and you talked about the cruise. You remember?"

"Yes, I remember."

"I wanted to confess something to you." Oh no! Here we go. I knew I would have to deal with this. I'm expecting the worse. If he done cheated on me with this girl, it's over!

"I know your husband. We met a while back. He's real nice," she admits.

"Yes, I know he can be very charming. Come on and sit down," I tell her. "What's on your mind?"

"Well, he told me that you were getting divorced, that you two were having a lot of problems. I believed him."

"I can't really say why he would tell you that, but I will admit that he and I have had our challenges. Marriage isn't easy. It isn't to be entered into lightly or dissolved without serious consideration."

"Well, I was so flattered that he was interested in me that I didn't discourage his attention. Now some of my church members think that he and I are sleeping together. But nothing happened. He called me a few times after that, but that was all. I came to your church to talk to him about it, but when I saw you and how well you spoke and...well, I couldn't. I just left." She wrings her hands in her lap while she talks.

I reach over and put my hands over hers to still them. "Look, I'm not mad at you. I think you have courage to even come and tell me what's been going on. I can't even begin to tell you what you should do about your church family except to give it time. Don't give them anything to talk about and that should cease. As far as Jonas, you leave that to me. If he calls you, don't answer or tell him that you can no longer talk to him. And just know that I would give you this same advice if it was someone else's husband or boyfriend we were talking about."

"Well, you're nicer than I thought you would be. This always happens to me. I get men throwing themselves at me, and I get treated like a tramp."

"Sweetie, you're a beautiful woman. Men are just going to be attracted to you. Accept that. Then what you do is develop some standards or rules that you are going to follow—some questions you ask right up front to eliminate or qualify that person being in your life. For one, are you married or attached should be first. If they hesitate or say yes, you thank them for their time and bounce. Roll out, like the kids say." We giggle, but I get serious with her again.

"Women are threatened by people like you, especially when they are so insecure in their own skin or their own relationships. I have to admit that I saw how my husband looked at you and I felt some kind of way about it, but I prayed about it and I knew God would bring it back around to be dealt with. I've always felt that my husband and I were God-ordained to be together. But unless we are both willing, nothing will come of it. We have to both be all in or it doesn't work. I know where I am, but he needs to decide. But you make it harder for him to make the right decision when you keep entertaining him because he makes you feel special."

"And you make him think he has a shot," Trish interjects from the doorway.

"Yes, Trish, I was just about to say that. Cherise, these are my friends Patricia and Aniyah. I'm pretty sure they heard what we were talking about, but I know they'll keep it to themselves, right girls?" I ask, with my eyebrow raised.

"I promise I won't say a word," vows Aniyah.

"Me neither," Trish concurs.

"Now, Cherise, if you ever need to talk, I'll give you my cell number and you can call me directly."

"That would be great. It seems like the only people I talk to are guys. Most women won't talk to me." Cherise hands me a piece of paper and a pen and I write my number on it.

"You should be used to that by now," Trish says, "I'm sure you've looked like that since middle school. And women haven't changed since the start of time. We are threatened when we see someone who looks better than we do. I admit, I felt that way when I first saw you," she reveals.

"But I don't try to ..." she starts.

"Exactly!" Aniyah and Trish and I say at the same time. We all have a good laugh.

"Girl, if I could look like that all the time without trying, you couldn't say 'boo' to me," I joke. "But, really, please call me and we can talk. I promise I won't trip. If you want to get together sometime, you have three people who accept you just the way you are." We stand and I give her a hug. She turns and hugs Aniyah and Trish. We walk her to the door and watch to make sure she gets to her car safely.

"Wow, she is so sweet. I knew I didn't like her!" Trish jokes. "She really is a nice person, though. I was expecting something else."

"Well, we should never judge a book by its cover. We're usually wrong when we do that, and the person is usually the total opposite of what we thought," adds Aniyah.

"That's how Trish and I met, so we can testify to that." I laugh as I remember our first meeting. I thought she was the biggest sinner. I never heard her cursing or anything, but she came real close. She used to smoke and holler and fuss at everybody. I avoided her whenever I saw her because I didn't want to do anything to make her mad at me. Most of my friends growing up were quiet and reserved, so I wasn't used to that. Then one day, I ran into her in the bathroom at church and she complimented me and told me that she admired my Christian walk. I didn't even think she was saved or knew anything about God. I thought she was just one of those "pew Saints". She took me by surprise. She told me she noticed my work in the church with Sunday school and singing and everything I was doing. I was shocked! She had so much word in her! As crazy as she is, God really loves that girl. So do I. Fortunately, she's mellowed out some over the years, stopped smoking, toned down her voice a little, but she still speaks the truth even when you don't want to hear it. I tell her she is God's mouthpiece, with the volume all the way up!

On my way home I wonder how I'm going to address the Cherise issue with Jonas. I pray about it and I feel like I should leave it for now. If I had had the audacity to do that, my experience with Keith could have ended differently, especially if I had known then what I know now. And I can't even imagine how crazy Jonas would act once he found out. Why? Why would he do that? Is it that bad? Am I that bad a wife? I know things aren't perfect, but are they so bad that you have to set yourself up with a replacement in case we don't make it? I think I feel offended, but what good does that do me? I could go home, throw this in his face and have a big blowout that would really affect my kids and my household. Or, I could try to let God handle it.

With all my praying and seeking God lately, you would think that option would come easy, but what I really want to do is go at Jonas. Just who does he think he is? I can't believe that I gave up on someone who seemed to really like and admire me just to stay with someone who's trying to replace me. I can hear Beyoncé's 'Irreplaceable' in my mind. "He must don't know 'bout me," I say. I look in my rear view mirror when I remember that the kids are in the backseat, but I see that they are asleep. When I pull up at home, I wake them and carry Mariah into the house. I take her upstairs and get her into her pajamas. She doesn't wake up at all. I kiss her, put her in her crib and turn out the light. I check to make sure Sammy and Gabrielle are in bed and then I go get myself in the bed. I put on my bed clothes and slide under the sheets. Jonas is already in the bed snoring. I reach over to get my journal to write in and I notice that it is not where I left it. What? I know he better not be reading my personal thoughts! I feel betrayed! I'm almost tempted to wake him up and ask him. "I'll fix you," I whisper and I write all about my talk with Cherise and how I feel about what she told me. I even elaborate on how hypocritical it was to be a man of God and in essence cheating on his wife in his heart. I totally ignored my own indiscretions, but this is not about me. Besides, I was trying to make a point. I may have embellished a little more than I should. I know this was probably not the 'godly' way to handle this, and I can't say that He led me to do this, but I am quickly becoming someone who doesn't like to be trifled with. I am tired of the games. Who does he think he's playing with? I make up in my mind to start a new journal and keep it somewhere he can't find it.

Sleep doesn't come to me easy, and I toss and turn for most of the night. After a couple hours of that, I get up and go downstairs. I walk around the kitchen and living room and den with my mind still troubled.

The only thing I can think to do is pray. "God, why is it that the more I try to do the right thing and stay in my marriage, the more Jonas does to make me wonder why I haven't left yet? Am I being naïve? Everyone is telling me to go, but I feel You telling me to stay. Are You punishing me? Am I punishing myself? Is this a test? What is it? I don't think I can take any more of this. God, please help me! I need to know why I'm still here with this man. I don't want to stay and give up the best of myself, and then when the kids are grown, he leaves me. Just make it clear. Give me a sign that this is Your will for me. Help me to trust You. Help me to stay in Your will. If it's something I'm not seeing, God, open my eyes. Wake me up. Make it plain. Reveal Your divine purpose in my life. In Jesus' name. Amen."

I drag myself back upstairs, turning off lights as I go. I climb back into bed and pull the covers up to my chin. I fall asleep as tears of frustration, hurt and weariness fall from my eyes.

Reversal of Fortune

For days Jonas has been walking around like he has a chip on his shoulder. He talks to me about the kids and when we have services, but that's all. That's fine with me. I haven't said much to him, either. I feel like there is a muzzle on me. When I want to say something smart, it just won't come out. Now, I can get a few good ones in anytime, but even though it comes to mind, it won't come out my mouth.

My first lady had me to reread I Peter 3:1-6. She told me something profound when we were sitting in her office after church on Sunday. "You know, Mildred, most self-esteem issues are based in pride. When women tell me that they can't submit to their husbands for whatever reason, I ask them do they like the way things are going in their lives now. If things are great, keep on doing what you are doing. But if they aren't, do something different. Maybe then you'll get a better result. This passage wouldn't be in the bible if God didn't feel it was important. Plus, if He didn't think you needed to be instructed in this area He would have left it out. It's mentioned several times for wives to submit, but it was clarified here what to do if your husband isn't acting right. You still have to submit, but do something extra, keep your mouth shut, and you'll see the result you're looking for. You just have to let go of pride, how you feel, how you think you should be treated and what you deserve; and just trust God. Keep your mouth off your husband. When I was young they used to say 'if you can't say something nice, don't say anything at all'. We need to use that in relationships, too. Stop speaking what you see and speak what you want to see. But you have to know what you want. Until it's clear to you, keep quiet."

So here I am, with my tongue bridled. I thought I knew what I wanted, but her words have made me really reevaluate what I want for my life. I still haven't narrowed it down, but I'm working on it.

Trish and I met for lunch again at our favorite spot, and she told me that she and Aniyah and Cherise were hitting it off real good. I am slightly jealous, but I'm glad I could bring them all together. Trish appointed herself Cherise's gatekeeper. Any guy that steps to her has to go through Trish. I feel for the poor brothers, because she won't take no junk, and so far, she hasn't let anyone in. The good thing is that Cherise really appreciates that. She says for the first time in a long time she has people in her life who really care about her and accepts her the way she is. Praise God!

When I get back to work, I spend the afternoon working on a letter that I plan on sending out to the addresses I started collecting from my morning commute. There are so many 'for sale' or 'for rent' signs up that I take a chance that some of those people may need advice or want someone else to handle those things for them. It was just a thought and I decided to act on it. I've had a lot of time to think since my mouth has been closed. Gabbi asked me several times at dinner if I was okay. Sammy asked me if I was mad at him. But I assured them everything was fine. Once Sammy realized he wasn't in trouble, he was good.

When I finish drafting the letter, I print out several copies and put them in envelopes to be mailed out. Everyone seems to be engrossed in their work this afternoon, so the office is quiet except for the radio playing softly in the background. Nora has her bible out and is reading it. We have been getting even closer since she accepted Christ and started coming out to J.U.S.T. meetings. She has a hunger and thirst to know more about God. I invited her to the next women's conference I was requested to do. My topic is "Fulfilling the Vision of the House--how fulfilling your husband's vision allows you to find your own fulfillment". I have been trying to get some insight on this, but so far nothing has come to me. One thing I realize is that we don't have a vision in my house. Jonas never shared with me what his goals for the future are. We've never even really discussed what we wanted for our children. I feel unqualified to speak on this topic, but I feel if God gives me what to say, it'll be what I need to hear as well as what He wants His people to know. As far as fulfillment, I'm finding I'm more content when I do what I feel God wants as opposed to what makes Jonas happy. If he was really following after God, then what I do should make him happy, too. Right? Well, I think so, but what do I know? I just hope this topic comes together for me in the next few days. I only have a little more than a week before the conference.

Gabrielle asked me if she could come with me. I didn't tell her about it because I didn't want it to get back to Jonas. I really just didn't want any more friction even though I was doing something he didn't approve of. But she overheard me on the phone with Trish (really, she was eavesdropping) and I couldn't say no. Gabbi's been wanting to be with me more often lately. I'm flattered and glad, so I've been taking her with me to different places and to my JUST meetings and letting her sit in some—usually the topics are pretty light. If it starts to get deep then I have her step out. Afterwards, she asks questions about the things she doesn't understand and I answer them the best I can. It's been great. I can see her starting to mature and think things through more. She has even been helping out around the house and with her siblings without me asking.

I'm all the more convinced now that Jonas and I have to get it together. Our children can't be casualties of a battle of wills where our marriage is concerned. And that's what it is--a battle of wills. He wants what he wants, and I want what I want. What I want to me seems to be honorable, and what he wants to me is unreasonable. I'm probably wrong and looking at it through my feelings of hurt, betrayal and fear, but I can at least see that he and I are not on the same page. I've been feeling like I need to confront him, but I can't get up the nerve. I will have to sometime, but I have to make sure the timing is right.

On my way home, I decide that I don't want to cook. I pick up the kids and take them to get whatever fast food they want. They choose McDonald's and we go inside to eat. Jonas hasn't been eating what I cook lately anyway, so I only feel obligated to feed my children. They give the cashier their orders and I give her my card. When she swipes it a little ticket comes out. The girl looks at me and tells me it won't go through.

"Can you try it again? I know I have money in that account," I tell her. She swipes it again and another little ticket prints out. "I don't understand," I shake my head as I take my wallet out. Fortunately, I have a twenty dollar bill in there for emergencies and I hand it to her. She counts out my change and hands it to me. I take my change and move over so she can wait on the next person. I feel embarrassed because of the stares from the people around me, but I know there is money in that account. I just deposited my paycheck less than a week ago. The only bills I paid were the babysitter and the water bill. I also got gas, but that was all. It should have been at least two paychecks worth in there because the mortgage bill is coming due. When they put our food on the tray, I pick it up and carry it over to the table where the kids are waiting. I let them get their food and I break off little pieces of my fish filet for Mariah and feed her. I'm still trying to figure out in my head where I miscalculated. *I'm just going to have to check my account statement. Maybe I made a mistake or transferred it to savings. I hope so because I have to pay the mortgage soon. I know Jonas ain't going to help with that.*

When I get home, Gabbi gets the kids through their nightly routine so I can spend some time on the computer. I pull up the internet and access my online banking account. Plain as day I see a transfer from my account to Jonas and my joint account.

"What in the world!" I yell. I can't even go confront him because he's not home yet, and when I call his cell, it goes to voicemail. I scroll through and see that he made the transfer a few days ago. "Why would he go and do that? He knows the mortgage is due." When I was sick, I made the ultimate mistake of giving Jonas my password because I needed him to pay some bills for me. And because I never saw him use it after that, I assumed he forgot what it was. Well, if this ain't the biggest wake up call, I don't know what is. I immediately change my pin number. I consider whether to call the bank and report it, but I need to find out what's going on first. I feel violated. I pick up my cell and call Trish.

"Hey girl. You won't believe what Jonas did," I bait her.

"What's going on? I know it ain't Cherise, because we've been hanging out a lot lately. She doesn't have time to mess with him."

"It's not that. I just tried to use my bank card and it wouldn't go through."

"Don't tell me! Please don't tell me. Did he take your money?"

"Girl, yes! He transferred it from out of my account to the joint account," I tell her.

"Can't you just transfer it back?" She asks.

"No, he withdrew it already."

"Do you want me to make a call? I told you this can all go away for you, just let me know. You can be collecting insurance money in a month."

"Trish, this is serious. That was my mortgage money!"

"Girl, I am serious! You can't keep letting him do that to you. Did you talk to him yet?"

"No, I just found out a few minutes ago, and he's not home yet. I could spit nails. Why does he do stuff like this? I would never go into his personal account and just take money out," I vent.

"You're a good one. I don't think I could put up with him and his little bags of tricks. One or both of us would be dead, believe that. Look, you find out what's going on. I mean it, Mill. Get up in his face if you have to, and let me know if you need me. If you need the money I can let you borrow it, but don't let him know that."

"Thanks, Trish. I don't know what I would do without you. And I will call you back and let you know what happens."

"You better. Bye Mildred."

"Goodbye." I hang up the phone feeling a little better, but knowing that Jonas and I are about to have the showdown of a lifetime.

I make copies of my account history and shut the computer off. I pace back and forth for a while trying to cool off. I want to come off angry but controlled. Right now I could pass for unhinged. I don't want him to know that he has that kind of control over me. I am so angry; I almost forget to pray about it. After the seventh or eighth trip around the den, I drop to my knees in front of the couch. "God, I need you so bad right now. I can't do this anymore. Please, help me. I don't want to feel this bad. You can't want this for me. I need you to move right now in this situation. I want to give him the benefit of the doubt, but not at my expense. If this is where you want me, then give me a sign, if not, end it."

Before I could get 'amen' out, the phone rings. I go pick it up. "Hello," I answer.

"Is this Mrs. Wilson?" A lady asks.

"Yes, may I ask who this is?"

"I'm calling from County Memorial Hospital. Your husband gave this number as his emergency contact."

"Is he okay?" I ask, knowing in my heart that they wouldn't be calling me if everything was okay.

"Your husband was in a very serious accident this afternoon; he was brought here to our trauma unit. We need you to come down right away. When you get here the doctor will fill you in on his condition."

"I have to get someone to look after the kids and then I'll be right there," I tell her, my voice trembling.

"I'll let Dr. Brown know you're on your way. When you get here, ask for me, Nurse Jocelyn."

"Okay, thank you for calling."

"No problem. I'll see you when you get here."

I hang up the phone and immediately pick it back up. I don't want to wake the kids up and get them all upset, so I call my sister in law and see if she can sit with the kids while I go to the hospital. County Hospital is about twenty minutes away from the house, but it seems like forever before I can get there.

When I walk into the emergency room over an hour later, there is a little bit of activity, but nothing especially unusual. I go to the admittance desk and ask for Nurse Jocelyn. A pretty Asian girl waves me over to these double doors that you need to swipe a card to get in. She swipes her card and the doors swing open. I follow her down this antiseptic hallway to another nurses' station where a doctor is going over a chart. When we get close he looks up and puts the chart down. He extends his hand to me. "Mrs. Wilson?" He asks. I shake his hand and nod, unable to speak.

"Your husband was in a pretty bad accident this afternoon. He had to be cut out of his car. There was some head and neck trauma even though he was conscious when he arrived."

"Is he going to be okay?" I ask, not knowing if I can handle the answer.

"He's stable for the moment, but we have to monitor him for any brain damage. He gave the responding officer your name and number, but he lapsed into unconsciousness shortly after arrival."

My legs suddenly felt weak. Dr. Brown and Nurse Jocelyn help me over to a small waiting room and sit me down.

"I don't want to say he'll recover with no problems. That would be ideal, but there is no way to know for sure. We have to watch and see what time will tell. He has a concussion and there is some swelling around his collar bone, but his spine seems to be undamaged. Once the swelling goes down and he wakes up, we'll know for sure what we're dealing with. We are also running tests to see if there is any swelling in the brain. We should have the results of those tests shortly."

"Can I see him?" I ask, not sure if I can handle it or not.

"Sure, right this way." He leads me down the hallway to a room just past the nurses' station. The curtain was pulled back and Jonas was lying on the bed, lifeless. There were machines beeping and IV's in his arm. I stand next to the bed, and my heart is beating so hard. Jonas' head is bandaged, and he has a brace on his neck.

"Oh, God," I cry. I feel guilty because I was just praying about our relationship and wanting out, and here is my husband, lying here unconscious.

"I'll give you a few minutes alone and then you can fill out the paperwork," says Nurse Jocelyn. She and the doctor step out, and I take a step closer to the bed. I put my hands on Jonas' arm as tears roll down my face. Now the whole battle of wills between us seems so pointless. Why does it take tragedy to bring life into focus?

"God, please don't let it end like this. I don't know what his condition is, but I pray You heal him. Whether or not we can work our differences out, please don't take my kids' father from them. Forgive me for not trusting You to do what You needed to. I was being selfish. Forgive me. Please let him be okay."

I can't do any more for him, so I turn and walk out the room. The nurse hands me a clipboard with all these forms to fill out. I go back to the waiting room and sit down. I pull my cell phone out and call my sister in law, and let her know about her brother. She tells me to stay as long as I need to; she'll watch the kids, but to update her. I then call our pastors and tell them about Jonas. They pray with me and tell me they are coming to the hospital. I call Trish and my family and they try to encourage me as well. While I wait on the pastors, I fill out the paperwork and hand the clipboard back to the nurse.

My whole body is numb. I sit in a fog wondering how I'm going to tell my kids about their daddy. I know Gabbi is going to know something's up when she wakes up in the morning, especially when she doesn't see me. I told Gina to call me if she has any problems with them.

That money seems so insignificant now. I just wish I knew what was going on in the spirit world. What is it God's trying to show me? I try to be a good wife. I try to do what's right. I know I'm not perfect, but I try to follow the word and live accordingly. I know troubles come and go, but why does it seem like trouble wants to camp outside my door? I get up and pace around the little room. Since it's late, there aren't too many people around this time of night, so I can spend time pondering what I'm going to do. I get a little notepad off of one of the tables and write down a list of things that I need to do—call Jonas' boss, call my boss and coworkers, call to drop out of the conference, call the kids' schools, call Aniyah to contact the women of JUST and have them pray. Anything else will have to wait until I know what I'm dealing with. I don't want to think about long term things until I know what's going on.

I put my list in my purse and my hand brushes against a bottle of anointing oil I got from a prayer meeting Jonas and I went to. He took a bottle too, but he leaves his on the dresser. I believe in the power of oil, so I keep mine handy. I take it and put some oil on his head, his neck and his hands. I ask God to bless him and raise him up, and I go back out the room just as Pastor Gilliam and his wife are coming down the hall. When I reach them, they hug me and tell me that everything's going to be okay. Strange, but I believe them. I am peaceful about it. I take them to Jonas' room. They pray over him, and we walk out to the waiting room. They ask me what happened. I tell them he had a bad car accident, but that I don't have any real details. I pull out my list and write—get info from police accident report. We talk for a while and they encourage me to trust God in this situation. Pastor Evelyn goes and gets me some coffee. Then, we all just sit quietly, each of us lost in our own thoughts. I know they think of Jonas as a son. This is probably just as bad for them as it is for me.

"Mildred, I know this is hard for you, but trust God. He won't put more on you than you can bear," Pastor Gilliam tells me.

"Yes, He'll work all this for your good. You'll see. He hasn't let you down, Mildred. Just stay faithful. Keep pressing and keep pushing forward. Jonas will be fine. God has him and you right where He wants you," Pastor Evelyn says. "And don't hesitate to call on us when you need to," she offers. They hug me and they leave, promising to call the church secretary and have Jonas added to the sick and shut in list.

I go back down the hall and look in on Jonas again. The machines are blipping and beeping that monitors his vitals. His face is peaceful, like he doesn't have a care in the world. "Jonas, if you can hear me, please get better. Even if you don't do it for me, do it for the kids. They need you. Please wake up," I plead with him. The only sound is the incessant hissing and beeping of the machines. At least he was breathing on his own. I go back down to the waiting room, and a nurse is walking Trish down the hall. "What are you doing here?" I ask her.

"Where else would I be, Sis?" She hugs me, and we go sit down.

"Any changes? How are you doing?" Trish questions.

"No, he's still out. I'm okay, though."

"Girl, I feel so guilty. I had to pray the whole way over here. I had just been talking about him and now look."

"You weren't by yourself. I was right there with you. I even prayed for God to do something. The next thing I know the phone is ringing," I admit.

"We couldn't have known, but it sure makes me want to watch my mouth from now on. I'm just sorry it had to come to this."

"Me too. But you know the funny thing?" I ask. "I'm more afraid of the kids losing him, but not for myself. I think I'm jaded. I feel bad for him. I don't know what I'm going to do if he doesn't wake up, but that's about the extent of it. Am I a bad person for feeling like this?"

"Mill, he's put you through a lot—mentally, emotionally, financially. Then, you find out about this accident. You're probably in shock. Give yourself some time to deal with this. I wouldn't start guilt-tripping just yet."

"Yeah, you're probably right. Thanks for coming, Trish. You know you don't have to stay; I'll be alright," I tell her.

"I know, but you're my girl. I'm here if you need me and you need me." She hugs me again and stands up. "I'm going to find some pillows and blankets. This place is cold! Do you need anything?"

"No, I'm good."

"Okay," she says and she walks off.

What a friend! I thank God again for her, and I sit back in the chair with my eyes closed. When I wake up, I have a blanket draped across me and Trish is sitting next to me with her own blanket pulled up to her chin. I get up and walk back down to check on Jonas. He's still unconscious. After a few minutes of watching his chest rise and fall, I go back to the waiting room. I take out my phone and call my boss and let him know what's going on. Next, I call Jonas' boss and give her the same information. I answer her questions as best I can and promise to update her when I can. I call Gina and make sure the kids got off to school. She tells me that she told them I had something important to take care of and that I would explain after they got home. I thank her and promise to call her back as the doctor comes down the hall towards me.

"Trish, wake up," I nudge her. She sits up and rubs her eyes, but she immediately stands up when she sees the doctor.

"Good morning, Mrs. Wilson," he reaches out to shake my hand.

"Good morning Dr. Brown," I shake his hand.

"Well, the results of the tests we ran show there is some slight swelling on the brain."

"Oh, no!" I immediately sit down and Trish takes my hand and squeezes it.

"It's not a good prognosis, but so far there's no bleeding on the brain. As far as damage, we have to wait and see. I know that's probably the last thing you want to hear, but I can't tell you anything beyond that. We have to see what we are dealing with once the swelling has gone down and he has regained consciousness."

The doctor talks with me a little more, telling me in medical terms that there is a possibility that Jonas could come out of this none the worse for wear or a mere shell of the man I knew. There was just no telling. Only time would reveal what we were dealing with. After he leaves to make his rounds, Trish convinces me to go home and get some real sleep. I give the on duty nurse all my contact numbers and I drive home with Trish following to make sure I get there okay. I go into the house, go upstairs, take a shower and get in the bed. Eating is the farthest thing from my mind. I fall into the deepest sleep and sleep for hours. Fortunately for me, people love me. When I wake up, Gina has already gotten the kids and is getting dinner. I decide to not put off the inevitable and call the kids into the den. I tell them about their father and Sammy takes it the hardest. He cries, and I just hug him and encourage him that his daddy will be okay. Gabbi just sits and stares at her hands. I know she has had some hard feelings for her father and she's probably feeling guilt like I am. I make up in my mind to talk to her privately after Sammy's gone to bed.

Gina says she'll stay with the kids again, and I get ready to go back to the hospital. I call and talk to the head nurse who says there has been no change other than putting him in a different room. When I get there, a couple of the deacons from the church are leaving. They lead the hospital ministry so it makes sense for them to be there. More than likely the pastors filled them in on Jonas' condition. I greet them and they wish me well and encourage me that Jonas will be okay. "God's got him," says the oldest deacon, Brother Grimes.

"Take care of yourself, Sister Mildred," says Deacon Howard.

"Thank you both. See you," I tell them as I go into the room. Jonas' bed is raised like he's sitting up. I can see bruises on his face where he hit the windshield. There are some small scratches on his cheek, and I lightly trace them with my finger. I pull up a chair and I sit and just watch him. I don't know what to say, so I just sit there. After a couple of hours, I get up and walk around to stretch my legs. I go back out to the waiting room and I see a cop standing there talking to a nurse. When she points to me I walk over to where they are standing. The cop introduces himself as Officer Smith. He tells me he was the first on the scene. Apparently someone ran Jonas off the road. Witnesses said that a black SUV was chasing Jonas for at least a few miles and then rammed him and forced him off the road into a concrete abutment. They had conflicting eyewitness accounts of the driver but were attempting to follow every lead. I ask him to please call me if he gets any more information, and he agrees. He also tells me where Jonas' car was towed. It was processed, and I can have it picked up or moved. I thank him and he leaves me to wonder why someone would run Jonas off the road. Did he cut someone off? Was it road rage? Was is random or were they after him specifically? I rub my eyes and sigh. There is just so much about Jonas' life I don't know. We have been so out of touch lately. I don't even know who his real friends are. Other than the elders at church and his family, I don't know who else I would call to tell about him. Who else would want to know? I feel bad that I don't even know my husband after all these years.

I muse about this as I return to my chair by his bed. Jonas told me one time years ago that I was getting to know him too well and he had to 'change up'. I asked him what he meant by that and he told me that he never wanted to be predictable. I remember shaking my head back then, but thinking back on it now, I should have told him that that was how trust was built. I don't trust him any farther than I can see him now, but that could have been nipped in the bud back then. I think it might be too late now. You can't turn back time. How do you undo fifteen years with someone? You can't just say 'do over' and then start fresh like nothing happened. All those experiences, tears, fears, good times and bad times don't just disappear. I want to let them go and move on, but it's so hard! Forgiveness in one thing, but I can't forget how he treated me and talked to me and abused me. I heard from Myles Monroe one time that if you don't understand the purpose of a thing then abuse is inevitable. But am I wrong for allowing it? Should I have made him see my purpose? And if I couldn't figure out my purpose, should it have been his responsibility to bring it to the light? He's the head, right? Why didn't he try harder? Why didn't I? Why was it so easy for me to allow all the bad stuff and put up with the verbal attacks? "God if you have any answers, show me," I whisper.

I used to be the most outspoken person. I had a smart mouth, and if you got on my bad side, you knew it right away. I didn't believe in holding on to stuff. I let it fly. I guess it has something to do with being a middle child. I felt like I had to do things to get noticed or to matter. But when Jonas came along, I turned into this wimpy, weak, subordinate version of myself. I thought I was just being submissive, because that's what the bible says, that women should submit. I really felt he loved me and wanted the best for me, so I was willing to fulfill my role. But as I sit here, I realize that the one he really loved was himself. He wanted something from me that wasn't already there. I admit I fell into that same trap. We were two incomplete people looking for someone else to complete us. The unfortunate thing is that when Gabrielle came along, we were no farther than we were on our wedding day. Fast forward two more children and fifteen years and nothing's changed. In some ways things are worse. The only common area is the children, and I am primarily responsible for them. There is really nothing holding us together but choice.

Maybe this whole accident was God's wake up call for us. Maybe he's showing me that the ball is in my court, and I can decide my future without fear of what Jonas will say or do. Right now he can't say or do anything. I have to let this marinate for a while. I stand and look down at him. "Bye, Jonas."

I turn and leave the room. Since tomorrow is Saturday, I'll be back up here first thing in the morning. I have to make up in my mind if I want the kids to see him lying there like that. I ponder the pros and cons on the drive home as I let the radio play, but I don't sing along like I normally do. I feel like I'm at a critical juncture. Any decision I make could change the course of my future. I'll let the kids come see their daddy. Maybe that could help him fight to regain consciousness. Hearing their voices could be good for him.

When I get home, I go look in on the kids and kiss them on their foreheads. I spend a few minutes talking to Gina and filling her in on her brother's condition. I also thank her profusely for being there for us.

"You would do it for me," she says. "Plus, I know you love my brother. I know how trifling he is, and you've put up with him all this time. You know, if it wasn't for you, I would have given up on my own marriage years ago," she reveals.

"Really? I would never have thought that. Why haven't you told me this before?"

"You know I don't do all that church stuff. I went because it's what we've always done. I didn't go expecting God to move in my life. But I thought if it's working for you, I would give it a try. My marriage did get better because I just did what I saw you doing, but I still didn't give my heart to God. But, believe it or not, I did that this past Sunday. It made everything so clear. I saw that all you did wasn't for Jonas, but unto God, because I know if you had your way, you wouldn't have done anything for Jonas. It had to be God. Jonas doesn't deserve you, but he's not all bad. There are a lot of wonderful things in him and some not so wonderful things; but that's my brother and I love him, good or bad. I just know if you leave it'll crush him."

After Gina leaves to go visit her brother, I sit and think about what she told me. I never got the impression that Jonas would care if I left or not. And what about her staying with her husband because I stayed with mine? Crazy, ain't it? You never know who's watching your walk. That was proof if there was ever any doubt. I decide then and there to go ahead and do the conference. It would be too late to replace me anyway. There's no telling who would benefit from seeing me persevere through all this. I want my life to matter, but not for me. If I can help other women achieve success, happiness and salvation, then everything I've gone through is worth it. And if Jonas and I could get on the same page, we would be unstoppable. I just don't know if it's too late for us.

Saturday I get up and prepare the kids for what they'll see at the hospital. When we get there, some of Jonas family is there visiting. His mom and his aunt are sitting in the only chairs in the room. I tell the kids to say hi to their daddy, and they do so with hesitancy, trying to avoid looking at him lying there lifeless. I tell my mother in law to stay as long as she likes while I take the kids to the waiting room.

"Mommy, why does daddy look dead?" Sammy asks.

"Well, he's unconscious. He can probably hear you, but he can't make himself wake up," I explain.

"Why can't he wake up if it was just a concussion?"

"His body won't let him. He just needs to rest and get better, and then he'll wake up."

"I hate seeing him like that," Gabbi says.

"Me, too," I commiserate with her. "I wish you didn't have to see him like that, but when he's up and back to normal, you'll see just how much God has blessed him. Sometimes God uses these moments in our lives to show how great He is."

When Jonas' family leaves to get lunch, the kids and I go back in the room to sit with him. I listen to Sammy as he tells his daddy about his classes, toys and video games. While he talks Gabbi thumbs through a magazine, and I try to stay awake. It's amazing how draining this all is. I make phone calls, update everyone as much as possible and try to answer their questions, but there haven't been any changes to report. I wonder how long it'll be before he wakes up. According to the doctor, there is still some minor swelling, but we can't predict what the outcome will be. "The brain is somewhat difficult to predict. I've seen more severe head trauma where the individual recovered completely without ever slipping into a coma. We just have to keep waiting."

In the meantime, I do everything I can to try to keep to as normal as schedule as possible. There's still church and work, school for the kids and, of course, the conference. While I sit here, I work on what I plan to talk about. It's hard because I really don't know what's going on in my life now. In essence, with Jonas out of commission, I don't have any vision. That's where my exhortation is centered around. Without a vision, the people perish. If there is no vision, how can you know where you're going or when you're off the path? And if I'm correct, the man should carry the vision and communicate it to the wife and family, so everyone can work to bring it to pass. I have been 'doing my own thing' for so long. I think this is the first time I've really had a chance to evaluate my progress. I'm not going anywhere! Why? Because I don't have a clue where it is I'm supposed to be going. I have dreams and desires and things I want to see and do, but overall, he should have a plan for our family and then we should work that plan. If he does his part, then I can do my part. Everything I want I should be able to do within that framework and vice versa. We both win. I believe that it would have eliminated a lot of the stress and frustration I've been feeling and put some of the responsibility of the household back on Jonas' shoulders where it belongs. I wasn't meant to carry some of the things thrown on me. For as long as I've been carrying it, I know it was only God that got me this far. Now it's time to get things back in order. I can see that now, but what do you do when your eyes are shut?

The conference was such a success, I can hardly believe how God is blessing me. The only thing I can't figure is why Jonas is still comatose. Pastor Evelyn told me to just trust God, that He was working on some things in me and to 'let patience have its perfect work, that you may be complete, lacking nothing.'

"Mildred, you've been praying to God to help you and now that He's working on it, you doubt Him. Know this, when you pray, God hears you. He always hears you. And just because He doesn't show up the way you think He should, doesn't mean He's not there."

"Pastor, I trust God. I do. I guess the truth is I don't trust myself to let Him work. I keep trying to do it myself because I want it to work out a certain way. Never in a million years would I have expected Jonas to end up like this just because I was a little unhappy," I open up to her after service Sunday, three weeks after Jonas' accident.

"Mildred, I could tell you've been unhappy for a while. What pastor and I did elevating you was unconventional. We both believe in you and your abilities; that was never an issue. But of course, there is protocol to these things. When God spoke and told us to do it, we had to act on it. Pastor and I talked it out back and forth what the pros and cons were, what kind of a backlash it could create with the elders and ministers, and how the congregation would react. But it was ordained of God. We had a couple of people come to us with concerns, but for the most part, it was a smooth transition. And look what God has done through you! He's not done yet. He's trying to get out of you what He put in you. Your sense of purpose and joy, He needs that from you. You've been so focused on your life, your husband, your children--and as well you should have been. But it's His time now. He wants you about His business. You are so strong and persuasive and compassionate, but you can be timid. You can't doubt yourself and still expect to win souls and impact the kingdom the way He wants you to."

I just sit here and allow her rebuke and love to wash over me and open me to God's heart, because I know He is speaking through her.

"Mildred, you still have a fear of being who you are that you have to overcome. God doesn't want you worshipping any idols, even if that happens to be your husband. Even if you don't physically bow to him, in your spirit you have bowed and subverted yourself to him so much that his will overrides what you know God's will is for you." My heart is beating so hard, I feel it down to my toes. It's amazing to me how God can just cut straight to the heart of things 'piercing even to the division of soul and spirit'. Listening to Pastor Evelyn, I feel like I should repent and give my heart to God all over again. It's a feeling so strong that it literally drives me out of my chair to my knees. She comes around her desk and kneels with me while I cry out to God. We stay like that until I can't cry anymore. I stand up, shakily, and Pastor Evelyn and I hug.

"Thank you, Pastor. I appreciate having you in my life."

"I just hope you still appreciate me after I finish giving you what God gave me for you," she says. "This was just a part of what He wanted you to hear. But we'll save it for another time. You need to go check on your babies, and I need to make sure Pastor gets his dinner. You be blessed," she hugs me real tight and kisses my cheek.

"Thank you, and you be blessed, too." I walk out and go in search of the kids. As I come down the aisle, one of the ushers tells me that Trish took the kids to dinner and for me to go home and relax.

"Well, praise God." I go on home and change clothes and climb onto my bed. I have been sleeping fitfully since Jonas has been in the hospital. I roll over expecting him to be there or I lie awake dreading a phone call that hasn't come. It's not wishful thinking, its fearful thinking. I don't want to be caught off guard, so I imagine the worst and hope for the best. I know that's the wrong way to look at it, but I'm trying to do better.

June 4

I can't sleep. I've been having some unsettling feelings for a while now. Jonas is still in the hospital with no signs of waking up. There's still brain function, and the doctors are puzzled that he's still comatose. Plus, it's starting to wear on me all the long days of work, home and kids, and then sitting with him. The children get out of school next week, and I don't know if I can keep up with this pace. I've started getting these weird phone calls, too. Someone calls, hangs up, calls back and then just breathes into the phone. I've reported it, but somehow the call can't be traced. I just pray it doesn't have anything to do with Jonas' accident. The police don't have any real leads because the car that ran him off the road didn't have any plates. The witnesses could only describe the car, but without at least a partial plate number or something, it's like finding a needle in the haystack. I'm also getting a bunch of bill collectors calling. Apparently, Jonas hasn't been paying the bills. I'm stretched so thin. I couldn't possibly borrow anymore from Trish. I owe her so much already. I don't know what to do. The money I got from the conference went to paying on the bills that were the farthest behind. I made arrangements for the water and phones, but I don't know how long I can keep this up. Jonas' bank won't give me access to his accounts other than to say there really isn't much in there. Where is all his money? Is that why he took mine? What's going on? I'm praying about it every day, and trust me, I believe God can work it out. I just need to know how long? I'm trying to remain strong for my kids and the church and Jonas' family, but I feel like I need a shoulder to lean on. Lord, give me strength.

Flashback

Since Jonas has been in the hospital, there haven't been too many speaking engagements after the conference. I speak at church occasionally, but everyone is sensitive to my time constraints with Jonas and the kids and all. I appreciate that, but I need some money. I don't want to be crass, but I really need the free will offerings and honorariums to supplement my income. Plus, my children have not stopped eating. Then there's pampers, household items, gas, and so on. Gabbi offers to keep her brother for the summer to help out, and I take her up on it. I still don't feel that comfortable leaving Mariah, but having Gabrielle and Samuel at home sure helps out.

I never realized how much out of the loop I was. Jonas' name is on everything but the mortgage. I have to pull teeth just to get information on all the different utilities, and forget trying to make changes. Because he's not dead and everything has pin numbers and passwords that I don't know, they won't change it over to my name. But if I send in proof of power of attorney, they'll tell me what's on it or the payment history. The first thing I would get rid of is the cable. The kids have plenty of DVD's to watch if they get bored, plus, there are lots of books they can read and board games. We really have to start economizing. Fortunately, Jonas is still on my insurance, so his medical bills are covered. When I first got my job that was the first thing I looked into because I didn't want to be caught needing it and not having it. Somehow, he later convinced me that since I was already carrying Gabrielle and Sammy and paying the family rate that I should just add him too, and he would take care of the house bills. I added Mariah when she came along, and we left it like that. Actually, I mentioned it to him once not too long ago about getting insurance through his job, but you would have thought I told him to jump off a bridge. He went ballistic. So that's why I left it alone. It was easier than arguing with him. At least I don't have to worry about any medical expenses on top of everything else. My check alone is not enough to cover everything, but I keep praying and keep pushing. I try not to dwell on it too much because it's starting to get to me. I wake up at night wondering which bill I need to focus on first or if there was something I didn't pay. The phone calls keep coming. I don't know who it is. I just hear breathing. Not the heavy, disturbing kind, but just normal breathing. Like whoever it is is listening.

At the hospital, I tell all this to Jonas. The doctor said he can probably hear me talking and that may help him come out of this coma sooner. So, I spend my time with him telling him about the kids, the house and what's going on at church and home. I tell him things that I never felt comfortable telling him before, when he could respond. It's rather cathartic.

"What happened to all your money, Jonas?" I ask him. "And why did you go into my account? Is there something going on that you haven't told me? I keep getting hang-up phone calls and breathing. It's scary. Do I have to be afraid for the kids? I need you to wake up and handle this, Jonas. You're supposed to be the head—the protector and provider." I check for movement. Other than his eyes moving behind his lids, he's completely still.

"God, I need help. I need you to send me some help. Please, help me get through this. I need you to keep my family going. I can't see how we are going to get through this, but I know it can't happen without you. Make a way out of no way. Send a miracle, God. In Jesus'name!"

When I get home, a car I don't recognize is sitting across the street. I pull into the driveway, and it drives off. I don't know whether to get out or go to my sister-in-law's house. I decide to go in the house, because whoever it was may not know where she lives. I don't want to put anyone else in jeopardy. I get out and check around the yard and the perimeter of the house. I grab the mail, unlock the door and go in to make sure everything is okay. Gabrielle takes Mariah into the den and she asks me why it took me so long to come in.

"Did you see anybody hanging around outside today?" I ask, ignoring her question.

"No, and we didn't go outside or open the windows like you said," she answers.

"Good, you can never be too safe. Plus, I don't want anyone to know you are here by yourself."

"Ma, is there something going on? You've been acting strange lately," Gabbi whispers so Sammy can't hear.

"Sweetie, what isn't going on?" I evade. "With your father being in the hospital and me working and you watching your brother for the summer, I just want to make sure nothing happens to you guys, okay? Now, help me fix dinner."

After dinner, I sit and watch television with the kids until Mariah falls asleep. I take her to bed and call Trish. We talk for a while as I lay across the bed, and she gives me her take on what I should do.

"I'd tell you pull the cord, but since he's breathing on his own, I guess you just have to wait and see what's going to happen."

"I know. It's just the waiting is so hard. And all these bills. I had no idea any of this was going on. I feel like a naïve fool." I punch my pillow in frustration.

"Mill, you can't blame yourself. He should have told you if he was having financial troubles. You are the helpmate. You know how proud Jonas is!"

"What purpose does pride serve if you end up on the street or in the dark? I have a baby in the house! I can't go without water and lights! What was he thinking? And if he was into something worse, he put my whole family in danger! If something happens to one of my babies I don't think I could forgive him."

"Well, let's hope it's just your imagination. As bad as Jonas can be, I don't think he would purposely endanger your kids. He is their daddy, after all." Trish defends.

"I can't believe you are sticking up for him! That's usually my job." I point out.

"I know. Crazy, ain't it? It must be all these prayer meetings I've been in lately. I guess God is working on me. He still has His work cut out for Him, though. I still get a few good ones in before I feel guilty. Must be all that Hell He has to fight through," we laugh and I ask her about Cherise.

"Now that's something I never thought I would do," she says.

"What do you mean?"

"I never thought I would be friends with a pretty girl—and actually like her. That girl is really the crazy one," she cracks.

"Anybody would have to question their sanity hanging around you for any length of time," I joke.

"That's not true, Mildred. I can be a good girl," she chuckles. "Anyway, Cherise is doing good. We had lunch at our spot the other day, and she told me about some new guy that started coming to her church. He's older, but I get the feeling she's attracted to him. Of course, nothing is going on. They've only said "hi" to one another, but I think she wants there to be something. She said he had the prettiest smile and these light eyes. Personally, I prefer my men like my coffee—hot and strong, no cream and no sugar."

"Girl, you are crazy! But I sure do know what you mean." We talk some more about nothing and everything, and we promise to call each other the next day.

I go check on the kids and they are in their beds watching TV, half-asleep. I set the sleep timers, turn off the lights and go back to my room and get ready for bed myself. Before I lay on the bed, I pull back the blinds and look out the window. "Just to be on the safe side," I think to myself. There are no cars.

I get under the covers and stare at the ceiling. I lay there until I drift off. The next thing I know, Keith is coming into my bedroom. I sit up and he's smiling at me. "What are you doing here? How did you get in?" I question him.

"You let me in, remember? I'm here for you," he tells me as he climbs into the bed. As he slides under the covers he puts his hands on my shoulder and shakes me. He just keeps shaking me and I try to push his hand off me.

"Ma, wake up!" Gabrielle puts her hand back on my shoulder and shakes me again.

"W-what?" I open my eyes and realize that she was trying to wake me up. I must have been dreaming. "Gabrielle, what time is it?" I ask trying to get my bearings.

"It's time for you to get ready for work. Didn't you hear your alarm clock?"

"No, baby. I must have been more tired than I thought. Thanks for waking me." I get up, turn off the alarm and go into the bathroom.

"I'll get Mariah dressed for you," she calls through the door.

As I shower and dress, I try to figure out why I would dream about Keith all of a sudden. Then it comes back to me. Trish told me that Cherise likes this nice looking guy with a nice smile and light-colored eyes. "That's where that dream came from." I say aloud. "Whoo! For a minute there I thought I was losing it."

I go downstairs and Gabbi has Mariah dressed and ready to go. I reiterate the rules again before I go out the door. After I drop off the baby, I spend the drive into work praying and saying my favorite scriptures out loud. Since Jonas has been in the hospital I haven't been consistent with my devotions in the morning. Like this morning, it's been hard to get up on time, let alone early.

At work, my morning is busy. We have more accounts and clients now, so everyone's days are spent working up to the last minute. Plus, I keep sending out letters to our current clients offering them a one-time bonus for each referral. I've gotten a lot of feedback from that along with the letters I sent out earlier. It seems like our accounts have more than doubled in just a few weeks' time. In spite of this, Mr. Hughes hasn't been in the office. Other than a few emails and phone calls, we haven't heard much from him. I go into his office every week and water his plants and make sure his desk is dust free, but that's all.

As busy as my days are, I still call and check on the kids several times as well as calling the hospital to see if there are any changes with Jonas. "Girl, you need to trust that daughter of yours. You don't have to call that many times," Judy admonishes.

"You gonna give her a complex," agrees Trudy.

"Well, if she were my daughter, I would probably call all day long, too," says Nora.

"I don't call all day long!" I protest. "Just once to see if they are up, once to see if they had lunch, once to make sure no one's been by and once to see what they want for dinner. What's so wrong with that?" I ask defensively.

"Nothing, but for all that calling, wouldn't it be easier to just bring them in to work with you?"

"Yeah," says Judy. "You've been like a mother hen lately. Is there something going on?"

"What makes you think anything's going on? I just want to make sure they are okay. This is Gabbi's first time watching her brother all day without anyone being there."

"But you do trust her, right? Or you wouldn't have agreed in the first place. You may make her think you don't trust her and that could cause some friction later."

"We just think you should call maybe once or twice and then let her call you if something comes up. She's a teenager. You want her to feel responsible without you patronizing her by calling her all day," explains Trudy.

"Mildred, I kinda see their point. But whatever you decide to do, you have to be comfortable with it," adds Nora.

I sit and ponder their advice and wonder if I should tell them about the phone calls and the car I saw outside my house. I can't prove anything so it's no point in getting anyone else as upset as I've been. I tell the girls that I'll try to behave, and I go back to my work. At three forty-five, I start packing up to go. My days just don't seem to go by fast enough lately. I run out to my car at four and hurry to pick up Mariah and get home. Again, a car is pulling away as I pull into the driveway. This time I try to get a description of the car. It's a black, four-door Lexus. It looks like only one person in the car, and I can't tell if it's a man or woman. My gut tells me it's a man. Why would a woman be camped outside my house?—oh, yeah, I forgot about Jonas' appeal. It could be one of his adoring female fans wondering why she hasn't seen or heard from him lately. I'm really going to have to check into this. I go into the house working the problem out in my head as I start on dinner. I don't have too much time to devote to it because it's Thursday, and I have to get to my JUST meeting. Aniyah is in charge of the appetizers this time, so that gives me time to get the kids fed, changed and get over to the church.

After a very entertaining evening with a nurse giving us women pointers on taking care of ourselves so that we can take care of others, I sit around with her and Trish. "You know, this is just what I needed. I've been running around so much that I haven't been taking care of myself lately," I admit.

"Yeah, Mildred. I haven't seen much of you lately. And when I call, you barely have time to talk," complains Aniyah.

"She's just going through one of those trying times that we all face at one time or another," Trish explains. "Besides, I know Mildred will let us know when it gets to be too much," she says pointedly.

"Yes, mother," I kid, and then say seriously, "Since you mention it, I haven't really been sleeping well lately."

"I've been noticing you look a little droopy around the edges," picks Trish. "What's going on?"

"Well, you know about the phone calls, right?"

"Yeah. Are you still getting them?"

"Yes, but not as often. But that's actually not what's bothering me now. I've come home a couple times, and there was a car parked across the street from my house."

"Mildred! You have to call the police!" Aniyah exclaims.

"I know, I know. But I didn't get a good look at the car the first time and this afternoon I couldn't get a good look at the driver. Whoever it is pulls off when I drive up."

"Well, I have a few people I can call. We'll take care of this tomorrow," Trish says matter-of-factly. "And in light of my new found deeper relationship with God, I'll make sure no one goes missing. Okay, Mildred?"

I laugh, "You are incorrigible!"

"Hopefully, this can be resolved by dinnertime tomorrow and you won't have to lose anymore sleep over it." Aniyah stands up and pats my shoulder.

"You really are handling a lot, Mildred. But you are handling it, and the other ladies are noticing it. I've heard several of them say how inspiring you are. If you need anything—anything at all—don't hesitate to call me. If it wasn't for you, I wouldn't be going through this upswing in my life and my marriage. I thank God for you." We hug and she grabs her purse. "I'll talk to you girls later. I told my husband I wouldn't be out too late tonight. Bye."

When she leaves, I gather my things. Trish and I straighten the chairs, turn out the lights and collect the kids. I lock the door behind us as we go towards our cars.

"Don't worry about a thing, Mildred," she calls out her window. "I'll take care of everything." I get in my car and close the door.

"What is she talking about, Ma?" Gabrielle asks.

"Trish is going to take care of something for me while I'm at work tomorrow, that's all," I answer.

When we get home, I get everyone settled for the night. It takes a while for me to fall asleep, but when I do I sleep straight through the night without waking up. Unfortunately, Keith invades my dreams again. I can see him, but I can't hear him. He's beckoning to me, but my ankle is chained and I can't find a key. I reach for him, but I can't move any closer. There's a gulf separating us. He takes a running start and jumps. I wake up. I don't know if he made it or not. "Oh, God! Why am I dreaming about him now? What's this all about?"

As I get ready for work, it hits me that Trish is going to handle my stalker situation today. My heart flutters in anticipation of what might happen. I wake Gabrielle and tell her to make sure she and Sammy stay away from the doors and windows especially. I also let her know to call me if she needs me.

As I drive to work, I wonder if maybe I should have taken them with me to work for the day. I don't want them to know everything that's going on because I don't want to scare them. And with their father not at home, I don't want them feeling unprotected.

"Lord, watch over my babies. Angels, keep them safe and place a hedge of protection around them," I pray.

At work I'm distracted. I have plenty of work to do, but I find myself having to redo something because my thoughts drift back to what's going on at home. I pick up the phone several times to call, only to put it back down. The girls tease me unmercifully, but I can't help myself. I don't want my babies to be in any kind of jeopardy, knowingly or unknowingly. Who knows how this could turn out? Maybe I should have called the police. By lunch time I figure no news is good news. If anything had gone wrong my phone would be ringing off the hook, right? Anyway, Gabrielle has been showing a whole lot of maturity lately. She should know to call if anything weird was going on. Besides, I need to call the water company and the gas company to get an extension before it's too late. Funny thing is they tell me my bills are current. I know I didn't pay them. Maybe there was a misapplied payment or something. I plan to go back through my bills at home and check into it. With that thought I dig back into my work, updating spreadsheets and emails, sending out contracts and paying bills.

I get so wrapped up in what I'm doing that I don't look at the clock until Nora stands up and puts on her coat.

"It's time to go already?" I jump up and start clearing off my desk.

"You were on a mission today," she teases. "You didn't even hear Judy and Trudy leave." I look over at their desks and see them cleared off.

"Wow, you are so right. I must have really been focused. Did they say goodbye?"

"Look on the floor around your desk," she giggled. There were balled up pieces of paper lying on the floor.

"Did they throw these at me?" I ask incredulously.

"Yep, and you didn't even feel the ones that hit you," she laughs. "Come on, Mildred. Let's go home."

"You're right. It doesn't make any sense to work that hard and not feel somebody hitting you with paper. But make no mistake about this— I will get my revenge! Those two are on my list." I set the alarm and close the door behind us as we go to our cars.

"See you Monday, Mildred," Nora waves as she closes her car door. I wave back and throw my purse into the passenger seat. Just as I start my car my cell phone rings. I grab it and look at the caller id. It's Trish.

"Trish. Hey girl. What's up?" I answer.

"Will the kids be alright for a little while? I need you to meet me at the mall."

"Yeah, I guess so. I can call and let them know that I'll be a little late. And let the babysitter know, too. What's going on?"

"I think it would be better if I left any explanation until we meet," she says cryptically.

"Are you trying to scare me or what? You got my mind jumping all over the place now."

"I'm sorry, but you just have to wait until I see you at the mall. How fast can you get there?" She asks.

"Twenty minutes."

"Okay, I'll see you there." She hangs up. I drive to the mall as fast as I can without being reckless. The last thing I need is a ticket on top of everything else. I drive around until I see her car, near the back of the parking lot under a light. She's standing outside her car next to a black Lexus waving me over. I pull in beside her car and get out. As I walk over to her, the driver's side door of the Lexus opens up and who should get out but Keith.

"Keith?" I say questioningly, recognizing the car that was across the street from my house. "You're the one hanging around outside my house?"

"Hi, Mildred. It's good to see you." My name still drips from his lips like honey. How can a man make saying your name sound like music?

"You didn't answer my question," I tell him, trying to keep my thoughts pure. I mean, he was stalking me and scaring me, right?

"I'm sorry. I didn't mean to upset you. I've just been keeping an eye on things for you since I heard about your husband," he explains.

"Why would you do that? Who told you I needed looking after? I didn't know you lived around here anyway. Why are you here, Keith?" I fire at him.

"Well, I just couldn't get you out of my mind. I didn't like the way things ended with us and so I asked around about you. I've known for a while where you lived, but when I heard about what happened I figured now was a good time to come and apologize and see if you needed help."

"You figured now was a good time to come with my husband safely out of the way?" I clarify for him. "I hope you didn't let my kids see you."

"No, I was careful. Mildred, you made it clear where you stand. I mean no disrespect. I consider you a friend, and I want to help. It can't be easy having to do everything yourself. I just want you to know I'm here for you. That's all. No strings."

"Trish, did he run all this by you? I can't believe you fell for this!" I turn and face her. She shrugs and says, "I don't get the feeling he's lying, Mill. When I came by the house he was leaving these money orders in your mailbox, he didn't try to drive off or anything. He just introduced himself to me and told me the same thing he's telling you." She handed me two envelopes—one marked power and the other phone

I look back and forth between the two of them wondering if there was some cosmic joke being played on me. Here I've been dreaming of this man, and he's sitting outside my house all this time. Paying bills! Now I understand about the gas and water. Well, I can't just stand outside in this parking lot. *So what you goin' do Mildred?*

"Keith, I appreciate you wanting to help me. And it's nice that you've been keeping an eye on what's going on with me..."

"But..." He interrupts.

"But I don't want any misunderstandings. I can't have people thinking something's going on, especially with Jonas incapacitated. It just doesn't look right."

"So we can't be friends?" He asks.

"You should know the answer to that."

"I think you should trust yourself and let me help you...as a friend. Patricia here can be our witness that nothing's going on. She can make sure we behave. If you want, I promise to not be alone with you, so you know my motives are genuine." He holds his hands up like a boy scout, looking just as fine and, yes, sincere as he wants to be. I hesitate, giving it another thought. I sigh in resignation.

"We'll try it and see what happens, but if it looks like it's causing more harm than good, I'm ending this arrangement."

"Agreed. Really, Mildred, I only want to help as a friend."

Lord, how do I explain this to the kids?

"So, if we are all done here, I need to get home and get dinner," I say.

"Mill, Keith and I were discussing that before you pulled up. Why don't we get take out and all of us have dinner together, that way the kids won't think anything strange about Keith being around. He can just be a friend of ours who's visiting. If he just shows up by himself, Gabbi especially, will think something's going on. What do you think?"

"I think my friend is conspiring behind my back, that's what I think," I say looking back and forth between them. "Well, since you have this all figured out, what are we having for dinner?" I ask them.

"Chinese!" they say in unison. I just shake my head and go back to my car.

"I guess that means you're buying. Trish you know what I like and get some chicken lo mein for the baby. I'll see you at home." I start up my car and pull off, heading home.

Wow! What a day! Who would have thought it would have ended like this? I've had enough fantasies and dreams about Keith lately without any hope of ever seeing him again and now he's here in the flesh. I don't know if I can handle him being here. "Lord, help me!" I yell. Seriously, I don't know if Keith being here is a help or a hindrance. I just know that I'm going to have to stay "prayed up" like the old saints used to say.

June 15

Dinner went surprisingly well. Keith behaved himself. I could tell the kids liked him. Mariah even let him hold her. She kept calling him 'Dada', but then she calls every man that. I just hope it didn't put any ideas in his head. I can't help wondering what would possess him to track me down. I hope he isn't one of those 'fatal attractions'. I'm kinda glad we don't have a rabbit. I would hate to come home and find a pot of bunny on the stove. After dinner, we all watched a movie together. Half way through, Trish said she had to leave and Keith offered to walk her out. I thought he was going to leave, too, but he came back in and stayed until the movie was over. After that, the kids got ready for bed, and he told them he enjoyed hanging with us and was looking forward to stopping by again sometime. That went over especially well with Sammy. He asked him to come back tomorrow and Keith agreed. I guess I didn't realize how not having his dad around was affecting him. Maybe this could be a good thing. I just hope everyone can keep it all in perspective—myself particularly. I can't deny that there is still a part of me attracted to Keith. He treats me well, speaks kindly to me, compliments me and gives me his focus—and not to mention FINE. I don't feel like I have to compete with anything for his attention. I get the sense that he would give me the coat off his back and the last dollar in his pocket if he thought it would make me happy. I wonder what it would be like for Jonas to treat me like that. I've been lying here wondering, if all things were equal, which man I would want to have in my life if I were given the choice. I honestly can't say. What would you do if you were in my shoes?

I get up early Saturday morning because I want to go by the hospital to check on Jonas. Once the kids and I get dressed and eat breakfast, we get in the car and make our way to see him. As often as I've been here, I just can't get used to him being here. Seeing him lying there is like seeing a grizzly bear, stuffed and mounted. You know it can't really hurt you, but it still creates fear from past encounters. It's like you're afraid it could come back and attack you. As we come up to the room, Sammy dashes ahead of us and starts telling his dad all about Keith. "We met a friend of mom's yesterday. His name is Keith. He going to come back and see me, maybe shoot some ball. He's nice, Dad. I like him. He watched movies with us and ate dinner."

"Okay, Sammy. Slow down. I know you're excited, but at least tell your daddy hello," I admonish.

"Hi, Dad. I hope you can hear me. Keith really is nice. I just wish you could meet him. You would like him, too."

"Hi, Dad," Gabbi says. She takes Mariah from me and lets her reach over the bed and touch Jonas' face. "Dada," she says.

I put my purse on the arm of the chair and I go uncover Jonas' legs. Since he's not moving I like to exercise his legs to keep his muscles from atrophying. I push his legs back and forth up and down several times. I also check for bed sores. I know the nurses are taking very good care of him, but I want to feel like I'm doing something for him instead of just watching him waste away. Plus, it helps pass the time. The kids pick up the remote and flip channels on the television until they find something interesting about beavers to watch. I move up to the top of the bed to work on Jonas' arms. I hum softly while I work. Every now and again I ask him can he hear me, watching for any signs that he does, but I get no response. We stay about an hour. That's about as long as I can endure Sammy asking me over and over about Keith—when is he coming? Is he bringing food again? Are we going to watch movies? When can we go to his house?—etc, etc. I tell the kids to turn the TV down and we say our goodbyes. Keith left me his cell phone number to call if I needed anything, but I just didn't feel right using it. So, I just go back home and tidy up. You know the chores you do when the real chores are done—baseboards, wiping doorknobs and light switches, or polishing and dusting. It's something to keep me busy and hopefully from fantasizing about Keith. I tell myself I'm not cleaning to impress him, either, but even I'm not convinced. After a light lunch with no sign of Keith, Sammy falls asleep on the couch. I let him sleep, and I go upstairs myself and play with Mariah. It's about her naptime, too, but she's fighting it. We bang on her toy piano and drum. I put her blocks on the floor, and she knocks them over before I can get them stacked up high. She laughs when I say "Uh oh," and I start over trying to stack the blocks. When she gets tired of that, she plays with my hands, trying to play patty cake. When she starts to yawn, I pick her up and sing to her. I hold her in my lap and she plays with my fingers as her eyelids start drooping. When she falls asleep, I lay her in her crib and go into my bedroom to watch a little television. I must have dozed off, because I wake up and Keith is standing over me, calling out my name. "Hmm," I say, dreamily. I've had this dream so many times before. I can almost tell you what's going to happen.

"Mildred, are you hungry? I brought pizza," Keith tells me.

"I was expecting something a little more romantic," I tell him.

"Romantic? Really? I thought we agreed to just be friends," he says, puzzled.

"Friends? Are you trying to play hard to get?" I tease, throwing caution to the wind—'cause I'm dreaming, right?

"Mildred?" Keith's forehead crinkles up.

"Hunh?" I sit up and look around, finally realizing that I'm not dreaming and that Keith is really in my room. "Uh, w-what are you doing in my room?" I stammer, embarrassed to say the least.

"I brought pizza. Gabrielle was changing the baby and told me it was ok to get you because you were watching TV. Sammy is already eating," he explains.

"Oh, uh, okay, I'll be right down," I tell him, stalling. I can't believe I was so clueless. I should have known.

"Are you okay?" He asks, taking a step towards me.

"Stop!" I hold up my hand like a traffic cop. "Yes, I'm fine. I'll be down in a minute. Okay?"

"Sure, okay," he turns to leave and I flashback to the cruise when I pushed him away. The last thing I want to do is hurt him, but this can't be good, right? Now I'm wondering what would have happened if I handled it differently—left the door cracked a little. You know? Maybe then my dreams would come true. But I'm awake now—and hungry. I fix my hair and go downstairs. I coach myself all the way down to act like what just happened didn't.

I walk into the kitchen and inhale the aromas of my favorite kind of pizza—sausage. How did he know? I grab a plate and a couple of slices and sit down on a stool at the counter. The little radio that I keep in the kitchen is playing music from the local gospel station. That's the only sound being made. Keith and I avoid each other's eyes and pretend that we're not trying to avoid each other's looks. Thankfully, the kids don't seem to notice. But it sure is a little tense.

After we eat, Keith takes Sammy outside to play catch. Jonas never really played outside much with him. He was always gone, watching TV or too busy. I straighten up the pizza mess and go into the den and sit down. Gabbi comes and sits down with me.

"Momma, do you like Keith?" she asks me. I don't really know where she's going with this, so I try to keep it loose and not read too much into it.

"Sure, Gabbi. He's nice," I answer.

"No, I mean really like Keith," she amends.

"Sweetie, you know we really shouldn't be having this conversation. Your daddy and I are still married. Whether we have issues or not is no reason for me to start looking to replace him."

"But, he's not waking up! He's been lying there for weeks. What if he doesn't make it? Then what? What are we going to do? How are we going to make it?" She fires at me, trembling. I put my arms around her and hug her tight.

"We're gonna be all right, Gabrielle." I console her. "It may look tough, but I trust God. I know He's going to take care of us."

"Don't you think that's why Keith showed up here now? Maybe God is getting him in place in case...," she trails off.

"Now, really. You shouldn't even stress yourself out about that. Don't start borrowing trouble. We have to stay positive. Hope for the best. Everything will turn out okay." I give her another squeeze. "Now let's sit here and enjoy the day relaxing and watching movies, okay?"

"Sure, but can I ask you one more question?"

"What is it, baby?"

"Would you at least think about Keith if something happens to Daddy? I like him and so does Sammy and Mariah." She obviously doesn't expect an answer, because she turns back towards the TV. I sit there pondering her question, and what would possess her to ask me that. Knowing how God is, I can't believe he would send someone 'just in case' my husband doesn't pull through. Especially knowing how tempted I could be. It would be a setup for failure, for sure. The bible says that God doesn't tempt us. I know he does all things well, and 'well done' is what I would consider Keith to be. But He also doesn't put more on us than we can bear. Keith is my burden, so I have to make sure I stay on guard. I vow to lay down some more ground rules with him once he and Sammy come back in. Now that my kids are involved I have to be really careful. I don't want them hurt.

After Keith leaves, the kids scatter and I get a few minutes of peace to talk on the phone. I put Aniyah and Trish on three-way and tell them what happened, fussing at Trish for not being there.

"Mildred, it's like the cruise all over again," says Aniyah. "Believe me, I know you said that he's just helping as a friend, but I don't think I could handle a friend that fine and not want something more."

"She's right, girl. You know I love my husband, but that boy will make you look twice--going and coming!"

"Trish, you are so bad! I thought you were behaving from now on."

"I am! I'm just acknowledging God as Creator—and wishing I could have breathed the breath of life into something that fine." We crack up.

"Girl! You better stop playing like that." We take a few minutes to let our laughter to subside.

"Seriously, guys, what should I do? I opened this door and now I want to close it, but without hurting anybody."

"Well, you already put him in his place about coming in your room and about calling before he shows up."

"Yeah, but please don't remind me of that. That was so embarrassing. I didn't realize how much I was fantasizing about him. I've been trying to live holy and still having these dreams. It's crazy!"

"That's how the devil works, Mill. As much as I joke and play, there are some things I just can't do. To do so would take me back too far. I've come such a long way that I refuse to go backwards."

"Trish is right. You know what I've been through and if it wasn't for God putting you in my life, things would be so different now. Because of you, my marriage is stronger. I love my new church now, and I can even tolerate my in-laws. But the biggest thing is I've finally forgiven myself. It's such a good feeling. I don't think anything can get to me now. So Mildred, you've already put the prayers out there. You've made your petitions known. Now, just trust God."

"Yeah, listen to Aniyah. Everything you're going through now is just to sidetrack you. You've impacted so many lives in the past few months that the devil has you in his radar. But you can't stop now. You have to keep moving—duck and dodge, girl. Don't let him pin you down. Even when it comes to Jonas," Trish advises.

"What you mean by that?" I ask her.

"Well, I know you go to the hospital almost every day, exercising his legs, sitting there for hours. It's like you're punishing yourself for what happened to him. You can't do that. I commend you for standing by your man, but you need to keep it all in perspective. There really isn't anything you can do for him but put him in God's hands and keep moving forward."

"But I haven't stopped moving. I wasn't getting the speaking engagements I was before, but I still got a few," I explain.

"Yeah, but Mildred you should be hosting or planning your own conferences. The idea for JUST is something needed not just here but everywhere," Aniyah says.

"Well, I have been jotting down some ideas that I have about that, but with everything going on, I haven't done anything more with it," I confess.

"Have you even mentioned it to Pastor Evelyn?" Trish asks.

"No," I admit. "I was trying to wait until I knew what was going on with Jonas."

"Well, you know the answer to that. God has him in a holding pattern until Mildred decides what she's going to do and then starts doing it. You can't keep using Jonas as an excuse for why you haven't fulfilled your calling. This is your time, Mill. What are going to do?"

I'm still pondering that question as the kids get ready for bed. I let my mind wander back to the conversation with the girls. I have to admit that I have been holding back. After seeing how much potential "JUST" has and how much the other ladies love it, I started thinking about an annual women's retreat. It would still have a lot of the elements of JUST, but we could go to like a spa location or a B&B and have a weekend of girl talk, pampering and fellowship. We could still have sessions at night, but maybe a little more informal to fit with the atmosphere. I've been putting off talking to my Pastor about it because of Jonas, but why? I should really put together a good presentation and give it to her. What could it hurt, right? I decide to start working on it tonight and give her the outline before church in the morning.

July 9

Pastor loved my ideas! She said she had always wanted to have our own women's conference, but that making it a 'retreat' was a wonderful twist. She said that it could do better at getting to the 'heart' of our problems and help us to overcome them for real. It's harder in a huge setting to get your individual needs met, but one on one or in small groups away from the problems makes it easier. She also said she was putting me in charge of it and that she wanted to have it before the end of the year. She said that God had been dealing with her in her quiet time about things He wanted done, and He was sending her someone to help. She had a feeling it was me, but she was waiting until I was ready to help.

I'm really writing because of something else we talked about. She asked me about Jonas. I told her he was still unconscious, but then she said she wanted to know how I felt about him as a husband. I was speechless for a few minutes. I started to give the usual, "oh, everything's good" or "we're doing okay" responses, but then I just cried. I poured out my heart. I told her about my ambivalence towards him, about how he talked to me, about my own insecurities. I even told her he didn't want me ministering with him. I spilled it all! And she said the strangest thing. "I was wondering when you were going to stop carrying all that around like I couldn't see it." My mouth fell open. I asked her if she knew, why didn't she say something. She said that it was my cross, and I had to trust God for myself. I had to decide what I wanted. Sound familiar, huh? She told me that I wasn't walking in my true "daughtership" (her word), that I was a child of God, and I had to know it and act like it before Jonas or anyone else could know it and act like it. As long as I was waffling, the devil was winning and gaining ground in my life. She said this was my time to grow up and be who God called me to be without interference. She also told me that I should throw off any weights (guess who?) because God wanted to take me to new heights and new levels. It had to be God, because as far as I know, she doesn't know Keith exists. Well, I guess I know what I have to do. Get busy!

Anchors Away

Weeks have been flying by so quickly. Before long the children will be back in school. I am still working on organizing the Women's retreat as well as, keeping my family going. It's been hectic to say the least. But I'm finally seeing some progress. We're going to the wonderful True Blue Snooze Bed and Breakfast in the mountains where there are hiking trails (mosquitos, ouch), fishing (ugh, worms), hot springs, and a licensed masseuse (aahhh). The best part is that we got a wonderful deal. I showed Pastor Evelyn the brochures after our last JUST meeting, and she was thoroughly pleased. If we contract to come back at least one more time, we could get another ten percent knocked off the price. Look at God! So it looks like our women's retreat will be annual for at least the first two years. After that who knows? If it generates enough buzz and interest, we may have to have a bigger venue. I look forward to having our own cruises and maybe having men sessions and women sessions and then coming together for night sessions (but in the good, Godly way, you know?) I was thinking about for just couples, but then after talking to Cherise, I didn't want to leave out single people. Speaking of Cherise, her number is coming up on my cell phone.

"Hey, Cherise. What's up?" I answer.

"Mildred, I really need to talk to you," she says.

"Okay. What's up?" I ask.

"I don't know if we should get into this over the phone. Can I come over?"

"Sure." I hang up and ponder what could be so important that she had to tell me in person. We have a J.U.S.T. meeting tomorrow. She could have stayed back and talked to me then. I hope it's not something bad. I have been trying so hard to maintain my focus; I really don't need anything upsetting the delicate balance that is my life. At least, not right now. It takes Cherise about twenty-five minutes to get there, and she's not alone. Aniyah is with her. I show them in and get everyone some iced tea. We go out onto the back porch and sit down.

"So, Cherise," I say getting straight to the point. "What did you want to talk to me about?"

"Well, you remember our conversation about the guy that I like?"

"You mean the sexy one with the pretty eyes?" I ask, smiling. "Yes, I remember. Did you finally get to talk to him?" Cherise stands up and walks to the edge of the porch clearly upset.

"Mildred, the guy is Keith," Aniyah tells me. You could have knocked me over with a whisper.

"Are you serious? I had no idea, Cherise."

"I'm sure. I just can't believe I threw myself at him and he turned me down. He told me that he thought I was attractive, but that he was interested in someone else. He slipped up and said your name and then it all fell into place," Cherise spills.

"What 'all fell into place'? There is no 'all' falling over here! There is nothing going on between me and Keith! He's just a friend. And really, I had planned to introduce you two thinking maybe you would hit it off even though he's a little older. I've just been so busy lately," I explain.

"Cherise is talking about a phone conversation she overheard. He was standing outside his car and she was parked next to him. Keith apparently was in a deep discussion about you with someone," Aniyah fills in for me. "He's been going to her church for a couple of months now, but he hasn't joined yet."

"Well, I don't know anything about that, but believe me Cherise, the last thing I need is for you to think that I would be unfaithful or misrepresent myself. I know it looks bad, but did Aniyah tell you that Keith is not allowed over here or around me without her or Trish being here?" I ask.

"No, she didn't tell me that," she admits. "It's just that I got so upset when he mentioned your name. He was talking about buying a house and settling down. He even mentioned having enough rooms for the kids," She sits back down and puts her hands in her lap. "I just got upset because I was really interested in him, and he acted like I didn't exist. What's wrong with me?"

"Nothing, Cherise. If he can't see that there is no future between us, and that there is a beautiful, intelligent woman who is interested in getting to know him, then that's his loss. Now don't get me wrong, I'm not chopped liver." I joke trying to get a smile out of her. "I think that Keith is trying to hold onto the past. I guess he thought maybe there was a chance for us, but I pushed him away before, and I'll do it again if I have to." I put my arm around her shoulder and give her a squeeze. "I think if you really like him, you should pray about it and let what happens happen. As far as all this phone call, I can't say what that's all about. I do know that he's been a great help to me. My kids miss their dad, and he just fills a void for them. He's helped me financially. I guess that's why I haven't really kicked him to the curb because of what it would do to them and me."

"Mildred, maybe you need to talk to him again and find out what his intentions are. You don't want this to go any farther than it has, especially because your kids are so vulnerable."

"I know. You're right, Aniyah. Cherise, are we okay?" I ask her.

"Mildred, you know I think the world of you. I can't stay mad at you. I was just a little hurt that's all. Besides, we can't let a guy come between us now—even if he is F.I.N.E! It'll mess up our friendship, the women's retreat, and everything."

"You got that right—on all counts! I plan on having a good time at the retreat. I really need this time away."

"Mildred, I keep forgetting how much you have going on," says Cherise.

"I guess we forget it because you're handling it so well," Aniyah says.

"I don't know if I would say that, but I am handling it. I have to do a lot of praying, that's for sure. Really, I probably would have given up if it wasn't for God."

"Why don't you call us more often? We really don't mind helping out when we can, you know. If you need babysitters or help with dinner or just time away, just call," offers Cherise.

"Yeah, Mildred. After all the help you've given me, it's the least I could do. If it wasn't for you and J.U.S.T. and most importantly God, my marriage wouldn't have turned around. Plus, I'm happy at church now. I learned how to put up boundaries around what goes on at home and who has a say in what goes on in my house. It's so liberating!" exclaims Aniyah. We laugh together.

"I'm so glad things turned around for you so fast. But you were in the right place for God to move. It didn't hurt that your husband was willing, too. That's the key. Unity can get a lot done in less time than doing things alone."

"So true. It's amazing that a year ago I wanted out. Now, I'm in love with my husband again like when we were newlyweds," she smiles.

"I'll have that one day. Just wait," Cherise declares.

"Me, too," I agree.

We say our goodbyes and I promise to call them if I need anything. I go into the study—yes, Jonas' study—and I sit and write out a list of everything that concerns me, from money to my kids to my marriage and my friendships. Anything that causes me any distress, no matter how small, I write it down. I even write down dreams that have yet to be realized or that I have pushed to the back burner. I sit there and go over it several times making sure I don't leave anything off. Then, I pray about it. I mean, seriously pray over it. I have worship music playing and the door closed. I am down on my face giving it all to God. For the first time in my life I really want Him to take it. I've said it many times before. I've attempted over and over to just let things go, but I never take my hands off of it. So I put that on my list, learning how to really cast my cares on Him and trust Him to work. I just cry out to God. I am so tired! Everything that I have been dealing with for so long, I just tell Him about it. My marriage, my children, my money, my ministry, my mistakes, my helplessness, my hurts, my confusion, my fears and myself, I lay it all at His feet. I didn't realize when I came in here that it would go like this, but for the first time in a long time, I have a throne room experience. I throw all of those cares off and I can feel God's presence so near. And the closer I'm drawn to Him the more unworthy I feel. I can't get low enough. I lay prostrate before Him and just cry and worship. I'm amazed that my mind can still process this experience and not leave His presence. I'm wondering why all those things I have carried for so long seemed so important. When I try to compare it to the glory I'm experiencing now, it doesn't even come close. It all seems so insignificant. I wonder why I ever wasted my time worrying about it. Next to the awesomeness of God, everything pales. I feel the weight of Him, but the weight of my burdens is gone. Everything is so clear. I don't really have answers or know the outcome, but it's clear that God's got it all under control. Wow! I feel so free and light. I want to stay like this always. Just magnifying Him above everything I've ever had to deal with. I can see past arguments between Jonas and me and they're fading away. The times that he didn't buy me presents for my birthday or our anniversary; the times he tried to make me feel small; the times he verbally attacked me; the times he didn't include me; the times he insulted my family or refused to spend time with us; the times he put others before us; every burden he put on me to try to break me; the times he looked at me with disgust and dislike; the times he told me he didn't like me or love me; the times I felt I deserved how he treated me; the times I pretended like everything was okay, when I knew it wasn't; the times I should have prayed about it and gave it to God, but didn't; the times I was so depressed that I didn't even like myself; the fear that Jonas would leave me; the fear that he wouldn't; wishing things could be different between Keith and me; wishing I'd never opened the door; worrying about bills and money; allowing all of these things and more to get between me and God—I can literally see it laying there at the feet of God. It is a huge pile! I have to look up to see the top of it. He is showing me how much I was carrying around—just how much stuff came between Him and me. I feel so ashamed and I repent. I thought all of these things were so important. I let all of these things, emotions and feelings become more important than Him. I know I go to church and pray and read my bible. I try to live a holy life. I try to be an example before my kids. I know God is still flowing in my life. I just got caught up looking for something I already had. Everything I need or could ever want is in God. What a revelation! Something that simple is the answer I've been searching for all this time. I just rejoice and praise God. Time doesn't even feel like it's moving, but I just bask in the forgiving and loving presence of my Father. I get the impression that He'll let me stay as long as I want to. I feel like I'm floating in a healing fountain. All my hurts and all the insults and offenses I've suffered are being healed. As I revisit each area, I realize I can touch it and there is no pain or residual hurt. Praise God!

By the time I am able to get up, it's two o'clock in the morning. I feel so light and refreshed. So many weights have been cast off. I feel like I am floating up the stairs as I go to check on my kids. Everyone is sleeping soundly. I go into my bedroom and slip into my PJ's. I lie across the bed and reminisce about the 'throne room experience' I had. I fall asleep reliving it and my dreams are sweet and peaceful—no Keith.

At five thirty I wake up without the alarm clock and I go back downstairs and spend some time praying and reading my bible. I feel like I slept all night long. I go get ready for work and get Mariah up and dressed. Gabrielle and Samuel are still asleep and I leave her a note letting her know to call me when she gets up. After stopping at the sitter's, I get to work without any hang ups. The drive to work is peaceful and quick. I pull into the parking lot and a car is already there. "Mr. Hughes is in the office today," I say. I turn off the car and get out.

"Good morning, Mr. Hughes," I say when I walk in, seeing him standing at my desk. He's going through the papers and contracts that I left from yesterday.

"Good morning, Mildred," he answers. "I see you have a lot going on over here," he says, stepping from behind my desk. "I'm gonna go on back to my office and let you get to work." He walks quickly down the hall, goes into his office and closes the door.

"What in the world was that?" I ask the room quietly. I put my things down and commence straightening up the papers that are scattered across my desk. Once everything is back into some semblance of order, I go make a pot of coffee. By the time it finishes brewing Trudy and Judy are walking in the door.

"Good morning, ladies," I greet them.

"Good morning, Mildred," they say in unison.

"You look all bright and chipper today," says Judy.

"Yes, you really do. If I didn't know better, I'd think you were expecting. You got that 'glow'," adds Trudy.

"Girl, those days are over! Mariah is the last hurrah for me," I laugh. As they settle in and get their coffee, Nora comes in and we greet her.

"Mr. Hughes sure is here early," she comments.

"He was already here when I got here," I whisper. "I walked in and he was going through the papers on my desk."

"What is all that anyway?" asks Nora. "Since those papers started piling up I've had more work than I can shake a stick at."

"Well, I was trying to make sure we all kept our jobs. I drafted some contracts and flyers and sent them out to people who had 'for sale' signs up or 'for rent' or who were advertising in the newspaper. The response has been good."

"Well, maybe that's what he's doing here so early. He's probably trying to figure out what's going on," Trudy surmises.

"All I know is, when he comes back out here I'm going to be looking like I'm working instead of chit chatting with you all," I joke as I go back to my desk and sit down. Truthfully, I don't have to pretend to work. I think I created a monster. Instead of limiting myself to just this side of town, I sent mailers all over. I wanted to make sure we had enough response to cover our bottom line every month. I wasn't expecting the deluge of new customers. Even the phones have been ringing off the hook from people wanting to ask questions about our services. Besides, the incentives didn't hurt. I even lowered the price a little. I didn't ask Mr. Hughes first, but I wanted to make sure we were competitive. I had several people tell me they were going with some other company, but our offers were more attractive. Thank goodness! I've been giving Trudy and Judy the rental properties and charging them with finding tenants. They've done an excellent job so far. I've even showed Nora how to do some of the reports and send them to Mr. Hughes. I wanted to make sure someone else knew how to do it in case I was out or too busy. The maintenance calls have also increased, but our guys do excellent work so there are not a lot of repeat calls. I've even gotten some good reports and commendations. I took the liberty of getting goodie baskets for the guys to keep them motivated and to thank them for their hard work.

They really enjoyed them. Since Mr. Hughes put me in charge of the petty cash fund, I used that. I consider that a legitimate business use that pays back in dividends. I made sure to scan the receipt and send it to him with an explanation. His email response was one word long—Okay.

At the end of another long and busy day, I wonder what is keeping me going. It must be the excitement of it all. I have to get prepared for another J.U.S.T. meeting tonight, so I cut out a few minutes early to pick up the baby and get home. Mr. Hughes left at lunchtime so I don't have to sneak out. Mrs. Emma is in charge of the food, so I don't have to run around picking up last minute items, but I promised to bring drinks which are at home in the pantry.

As I pull up in the driveway, Keith's car is parked out front on the street. He must have just gotten there, because he is still sitting in the car with it running. I get out and take Mariah out of her car seat. I take her in the house and put her in her playpen with her Elmo toy. I tell Gabrielle to keep an eye on her and go back outside. Keith is on his phone standing beside my car. He smiles and waves as I walk towards him. I stand there for a few minutes waiting for him to finish his call.

"Hi, Mildred," he says. "I'm sorry I just came over without a chaperone, but I really needed to talk to you. We can stay out here if you don't mind."

"Okay. What's going on?" I ask him.

"Well, I haven't been totally honest with you about some things and I want to set the record straight," he confesses. *Uh oh! Here we go again.*

"Alright, Keith. Go ahead," I say, cringing at what can only be bad news.

"Well, it goes back to the cruise. You know when we ran into each other?"

"Yeah, I remember," I tell him. *That day is forever etched into my brain.*

"Well, I actually followed you to that room," he admits.

"What! So it wasn't an accidental meeting," I say, astonished.

"No, it wasn't. I saw you when I first boarded and I promised myself that I would get to know you."

"What are you talking about?" I ask, confused.

"There was just something about you. I saw your ring, but I thought that since your husband wasn't there, then maybe I had a chance."

"Had a chance? What was it you had a chance to do, Keith? Are you saying that everything you told me about your wife, being my friend and wanting to help out was a lie?!"

"No, Mildred, that was all true. I loved my wife. She was my best friend, but she's gone now. I guess I just needed.... "

"So you were just trying to get me in bed?!" Frustrated, I turn my back to him and fold my arms. So many emotions are running through my head. One on hand, I've never be the object of anyone's lust before. I'm sort of flattered. Then on the other hand, I am not that kind of lady. What kind of signal was I giving off for him to even think I would succumb? Did I look that desperate?

"Keith, you know this can't go anywhere, right?" I ask, turning back around.

"Mildred, you just reminded me so much of her. Your husband…he won't appreciate you the way I do."

"But you can't honestly think that this is going anywhere? What kind of person would that make me?"

"You said yourself that things weren't great between you. I can love you and treat you the way you should be treated. You're an amazing woman, and you deserve better. Let me take care of you." He reaches out and puts his hands on my shoulders.

"Keith, I think you should go back home."

"There's nothing for me to go back to. I was kind of leaning towards staying. That was my realtor on the phone. What do you think about that?" He still has his hands on my shoulders, so I step back and he drops his arms to his sides.

"I think if you plan on staying here you should find a nice single young lady and settle down somewhere on the other side of town."

"Mildred…," he sighs.

"Keith, I'm married and as long as I am, there can't be anything between us. I appreciate everything you've done for my family, but it has to end here. I'll find a way to pay you back." I turn to walk away and he grabs my hand.

"Look, I know it wasn't proper for me to fall for you, but don't you think it was fate that brought me into your life? I mean, it can't be coincidental."

"I don't know if it was or not, Keith. I do know that my children have been through a lot and I don't need to cause them any more grief."

"You don't think me leaving without an explanation will cause them grief? Come on, Mildred. The things you told me about your marriage haven't changed. You're here by yourself trying to be a mommy and a daddy. I can help you."

"Look, I appreciate everything you've done for us. I do. I know my marriage isn't the best. It's hard to explain it to you, Keith, but I see things differently now. I don't know how it's all going to work out, but I know it will. I think you are trying to replace that empty hole in your heart with a fantasy. You need to get closer to God. Only he can heal your hurt. I'm not the one for you."

"Don't you remember what Marla said? She said you would have a new man. Here I am, Mildred. I'm right in front of you. You know I'll treat you the way you deserve to be treated."

"Marla never said that you were the man, Keith. God could be working things out right now in Jonas. I have to allow Him to move. Please, don't drag this out unnecessarily. Thank you for what you've done for my family. I don't know how to repay you, but I will and I do wish you well. Goodbye." Once again I turn and walk away from him. I go into the house and he stands there a few moments before he gets into his car and drives away.

I go to the window and watch him until he's out of sight. "Lord, I hope I didn't make a mistake letting him go," I whisper.

"Mom, what were you and Mr. Keith talking about?" Gabrielle asks as she walks up behind me.

"Well, he said he's thinking about getting a place here in the city," I tell her.

"Oh, that would be great, and then we could see him all the time. I think he's nice. Don't you have your meeting tonight?" Gabrielle asks as I continue to stare out the window.

"Yes, but we are going to stop at the hospital first, so let's hurry so we won't be late." I turn from the window and look at Gabby frowning. "Aren't you a little excited about seeing your dad?" I question her. "I know it's hard with him just lying there, but at least he's still alive and there's a chance he'll be the same when he wakes up."

"Is he going to be the same? I mean, is he going to remember us and everything?"

"I hope so. I wouldn't want him to have any brain damage or amnesia."

"No, I guess I mean is he going to act the same way or is he going to be nicer. Because if everything is going to be the same, then I hope he doesn't wake up!" She plops down onto the couch.

"Gabrielle!" I reach out and take her hand and sit down beside her. I put my arms around her and squeeze her tight. "I understand how you feel, sweetie. I don't want to go back to things the way they were, either. But I believe that God is already changing things. I really don't think it's going to be business as usual. We have to make sure that we are different people and that we behave like the women of God we are."

I sit and hold her for a few minutes and remember when she was born. I was so excited and captivated by her tiny hands and feet.

Becoming a mother changed so much for me. I put a lot of my dreams aside to care for my children. For a while it was okay, but the last couple of years there's been an emptiness and a restlessness growing inside me. I am just starting to get used to being independent and making my own way again, even if it's been a little bit of a struggle. I don't want to fall back into that same old pattern of putting myself on the back burner and letting Jonas do whatever he wants while I sit around upset because it's not me.

"Sweetie, if we maintain our course, things and circumstances have to change to fit us. We can't allow ourselves to fall back into old habits and old ways of thinking. If we can do that, then we'll be okay. Understand?"

"I think so. Thanks for not getting mad at me. I really do love him."

"I know you do. So do I. This can just be between you and me. I won't tell."

August 2

My ears are still burning. After I went to the hospital to sit with Jonas, I went to the J.U.S.T. meeting. We've been having them every week after the women voted unanimously. It started off very well. We were talking about love and marriage. Maybe we should have picked a different topic. Other than a few people, no one really knew about my relationship with Jonas—so I thought. A couple of the elders from church were there along with the usual group and they proceeded to grill me about my relationship with my husband. They wanted to know if I was praying for him. I told them of course I was. Then they wanted to know if he didn't wake up what I would do. I really hadn't thought that through, so I told them that. Not good enough. They accused me of being hypocritical and cheating on my husband. What? I asked them where they got their information from and one of them said that Keith was at the hospital when they went to visit Jonas and they overheard him saying that I belonged to him now and that there was nothing for Jonas to come back to. My God! What would possess him to do that? Maybe I didn't cut those ties soon enough. I had to explain to everybody about my relationship with Keith, but I could tell that they still had some doubts, so we got raw up in that meeting. I told them for the first time about my marriage and the funniest thing happened. Everybody started opening up about their own experiences. Some of the ladies were in physically abusive relationships, some had husbands who were alcoholics, some were verbally abused and a couple of the ladies were married to cheaters. One even admitted that her husband was on the DL—if you know what I mean. Who would have thought that my opening up about my situation would allow others to get free? We prayed up in that place. We loved on one another and comforted one another. At the end, those two busybody elders left out of there with their faces balled up. Here's the kicker—Pastor Evelyn was there! They tried to tear me down in front of her and it backfired! Those were the two individuals that took issue with my being elevated. After that meeting, I got more love and hugs. I even got a commitment from all of the ladies that they were going to the retreat, even if they had to bring sleeping bags and bunk on the floor! We promised to go more in depth there about our individual situations and really get healed spiritually. I got the biggest hug and smile from pastor before she left. All she said was, "God is well pleased." To God be the glory!

The phone ringing wakes me up at about four in the morning. "Hello," I say, cautiously once I see the hospital's number on the caller id.

"Mrs. Wilson, this is Nurse Rosalind. I'm sorry to wake you, but your husband has just regained consciousness."

"What?" I say, barely registering her excited voice. Jonas is awake! I don't know what to say. In my hesitation Nurse Rosalind thinks I'm too overjoyed to speak.

"It is a miracle isn't it! The doctor is looking him over now. Should I tell him you are on your way?" she asks.

"Uh…yeah. Yes, please. That would be great," I say, lamely faking enthusiasm.

"Okay, Mrs. Wilson. I'll let him know you're coming. Goodbye."

"Goodbye," I say. I place the phone back on the base and I sit with my legs dangling over the side of the bed. I feel like my world just came to an end. Is that wrong? It's like the best roller coaster ride in the world just pulled into the gate, and now I have to get out and let someone else take my seat and enjoy my ride. I'm not ready for it to be over! I want another turn. I'm not ready to get off. Now I know exactly how my daughter feels. I'm not sure I wanted him to wake up, either. Does that make me a bad person? Or just real?

I get to the hospital and walk down the hallway towards Jonas' room. I'm still a little out of sorts by the news. I walk into the room and the doctor is talking with him about what he should expect from here on out.

"Jonas. Hi," I say, stopping next to the bed rail. "I can hardly believe you're awake." He looks just the same--like he just woke up from a nap. Of course, he's a little skinnier, but that's about all.

"Mildred." His voice was raspy, but it still had a 'tone' to it—that 'I'm-only-speaking-to-you-because-someone-important-is-in-the-room-and-I-want-to-impress-them' tone. I don't know why I hoped it would be different. I would think after that much time comatose something would have changed in him.

"So, Doctor, how is he?" I ask.

"He's fine. We'll run some more tests later, but so far it looks like he'll make a full recovery."

"That's wonderful. Praise God!" I say.

"Yes, it certainly is a miracle. It didn't hurt that you came to visit so often. With you massaging his legs and arms, there was hardly any loss to muscle tone." He turns to Jonas and says, "You sure are fortunate to have this young lady in your life. Not too many wives would spend the time she did caring for you, especially with those beautiful children you have. I'll be back to check on you later." He turns and smiles at me and leaves the room.

I look down at Jonas and he's not smiling at all. Just staring at me.

"Jonas, how do you feel?" I ask, trying to break the tension in the room. All the while I'm telling myself, "Don't let him take you back there. You've come too far."

"How do you think I feel? Why would you bring them up here to see me lying here like this? You trying to make me look weak?" He rasps.

"Of course not, Jonas!" I respond defensively. "I wanted them to see that you were still alive. They needed to know that you were going to be okay. Sometimes seeing is believing."

"There you go thinking you got all the answers again. The last thing they needed was to get the idea that they couldn't rely on their daddy. Thank you very much for undermining me to our kids." He turns his head from me.

"Jonas, if that's what you think, then I'm sorry. But..."

"But, nothing. Just leave, Mildred. I need some peace and quiet."

I stand there debating whether to leave considering he just came out of a coma or stand up to him. My better judgment wins out and I decide to leave.

"Okay, Jonas. You get some rest. Bye." As I go out the door I hear him whisper, "Good riddance!" I hesitate for a fraction of a second and then I continue on down the hall and out to my car. Once I get inside, I just sit there for a few minutes and replay what just happened. You wake up from a coma, blessed to be alive with the activity of your limbs, clothed in your right mind and you're upset because I brought your kids to see you? On one hand, I see his point. On the other hand, I would have worked all that out after giving God praise that I'm yet in the land of the living. But I guess to some people, image is everything. I should have been expecting that. I should have at least been prepared for that, and then I wouldn't have been thrown like that. But what really bothers me the most, is how fast I regressed back to the scared, subservient little wife. I didn't break down, but I backed off—again.

"How long, Lord!" I cry out. I feel like the martyrs in the book of Revelations. I wonder when I'll be avenged. "God, give me strength!" I put my keys into the ignition and pull out of the parking space. The whole drive home I rehearse what to tell my kids. I don't want them to see how upset I am, and I definitely don't want to fake the funk, either. So, I cheat. I call my sister in law—who graciously came over to stay with them—and I give her permission to tell the kids. Then I convince myself that the Holy Spirit dropped that into my spirit. I would never have thought that one up. It freed me. I decide to drop into work. I already called in and left a message that I may not make it in, but I guess I need a distraction.

Of course there is no one there when I get there because it's still early. I forego my cup of coffee and just sit at my desk looking at the contracts and papers stacked in the center and wonder did I make a mistake. The response I've gotten is starting to get a little overwhelming. I input the figures and we are turning over a very healthy profit, even with paying out incentives or the slight price reduction. So far, Mr. Hughes hasn't responded to the reports I've sent him, but I know he'll address it sooner or later. I'll probably need to start coming in earlier for a while to keep up with everything. At least until school starts. By then I should have a better grip on things. Plus, now that Jonas is awake I won't have to take time going to the hospital once they let him come home.

I turn on my computer and check my emails. The very last one was sent at two thirty-four in the morning from Mr. Hughes. It said that he wanted a meeting with me first thing Monday morning. That's all. No subject or explanation. *Uh-oh,* I think to myself. I hope he isn't upset with all the changes I made! This could be the end of my job! My day is just getting better and better. Well, in for a penny, in for a pound. I've come this far and I might as well see it through to the end. I dig into the pile and send responses and incentive checks and input contract terms and figures into spreadsheets until my wrists start to hurt. By then, while I'm rubbing my wrists, I finally notice the girls at their desks working. When did they get here? How can I be so completely absorbed that I don't notice them?

"Good morning, everybody," I say.

"You finally noticed us. We feel so honored," teases Nora.

"I think you've been hanging around these two too long," I quip back.

"Well, we've only been here a couple hours!" exclaimed Trudy.

"Yeah, I thought we were closer than that! We feel neglected lately! You come and go and barely speak to us when you're here. We're starting to think you don't like us anymore," Judy says, pretending to wipe her eyes.

"You will always be my girls. You know that," I say standing up and coming around the side of my desk and leaning against it.

"Seriously, Mildred," says Judy, "why didn't you tell us about what was going on between you and Jonas?"

"I just didn't want you guys to think less of me for putting up with it. I hear how you talk about girls you know who let their men run all over them. I didn't want you to think that of me," I confess. "I should have been honest from the start, but I also don't like telling my business. And I thought that things would have been different by now."

"Different how?" Nora asks.

"Well, I've been praying for our situation to change for a while, and I expected God to change it. But this past eight months have shown me that it's not up to God, it's up to me and Jonas. We have to be willing to make the changes. I was. So far, he hasn't shown me he wants to change. Now I'm at the point of having to make a decision. Do I still want this or not? I know I don't want things like they are, but am I willing to put more time into waiting on Jonas or do I go? That's kinda where I am now."

"Honey, that doesn't make me think any less of you at all. To be frank, I always thought you were above us. It's good to know you go through things just like everybody else. It's encouraging, because even though you have to make hard choices, I know that if you can get through all you've been through, then I can make it too." She comes over to me and hugs me and Judy and Nora follow suit.

"Thank you, girls. I really appreciate you. Since we are being open, Jonas woke up last night," I tell them.

"Really? That's great!"

"Wonderful!"

"That's incredible news, Mildred. But why are you here working instead of with him or with your kids?" Nora asks. She takes one look at my face and says, "Never mind. It's still wonderful news, though."

We go back to our desks and sit down. "I needed to come in and clear my head and try to get back some of the freedom I've had since he's been in the hospital, to answer your question, Nora. I don't know how to feel. I just wasn't up to going home and dealing with the kids' questions or having to fake excitement about their daddy being awake."

"Girl, it's okay, we understand. You need a moment for everything to sink in," consoles Judy.

"It's a lot to take in, so take it in," admonishes Trudy.

"If you want to stay all day, that's fine, too. We'll even let you ignore us again," Trudy says, with a serious expression. We all laugh and I feel fortunate for the people God has placed in my life to encourage me and keep me going.

Home Going

When I leave work, I go by the hospital. When I get to Jonas' room he's sitting up and talking to the pastors. When he sees me he says, "Mildred."

"Hi, Jonas, Pastors," I answer.

"Sister Mildred, it's so good to see you," says Pastor Evelyn. "Jonas was just telling us how you've been taking such good care of him. He's been bragging on you since we've been here," she says, with a twinkle in her eyes.

"Well, Pastor, it was the least I could do." I try not to look surprised that he would say anything positive about me.

"I think it was a good idea to bring your children to visit. You've given them a lesson in faith that will carry them far. To see you minister to your husband and pray for him and for God to move and answer your prayer is a great example to them in trusting Him," Pastor Gilliam expounds. "Your faith is encouraging Sister Mildred."

"Thank you, Pastor. I appreciate that."

"So, Jonas," Pastor Gilliam turns back to him, "you must be excited about going home tomorrow."

"Yes, sir, I am," he affirms.

Tomorrow? I don't think I'm ready for that, yet. I was hoping I had a few days to get myself together.

"Mildred?" Pastor Gilliam says.

"Yes? I'm sorry. What did you say?" I struggle to focus on the conversation in the room and not the one in my head.

"I asked if you told the children yet," he repeats.

"No, sir. They know their daddy's awake, but they don't know he's coming home tomorrow. Actually, this is the first I'm hearing of it myself," I explain.

"Well, the doctor feels there's no reason for me to stay. As soon as he gets the results back from a couple of tests he ran this morning—and the results are what he's expecting them to be—he's going to release me," Jonas says, and if I may say so, rather smugly.

"That's wonderful," I say, with a smile pasted on my face.

"Mildred, let's go sit outside and let these two men talk," Pastor Evelyn takes me by the arm and escorts me outside.

"Sure, Pastor," I say as we walk into the hallway. She leads me down to the waiting room, and we sit in two chairs facing the direction of Jonas' room, which I feel is on purpose.

"Mildred, are you okay?" She asks me.

"I guess so. Why do you ask?"

"I'm just picking up something from you. I know you and Jonas have your issues, but I just want you to make sure you keep your heart pure. And your thoughts."

"My thoughts? I was just taken by surprise that they would let him come home so soon after being comatose for so long," I say defensively.

"Mildred, I just want you to make sure that you do all you're supposed to do. That's all anyone can do. Don't let your feelings get in the way of doing what the word says. Above all, you have to keep your heart pure. Whatever you do, do as unto the Lord. Take your personal feelings and Jonas out of the picture. Keep your heart and mind on pleasing God and you'll get through this. He's trying to draw something out of you. You are so much stronger than you realize and much more important than you give yourself credit for. You matter, Mildred! Don't let anyone or any situation make you feel less. You are more than capable of dealing with anything the devil throws at you. That's why he's fighting you like he is. Sometimes the best weapon he has is those closest to you. You are going to have to step up your prayer and fasting so you can see a breakthrough in your life. Don't go out without a fight! Show the devil whose he's messing with," she admonishes.

"Pastor, I hear you. Just continue to keep me in prayer. Pray my strength," I say.

"It's not time to back down, Mildred. It's time for you to fight! Don't give the devil an inch. You back down, and he'll take you out. Remember that. Don't ever forget that. You're not fighting against Jonas, but you're fighting for him. If you love him and if you've ever loved him, you need to fight all the more. This is not so much for your marriage, but for his soul."

As I listen to my pastor, I feel the warmth of the spirit of God in my chest. I know she's right. I have to win. I can't let things go the way they've been going. It's time for me to stand up and be the woman God called me to be. What do I have to lose, right?

Pastor Evelyn prays with me, and we talk until Pastor Gilliam comes back down the hall. As they leave, I take a deep breath, square my shoulders, and walk back to Jonas' room. Now that they are gone, I'm sure that he'll be back to his normal self, but I resolve to not let it get to me. I walk into the room and sit down in the chair next to the bed.

"What do you want?" Jonas asks.

"What time are they trying to let you go tomorrow?" I ask him.

"Why?"

"So I know what time to pick you up, Jonas. I want to make sure I get someone to watch the kids," I explain.

"Don't worry about it. I'll get someone to come get me," he says stubbornly.

"Why would you do that when I'm telling you I'll be here to pick you up?" I ask, feeling my old frustrations rising to the surface. Why does he have to try my patience like that?

"And why would you come get me when I obviously don't want you to? Answer that," he lashes back.

"You know something, Jonas. You're blessed to be sitting up in that bed talking to me at all. The least you can do is show me some respect and consideration," I fling back.

"I only respect people who deserve it. And you don't!"

"I'm sorry you feel that way, Jonas. I am. But don't get me twisted. I've let you treat me like a doormat for too long. Don't take my meekness for weakness. I am your wife, even if it's just on paper. You made a vow to me before God and man, and as such, you are obligated to treat me the way the bible says. If you choose not to, it's not me you have to answer to, but God. So, instead of wasting my time with your childish outbursts and temper tantrums, tell it to God. Because this is the last time you're going to disrespect me and think I won't have something to say about it." With that said, I gather my things and walk to the door.

"I'll be back in the morning to pick you up. Goodbye!" I turn, walk out room, down the hallway and out to my car with my head held high, but all the while I was shaking inside. I couldn't believe I just did what I did! I sit in my car gripping the steering wheel, trying to get my heart to stop racing. I pull my cell phone out and dial Trish's number.

"Girl, you will never believe what just happened!" I blurt out and soon as I hear her voice.

"What? What's going on?" she asks.

"I just told off Jonas! I can't believe it. I just told him save the drama for his mama!"

"You did what? Hold on, Mildred! Tell me from the beginning."

So I proceed to tell her the whole exchange. "I'm so proud of you, Grasshopper! You are finally a woman!" she laughs. "Mildred, for real, you should have done that a long time ago."

"I know! But I was just so...I don't know. I think I was trying to be submissive and pious and virtuous and whatever, but he got away with being a bully. I refuse to be a victim anymore. I deserve to be treated better than that. I know people who don't like me that treat me better than he does. Now, what does that say about him?"

"Really, what does it say about you, Mildred? You've been beaten down so long that you think all you are supposed to see are his feet. But it's time for you to stand up—not just to him, but to yourself. Challenge yourself and see how far you can go. I've been waiting a long time for you to come to yourself and see your potential."

"Well, I guess I've come to a point of no return. There's no way we can go back to the way things were. And I don't want to," I say defiantly.

"Good. And when you go in there tomorrow, stand your ground," she admonishes, "Cause he's probably laying there thinking how he can tear you back down and reestablish the status quo. You challenged him, and he wants to regain control. Don't let him bait you," she warns.

"I won't," I reply. "Girl, I'll talk to you tomorrow. I've got to get home."

"Okay, Mill. Stand strong and fight the power!"

"You are so crazy! Bye!" I laugh.

"Goodbye."

We hang up and I drive home. I feel pretty good—better than I have in a while. I know it's more than just talking to Trish. I stood up for myself. I can see that I value myself, even if Jonas doesn't. That doesn't even matter like it used to. I'm important to me! If he has a problem with that, then that's his problem. I'm not trying to strip his manhood away or belittle him, but show him that he doesn't have to make himself look bigger by stepping on me.

In the morning, I leave the kids with my in-laws, and I go to the hospital to pick Jonas up. The nurse is waiting for Jonas to finish signing his discharge papers, but he is still in his pajamas. I put his duffle bag on the bed with his change of clothes in it, and I sit down and stare at the television. When the nurse leaves, he grabs the walker next to the bed and stands up to go into the bathroom. Without a word, I get the duffle bag and carry it into the bathroom and place it on the sink. Jonas goes in and closes the door. When it shuts, I heave a sigh because the tension is so high in the room. I can tell that he was trying to ignore me, and I get the feeling that he did something, but I don't know what, yet.

I sit there and listen to him struggling to get dressed. As much as I want to help him, I know he'll just reject it, so I force myself to sit there. Twenty minutes later, as he's coming out of the bathroom, his brother-in-law Duane comes in the room.

"Hey, boy! Good to see you up and around. Hi, Mildred. I thought you had a meeting today?" He spills out.

"No, I didn't have a meeting today. Where did you hear that?" I ask, even though I already figured it out.

"Oh, Jonas told me you had a meeting and asked if I could pick him up," he admits, while Jonas is avoiding looking at me.

"No, I think he may have just got the dates mixed up, but thank you so much for coming," I say, sweetly.

"No problem. It's the least I could do."

"Well, I appreciate it. I hate that you came all this way for nothing."

"It's no big deal. I can at least help you get to the car," Duane offers.

"That would be great. I accept." So we get Jonas into the wheelchair that the nurse brings for him. Duane carries the bag while I push Jonas down the hall and out to the car. Once we get to the door, Duane puts the duffle bag in the trunk and I help Jonas up. He leans extra hard on me as he walks the two steps towards the car. When he sits down, he almost pulls me down with him. He's acting like some little helpless puppy in front of his brother-in-law, but I see the smirk on his face. He's trying to hurt me on purpose because his little ploy didn't work. That's okay. I got this. I reach into the car and grab the seat belt and pull it around Jonas and strap him in. Then I pull it real tight. "Don't want you sliding all around and reinjuring yourself." I tell him, loud enough for Duane to hear.

"That's some wife you got there, man. You sure are blessed!" He tells Jonas. "I'll see y'all later. Take care bro'," he waves and walks to his car.

As I walk around the car and get in, Jonas un-straps his seatbelt and re-straps it looser. I see his little smirk is gone, and his eyes have that steely look to them. I just put my keys into the ignition, start the car and turn up the radio. I sing the whole way home while Jonas stares out the window.

At home, Jonas doesn't wait for me to help him. He just gets out the car and walks to the door. He's barely struggling, so I know that little act was just for me. I unlock the door, and he goes in the house. He heads straight for his office, walks in and closes the door.

"Well, welcome home, Jonas. It's so nice to have you back," I yell down the hall. I know I shouldn't provoke him, but I guess I'm just flexing my newfound muscles. I put his things in the laundry room and go upstairs with his follow-up papers. Since he doesn't want to tell me anything, I'll just read it for myself. He has physical therapy twice a week for three weeks, but no real limitations. That's good, so he'll try to push himself to get back into his normal routine so people can talk about how 'strong Brother Jonas is' and 'look at God.' Although, he will probably try to get some of the credit himself.

I put the papers on the nightstand and force myself to try to let go. I sound like a jealous person. I'm not, but I've seen similar behavior from him before and based on his actions, I don't expect to see anything different. But…there is still power in prayer. I get my oil out and anoint everything—the bed, pillows, nightstand, lamp, remote, pajamas, doorknobs, door posts, dresser, brush—whatever I can get my hands on. I mean I'm not about to go back to the foolishness. I pace around the room praying, not really paying attention to anything. I hear a noise at the door and when I turn, I see Jonas' back and he is retreating back down the hallway. I continue praying in the spirit until I feel peace inside. I go downstairs, grab my keys and cell phone and go out the door. I walk down the driveway and onto the sidewalk. I walk at a pretty brisk pace with my arms pumping and the further away from the house I get the more I feel God's presence. I feel stronger.

I remember, before I had Gabrielle, Jonas and I would tussle together on the floor and he would tell me he had to stay in shape to keep up with me. He talked about how strong my arms and legs were, and anybody who thought they could take me would be sadly mistaken. I wonder if that's what God is saying to me now, but in the spirit. Whatever the case, I'm going to heed the prompting of the spirit. It seems to me that I still have some fighting to do and I need to be in good spiritual health.

I decide to walk for an hour and then go home and fix Jonas dinner. As I walk into the house, I hear him yelling down the hall. The only thing I can make out is "… and don't call my house again!"

"Who in the world is he yelling at?" I ask myself. "He just got home, shouldn't nobody be calling here upsetting him that quick."

I knock on his study door, "Jonas, you okay in there?" I ask him.

"I'm fine! Now gone leave me alone, I got work to do!" He yells through the door. I step back to do just as he says, but I catch myself. I reach out and turn the doorknob and push the door open.

I step into the room and Jonas looks up at me in surprise. "You just got home, Jonas. What work you got to do?" I ask him. "What you need to do is go get some rest. Come on now." I go around the side of his desk and take him by the arm. "You go lie down in the den and watch television and I'll fix you some dinner." If I could tell what he was thinking by looking at him, it would probably contain a few choice words. But he stands up and lets me guide him to the couch. I hand him the remote, flash him a big smile and walk out the room. I hear him mumble under his breath, and I turn back around. "What was that? Do you need something else?" I ask pleasantly.

"Go do whatever it is you got to do and leave me alone," he barks at me.

"Alright, but if you need anything, just let me know," I tell him, sweetly. In the kitchen I can hardly contain myself. I giggle to myself as I take out leftovers to heat up. The kids should be home any moment and I know they'll be excited to see their dad. I know I should behave, but after all he's put me through. Well, I do have to remember that God doesn't like ugly. As much progress as I've made, the last thing I need is to go back to that place. What we had was pretty ugly. This is just my way of coping, I guess.

Dinner is pleasant enough with the kids asking their dad a lot of questions about what it was like to be in a coma and if he could hear them talking and what it felt like and on and on. I could tell even Gabbi is happy to see her dad. And for once, he acts like he is truly glad to see and spend time with his children. Maybe this had to happen to get us to this point.

After straightening up, I call Trish and tell her about our day. "So, is he acting any better?" She asks me.

"Not really. I just ain't trying to let him get to me, that's all. I've been real nice and pleasant. He did act really good with the kids, though," I admit.

"Well, that's something, I guess. Have you gone off on him for real, yet? Cause all this pleasantness is just a cover for what you know you should do," Trish admonishes.

"Come on now. You know he just got home. I'm trying to eliminate drama, not have a full on blowout. I'm trying to move past all that, Trish."

"I understand all that, but you need to confront him now before he gets back up to full strength."

"But that's like kicking a man when he's down. That's cheating!"

"You want to win don't you?"

"Sure, but what's the point of winning the battle and losing the war? Ultimately, Trish, I want the war. I want the spoils, the bragging rights and everything that comes with winning. The only way I can have it is to do things God's way."

"I hear you. I'm just not sure I can watch you get beat on and torn down again. I won't sit by quietly this time! I'm gonna fight for you, Mill! Maybe not in the natural, but in the spirit world, it's on! He's had too much time already tearing you down. Now when you're about to really make a push for the Kingdom, here he is trying to stop you again. It ain't right, Mildred. It just ain't right," Trish fusses.

"Well, like you said, it's on in the spirit realm. I'm not fighting Jonas. I'm fighting every spirit and principality on assignment trying to delay or stop my purpose from being fulfilled. And they are familiar with me. They know my weak spots, which buttons to push, the best times to strike, what food I like. They've been studying me for fifteen years. I can't lose this, because I'm on the front line. The next line has my kids on it and I won't let the devil have them without a fight! My winning this insures their victory."

"Girl, this is some serious warfare! Now I see why I've been in all these prayer meetings. It wasn't to clean me up, but to help you fight in the spirit. You can count on me, Mildred. I'll definitely be praying for you—and your family."

"Thanks. I really appreciate the support." We say our goodbyes and I go get ready for bed. Jonas decides to sleep in the study. He claims it's because the steps are too much for him right now—even though I saw him upstairs earlier, but I didn't call him on it. When he worked long hours on the computer for work (or not) he would fall asleep in the chair, so he bought a daybed to put in there for those times. I don't argue with him. I just bring him some pillows and blankets and tell him to call upstairs if he needs anything. I get myself in the bed and stretch out on my back. I don't hear a thing until the sun comes up.

August 20

Church was what I expected. Jonas took the stage amidst applause and praises to God, like he was a war hero come home. And trust me, he milked it for all it was worth! It took everything in me not to roll my eyes. I had to repent to God because I thought I would handle it better, but there are still seeds of bitterness there. I spent all this time taking care of this man who treats me like dirt, and I don't get a "thank you" or "I appreciate you". It just doesn't seem fair! To top it all off, I got my hair in braids yesterday so it would be easier to handle and pretty much stay fixed, and he told one of the deacons that I was trying to be "ghetto" and that I did it out of spite. What?! The only time he ever commented on my hair was to tell me what he didn't like about it, so I shouldn't be surprised.   I'm just tired and drained. I've been trying to give him what I don't have. He's taken so much from me without putting anything back. I think I want so much more than he has the capacity to give me. I want a husband who loves me like Christ loves the church, who puts me first, who honors me as the weaker vessel, who spends time learning me, who treats me like a queen, who talks to me and cares about my feelings. I need a husband who lets me be who I am and is not threatened by that. I don't need someone to try to change me, but who prays for me. I can't tell you the last time Jonas prayed for me. If anything, he prays about me—Lord, change her! I've admittedly had a few of those prayers myself, and trust me, he got worse while I was the one who changed! I just pray God helps me through this time and that it doesn't last long. When we got home from church the phone was ringing. Jonas nearly knocked me down trying to answer it. I have a feeling that there's more going on here than meets the eye. When I confronted him about it, he just played dumb. I got your "dumb" act and I raise you "discernment". Whoever she is, she don't know me very well, does she? As for Jonas, I think we all know that he doesn't know me at all.

Bright and early Monday morning I go into work. Since Jonas is home, I feel a little better about the kids being there, but I still drop Mariah off at the sitter's. I want to spend some time praying before everyone one gets in the office, but Mr. Hugh's car is already in the parking lot. "Uh oh," I say. "This can't be good!" I sit in my car and gather my thoughts. I hope I still have a job at the end of the day. The way things are going I just don't know what to expect.

"Lord, I pray for favor. Go ahead of me and prepare my way." I get out of the car and go inside. There's a note on my desk telling me to come back to his office around nine o'clock. Wow! I have to sit here for two hours stewing in fear. I'm sure by then I'll be good and done—fork tender, as they say. At least it'll be easy to tear me apart if that's what he plans to do. It's the not knowing that's the worse. I'm almost afraid to do the work on my desk because that has to be why he wants to meet with me. As I sit there pondering my predicament, the girls come in one after the other. In my distress, I didn't notice that they had notes on their desks, too. Apparently this is bigger than I thought initially.

God, what have I done? I hope I didn't get them in trouble. I couldn't bear it if I cost them their jobs.

At eight fifteen, Nora goes back into Mr. Hughes office. Judy and Trudy and I sit there pretending to do work, avoiding looking at each other. When Nora comes back to her desk fifteen minutes later, Judy gets up and goes down the hall. I try to get Nora's attention, but she won't look at me. This is looking really bad. I give up all pretense of trying to work and I sit there with my head on my desk. At eight forty-five, Judy comes back and Trudy takes the walk down the hall. No one is talking. There's just the sound of paper shuffling every now and then, but for the most part, it's quiet. At eight fifty-nine, I get up and make my way down the hall. Just as I reach the door, it opens and Trudy comes out. She pulls the door closed behind her and says, "Mr. Hughes says to give him a couple minutes."

"Oh, okay," I respond. I turn around and go back to my desk. As I sit back down, the other girls get up and go back to Mr. Hughes office.

"What is going on," I whisper. "If I'm fired, why drag it out. This is like American Idol. They know who's gone at the beginning and they make you wait an hour to tell you. That's just crazy!" While I'm musing, the intercom on my desk buzzes. I jump because this is the first time he ever used it. I'm surprised it works! I press the button. "Mildred, come on back," says Mr. Hughes.

"Yes, sir," I answer. Once again I make the trip down the hall. When I get to the door, I take a deep breath, reach out and grip the doorknob. I turn it and push the door open.

"SURPRISE!!" Everyone yells.

"Oh my God!" My mouth drops open. The whole office has been redecorated and there are balloons and banners saying 'Congratulations, Mildred' on them.

"What is all this?!" I ask bewildered.

"Well, I just thought my new manager might want her new office fixed up," says Mr. Hughes.

"What are you talking about?"

"Mildred, I'm promoting you," he says.

"I'm not fired?" I ask, incredulously.

"Why would I fire you? You have made some very good decisions these last few months and it has increased the profitability of this company. I would be a fool to let you go."

"Congratulations, Mildred!" Nora hugs me, followed by Trudy and Judy.

"You guys were in on this?"

"We were sworn to secrecy. Besides, we wanted to remain in the good graces of our new Manager."

"This is so unbelievable! I am so surprised! I thought you were firing me," I confess.

"You have shown the kind of initiative that any boss would love to see in all of his employees. And you did it without getting my approval. It paid off. I knew there was something about you I liked. You value your job, and I trust your instincts. I went over every report you sent me and it made good sense what you were doing. That's why I never intervened. I am honored to have you run this office and the new one I plan on opening up across town," expounds Mr. Hughes.

"What? Two offices! I'm managing two offices? This is so crazy!" I exclaim.

"Judy and Trudy are going to relocate to that office when it's opened and they'll report to you. You can have this be your headquarters and just commute when you need to. You hire the extra staff you need, promote or whatever and I'll just be a shadow overseeing everything in general, but it's yours to run. Mildred, I have faith in you. Congratulations! Girls, you can keep the party going and I'll see you later." With that, he gets his things, hands me an envelope and leaves us in my new office to celebrate.

"This is incredible!" I walk around the desk and sit down in my obviously expensive desk chair. The girls are looking at me and smiling and I just shake my head, trying to take it all in. "This is so surreal, guys. You can't possibly imagine what I'm feeling right now. It's overwhelming!" I survey the changes in wallpaper and paintings and area rugs. "How did you do this without me knowing?"

"Mr. Hughes got a crew to come in Friday after we left and they worked through the weekend," Nora answered.

"Forget that! What's in the envelope?" Judy asks.

"Oh, yeah," I say as I rip it open. There is a letter inside, a key and a check. I look at the check and I almost faint. It's a very sizable bonus check! I unfold the letter and read it, tears welling up in my eyes.

Mildred,

Words can't really express how much I appreciate your loyalty and dedication to this company. There is no way I could ever repay you for what you have done. This check is just a token of my thanks and the key is to my vacation home in the hills. Feel free to use it whenever you like. I keep a cleaning company on retainer. Their card is in the rolodex on your new desk. I also have the great honor of increasing your salary, but your value to me increases greater in every other way. I look forward to our continued success and I want to say thank you again. Be blessed.

Yours sincerely,

R. Hughes

"Wow, I feel so special. This is the nicest thing anyone has done for me in a long time!" Nora hands me a tissue and I wipe my eyes. "Well, enough of all this blubbering, we're supposed to be partying!" I stand up and dance back to my old desk and turn on the radio. I turn the music up and we celebrate the rest of the day. We order in at lunch time and after all the maintenance calls are assigned I give us all the rest of the afternoon off. I praise God all the way home. When I pull up to the house, a strange car is in my driveway. I get Mariah and our bags and go into the house. I hear talking coming from the study, but the kids are nowhere around. I take the baby upstairs and put her in her crib with her Elmo doll and I go back downstairs.

I stand outside the study door and put my ear to it. I hear Jonas' voice and a female voice arguing.

"How long do you think you can keep this from your wife? You owe me. And I want my money!"

"You not getting another dime from me until you got proof that kid is mine!"

"I don't have to prove nothing! I can just show up at church one Sunday and your sweet little gig will be over. How do you like that? No more Mr. Preacher, Mr. Bigshot. You'll be a disgrace to everybody. Everybody will know you cheated on your wife. You act like you're so holy and you're better than me, but you're not!"

At this point, I've heard enough. I open the door and they both jump. "What's going on here?" I ask, even though I have a pretty good idea.

"What you doing home so early?" Jonas asks me, evading my question.

"When you answer my questions, I'll answer yours. What is going on, Jonas? Who is this?" I look at Jonas and wait for a response. He can barely hold his head up.

"I'm Monique and Jonas is my boy's daddy," the young lady speaks up. "We were just discussing child support payments that he owes me."

"Well, Monique, first of all, I was talking to Jonas. Second, you are not getting another dime until you bring proof that Jonas is the biological father. I don't take too kindly to extortion, so you better hope he is or I will file a suit for the money he's given you so far. And if you so much as cross my doorstep again with this foolishness, I'll have you arrested. Now get your things and go."

"Excuse me?!" She yells.

"I don't believe I stuttered. And by the way, don't you call here again tying up my line and breathing on my phone, you hear? Now get out!" That must have been straight from the Holy Spirit because she just rolls her eyes, sucks her teeth, picks up her purse and stomps out the door. I follow her, but I say to Jonas, "I'll deal with you when I get back."

I follow Monique to the driveway and watch until she drives off, tires squealing. Then I come back into the house to confront Jonas. He's sitting on the daybed staring down at his hands.

"Mildred, I..." he starts.

"Jonas," I cut him off. "I don't want to hear any excuses. You were wrong. I know it. You know it. But most importantly, God knows it. I don't want to hear you slipped, she tricked you, and I wasn't there for you or any of those lame excuses men give women when they can't control their urges. Don't expect too much from me right now, because I don't have anything to give you. You can thank yourself for that. You took everything I had—my love, my compassion, my trust, my loyalty, my respect—and you didn't replenish it. With this one act, you threw it all back in my face. I don't know how to feel right now! I am so mad at you! I can't believe you would treat me like you've been treating me all this time and you were the one living foul!" I yell.

"Look, you don't understand..."

"Don't understand what, Jonas? That you treated me like trash, like I wasn't worthy to breathe the same air as you. You have been so mean to me! And I let you! I can't believe I let myself think I was less than you! You've spent all these years making me feel like you had some inside connection with God and that I wasn't worthy enough to be in on it, too. But the truth shall set you free. Don't think all this was for you, that everything I've gone through was just coincidence. It wasn't. It was to make me into who God created me to be. Everything we've been through was to help me to realize my own connection to God. I am the daughter of the Most High God. You no longer have power over me, Jonas. You don't get to dictate how I feel and what I do. And if you don't tell the pastors about your indiscretions, I will. You need to find somewhere else to live, too, because we're through!" With that, I storm out the room and go upstairs to check on Mariah. I see that she fell asleep and I pace back and forth in front of her crib.

I can't believe what just happened! Jonas was unfaithful to me! I want to scream, but what good will that do? It won't change the past or make it all magically disappear. It's not like the suspicion wasn't there. "I'd love to take a bat and bust his head open," I say. But what that'll get me is time behind bars, and right now my kids are going to need me more than ever. I really thought that God was maturing me so my marriage could get better. I thought the changes I was making would force Jonas to change, too and then we could work things out. I had no idea it would come to this. Even though I kept vacillating between wanting out and wanting change, I still secretly hoped change would come. What a day!

Revelation

By Sunday, the whole church has heard about Jonas' apparent fall from grace. I called the pastors the night he left and told them what was going on in the event it got out. Apparently, Monique thought spreading it would get her what she wanted, but she's not very bright. You can bet she won't get a penny now--at least not from me. She's taken enough of my money. Jonas was trying to keep this quiet, but anybody knows that once a person thinks they got you, they get greedy to the point that you could never give them enough. I get a lot of "we're praying for you, sister" from the church members, but I just want it all to go away. My kids miss their daddy, even Gabrielle. She knows what happened, but that's still her dad. We talked about it a little and I told her that even though I was hurt by his betrayal, that I forgave him. That was hard to do, but I can't hold onto hurt and expect God to bless, can I? I definitely don't want to teach her unforgiveness.

Out of everyone, Trish surprised me the most. She told me to really seek God before I made anything permanent. "Get by yourself and consecrate yourself, Mildred. You want to make sure whatever you do, you are spirit led to do it. Or you could be setting yourself back."

I'm taking her advice. I decide to use the key Mr. Hughes gave me to go away for a few days. I want to take the kids because of all the backlash with Jonas, but I send them to stay with my parents instead. That way, they'll be away from the drama, and I can still get alone to clear my head. Because I have nothing but the address and no clue what to expect, I bring my radio, CD's, my bible and some reading material with me. I listen to my bible on CD on the drive down. I started out with the radio, but every song reminded me of the test I found myself in and I just didn't want to deal with it right now, so I listen to the voice of the narrator as he reads the book of Matthew. I plugged the address into the GPS and so every few miles it chimes out directions that help to break the monotony.

I think about how less than a week ago I was feeling strong and in control. Now I just want to cry. I started packing up Jonas' things two days ago to reinforce my decision to put him out. I found some adult videos in the closet and DVD's in the nightstand next to the bed. That just goes to show how clueless I was. He never wanted me to touch his stuff—that should have been clue number one. Hindsight is always twenty-twenty. I just threw them in the trash. The DVD's were actually copies. I wondered who was comfortable enough to give him those knowing he was supposed to be a man of faith. Who did he feel comfortable enough with to ask for them? How come he did knowing it would (or should) affect his witness? I mean, how can you preach to me when I know I just gave you some porn? Am I the only one getting this? I am no longer naïve, gullible Mildred. My eyes are wide open now. Everything is not black or white, but shades of gray where he is concerned. It should be hot or cold, yeah or nay, but when you're trying to get away with something you tend to stay in shadowy places. When the light comes, darkness has to flee. The spotlight is on him now, not only him, but me as well. I feel everyone looking at me to see what I'm going to do. Hopefully, this time away will help me solidify what my next steps are going to be because I honestly don't know.

Truthfully, it's been a long time coming. If the blatant disrespect and the underlying hostility wasn't enough to send me packing, it had to be something big like betrayal. I would try to convince myself that he loved me. There were times when we had conversations he would tell me that he loved me, but didn't like what I was becoming. Like, I was mutating or something. In life everything changes and evolves. You adapt. But apparently, I was some type of monster that he felt plagued to deal with. Like a scar he couldn't get rid of. Well, scars are simply reminders of careless mistakes you've made or injury caused by an accidental or purposeful action. They don't hurt, they just let you know what not to do next time. You learn from them and you move on. But if you keep treating the scar like a wound, then it will never heal and you'll never learn from it. That's like keeping your hand in the fire even though it's burning. It doesn't make much sense to me. It does sound a lot like unforgiveness. Causing yourself hurt and blaming it on the other person. I really have to make sure I don't fall into that trap. It's just that, if Jonas was that unhappy with me, why stay and make himself and me miserable? Just leave. Now so many people are suffering. Lord, we sure can mess things up!

If I weren't so preoccupied with my circumstances, I would notice the beautiful scenery around me. I can see why Mr. Hughes would have a vacation home up in the mountains. The fresh air, trees and the mountains in the background are enough to make you forget your troubles. After about four hours of driving, I pull over and I stand outside the car to stretch my legs. I have about another hour to drive, but since I'm in no hurry, I take time to look around and appreciate the natural beauty of the area. There are not a lot of cars around. I've practically had the road to myself for the last couple hours.

I walk over to a huge rock outcropping and lean against it as I relive the last few days of my life. On one hand, some good things have happened for me and on the other some pretty bad things have as well.

All of them have impacted my life drastically, the good and the bad. I guess that's why I feel a little off kilter. I want to be happy, and I want to scream. I want to jump and shout for joy, and I want to punch somebody. I prayed to God to help me because I was feeling so strange, but when I pulled out my bible to get a word, it fell open to Psalm 19. I don't think it was coincidental, either. When I read verses 12-14, I felt a burning in my spirit. 'Who can understand his errors? Cleanse me from secret faults. Keep back Your servant also from presumptuous sins; Let them not have dominion over me. Then I shall be blameless, and I shall be innocent of great transgression. Let the words of my mouth and the meditation of my heart be acceptable in Your sight, O Lord, my strength and my Redeemer.'

I thought I would get a word telling me that I was right to be upset and that Jonas was going to get it, but God is dealing with me, instead. I hear Pastor Evelyn telling me to keep my heart and thoughts pure. I shake my head, stand up and make my way back to the car and pull back out onto the highway. I haven't given up my musings, but I do want to get to my destination before it gets too late.

I arrive at the mansion—that's really the only word that would fit. This place is gorgeous! The landscaping is majestic. There are flowers bordering the long driveway. There is a fountain in the middle of the grounds. It has an angel playing a harp with water shooting up all around it. How lovely! I go up the stairs, straining to take in everything at once. I pull my key out and open the door. For some strange reason my hands are shaking as I push open the door. "God have mercy!" I gasp as I walk into this huge foyer. There are ornate mirrors all along the walls and marble floors. It's so spacious and airy. There is a large chandelier hanging from the ceiling. I reach for the switch and turn it on. I feel like Belle in *Beauty and the Beast,* when she is touring the castle. In spite of its majesty, there is still a down home feel to the place—like it's 'lived in'. The furniture is well kept, but there are no plastic seat covers.

"Mildred, you have entered the big time," I tell myself. "Ain't no way I would have brought those kids of mine up here. I'm not trying to pay for none of this stuff!" I continue my exploring through every room in the house. There are expensive vases and antique pieces throughout. The kitchen is immaculate—not a fork out of place—and no food, either, I notice. The bathrooms are regal. I could spend some good quality time in there—you know, soaking, I mean. The master bedroom has one of those old fashioned tubs with the claw feet, but with a modern touch. Someone must have paid a fortune for an interior designer, but it was worth it. The colors are soft and calming, earthy without being boring, with splashes of boldness like burgundy, turquoise and emerald. I choose the bedroom to the left of the spiral staircase with a view of the backyard. There is a mountain in the distance and a small courtyard below the balcony. "Perfect," I say as I stand in the walk-in closet that is about as big as my whole bedroom back home.

I go back outside and get my things and take them up to 'my room'. Then I go searching for a phone book to see what stores are nearby. I do plan on eating a little while I am here. I feel like I should fast, but not a total one—a Daniel fast. While I'm trying to find the book, I call Trish on my phone to let her know I made it safely.

"Well, that's good to hear. I was a little worried about you going off by yourself. I wish you would have let me come with you," she fusses.

"I know, I know. Now that I am here I wish you could be here to see how beautiful it is. But I still feel I need this time alone—just me and God."

"Promise you won't spend the time crying and blaming yourself or pacing and plotting. Or I just might have to drive up there," she threatens.

"Don't worry. I won't be plotting anything bad or even blaming myself. I can't promise I won't cry or pace though. This place is huge and there is plenty of room to pace. I may even lose and few pounds going from one side to the other," I joke. "I told you I'll only be a few days. If I'm not back you have my permission to come and drag me back. But I promise you won't want to leave. It is really a gorgeous place," I tell her.

"Well, you just make sure you call me at least once a day and right before you get on the road to come back, okay?"

"Sure, I can do that." We hang up and I go through the drawers in the kitchen, still hunting for the phone book. When I get to the third drawer, the doorbell rings—actually, chimes is more accurate.

"Who in the world could that be?" I ask myself, walking warily to the door. When I open it, there is a petite woman on the other side.

"Hello," I say looking puzzled.

"Hi, I hope I am not bothering you. I know you just got here, but are you Miss Mildred?" She asks.

"Yes, but how do you know my name?" I questioned her.

"Mr. Hughes said you might be stopping by from time to time. I'm Sarah. I stay in the cottage at the edge of the property. I saw you pull up. My husband and I take care of the place in exchange for housing. Mr. Hughes is a very generous man."

"He is that," I agree. "Why don't you come on in, Sarah. Maybe you can help me find a phone book or direct me to where I can get some food." I back up and let her walk past me into the foyer. She proceeded down the hallway and into the library. Opening a drawer on the desk, she tells me that the phone book is probably older than Moses.

"The good thing is, most of the places around here have been here forever, so the numbers haven't changed."

"Well, that's good to know. I'll probably be here at least four days. Maybe it's better if I just eat out. That way I won't have to worry about throwing out any leftover food. Are there any good local spots?"

"Sure, if you don't mind salt, grease and pork," Sarah jokes.

"Well, why don't you show me around later and I'll treat you and your husband to dinner?" I suggest.

"That would be great. We do have to be back for bible study at six-thirty, though."

"Ok. Give me an hour to get myself together and I'll be ready to go. I just might even go to bible study with you."

"Sure, I'll go let my husband know, and we'll come back up in an hour." She lets herself out, and I go freshen up. Once I feel presentable, I go back downstairs to the sitting room to wait for Sarah and her husband. I have my purse and bible, so I decide to read a little. I go back to Psalms and try to get understanding of the passage I had read earlier, trying to determine what God was trying to tell me. Have you ever read the bible when you were having trouble sleeping? Did you fall asleep as soon as you opened it or did you get a least a couple verses in? All I know is there is some lumberjack standing over me saying, "Ma'am, ma'am?"

"Ahhh!" I scream. I jump up trying to get away from this guy in a plaid shirt and overalls.

"Mildred, it's just us," Sarah explains.

"Sarah, I'm sorry, you all startled me." I clutch my chest and look back and forth between Sarah and her husband.

"This is my husband Jim. Jim this is Mildred." He hands me back my purse and keys that fell to the floor when I stood up.

"Sorry, ma'am. We didn't mean to scare you."

"That's okay. I didn't realize I fell asleep. Why didn't you ring the bell?" I ask.

"We did, but you didn't answer, and we heard this crashing sound… that's why we came in," Sarah explains. "It must have been the sound of your bible falling and knocking over the vase. We do have a key because we come up and dust and clean sometimes."

"Wow! I am so sorry. I can't believe I didn't hear that! I guess I owe Mr. Hughes a vase. I hope it wasn't an antique." *Or there goes my bonus.* Sarah rushes to get a broom and dustpan and gets up all the glass. Once the mess is cleaned and they assure me the vase was a knockoff, we head on out. We get into their pickup truck with me in the middle. They take me around to the most beautiful places. They show me the stream that runs along the back edge of the estate. It is so peaceful and pristine. Then they drive me to the town and show me all the attractions—both of them.

"I guess it kind of has to grow on you," Sarah apologizes when she catches a glimpse of my expression.

I just stare out the window at the rock in the middle of town that sort of looks like Swiss cheese. Apparently, there is a great story behind it. I just smile and nod and try to fix my face. I have no clue where I am or how to get back, so the last thing I want to do is offend anyone.

"So, where is this restaurant you've been telling me about?" I ask, trying to lighten the mood.

"Well," says Jim, "it's just down the road a ways. My uncle owns it. We have time to get the daily special and still get to bible study on time."

What's the daily special? I wonder, as we pull up beside what looks like a little log house. We get out and go inside. While Jim and Sarah are saying hi and introducing me to his uncle, I inhale the most pleasant aromas and my stomach just growls. Turns out most of the food cooked and served here is grown locally. The daily special is a most delicious southern fried steak dinner with collard greens, macaroni and cheese, corn bread and sweet tea. There goes my fast. I had to go peek into the kitchen to see if any of my people were in there! It was so good!

After we say our goodbyes and I thank Uncle Ray—that was his name—we go a little ways outside of town to the church for bible study. I admit I am a little nervous because I feel out of my comfort zone, but I am curious. What I don't expect is to see so many people or how huge the church is. It looks like one of those megachurches out here in the middle of the mountains. Hundreds of people were in attendance.

"Where are all these people coming from?" I ask Sarah. "I would never have guessed this was back here," I admit.

"Yeah, isn't it great?" Sarah gushes. "The next town is about twenty miles away, and most of the members live there. There has been a real population boom the last five years. Our pastor just moved out there, but his family owns this land, and he built the church on it as a memoriam," Sarah explains.

"Once he did that, people started coming from all over," Jim added. "This is the largest ministry for miles. I think you'll be pleasantly surprised once we get inside." He parks, and we file out and follow a group of people walking into the building.

It is really a nice place. Not what you would expect. The sanctuary is huge and well appointed. We take our seats, and I gawk until bible study starts. It is more like a service. The choir sings, and they are awesome! The praise and worship leader is so anointed, and the power of God falls in that place. I forget where I am and that I am a visitor. I am so at home in the spirit. When the pastor finally comes out, I am so ready for the word. With so many people in there, I know he doesn't know me, but it feels like he is talking just to me. He speaks about the will of God, and how sometimes we do what we want and convince ourselves that it was God's will for our lives. He said that God doesn't put more on us than we can bear, but that when we make wrong decisions and choices, that's when God's grace comes in to help us endure those trials. God doesn't waste anything that happens to us—every hurt, scar, bad experience, wrong choice—He works it all for our good. It helps us to grow, get stronger and develop more trust that God would bring us out. That's how faith grows and gets strengthened, in the tough times. As we go through those difficult situations, God is with us, guiding us, teaching us, molding us and getting us to our expected end.

After service, my new friends take me up to meet the pastor. "That was such a good word, Pastor Bryant," I say, shaking his hand. *Why does he look so familiar?*

"Thank you. I'm glad you're here. It's always nice to have visitors, especially on bible study nights. It's encouraging getting positive feedback from someone so well-versed in the word. I really enjoyed your ministry this past April."

"The cruise! That's why you look so familiar. You were playing the piano, right?" I say excitedly as memories start to surface.

"Yes, that was me. One of my hobbies. I was really impressed with how you handled everything. God really moved!"

I blush and say modestly, "It was an honor for me and such a wonderful time. So many doors opened for me after that. I was a featured speaker all over. I started a women's group. I even got promoted on my job! God really blessed me," I reveal.

"That's great to hear. Tell me about your women's group. I've been wanting to start one here, but I don't have anyone to really spearhead it. Maybe we can set something up where you could bring it here quarterly."

"That's an interesting proposition," I say, nodding. "Well, the group is called Just Us Sistahs Talking or J.U.S.T. for short. We talk about what concerns us as women while helping one another find real solutions, support and fellowship as we navigate through whatever those issues are." I explain.

"I would love to have that here! I think the women would come out and support it, considering the lack of social outlets."

"You know I was thinking earlier how perfect this area is for retreats. Maybe we can make it work, Pastor Bryant."

"Call me Michael."

"Ok, Michael," I smile, shyly.

We talk on for a few more minutes before we realize that Jim and Sarah are fidgeting and there is a long line of people still waiting to shake the pastor's hand. "It was nice talking to you," I say, again shaking his hand and giving him one of my business cards. "We'd better go so you can greet everyone else. Bye." *I can't believe how down-to-earth and easy to talk to he is.*

Jim, Sarah and I talk non-stop all the way back to the mansion. They let me out at the door and I go inside, feeling full and light at the same time.

I realize that Jonas hadn't crossed my mind the whole night. "This is just what I needed," I say. I get into my pajamas and crawl into bed. I pull out my notebook and start writing. After Jonas moved out, I decided to compile the whole experience into a book of sorts. I wanted to have an outlet and vent so I wouldn't hold it all inside. As I write, I feel such a peace. Sleep comes quickly, and I don't wake until dawn. It's the sound of my own snoring that rouses me. I sit up and stretch. I throw my feet over the side of the bed, slide on my slippers and go out onto the balcony. The sun is just peeking over the trees. Looking at nature, the birds flying high up in the sky, the deer at the edge of the trees, the spider crawling on the banister, I get a feel for how alive everything is, and I feel that same life flowing through me. It's like all of a sudden, I've been reanimated. I have lived a dead existence for so many years—alive, but not really living. I have been trying to make other people happy and neglecting my own happiness. I really try to think back over the past fifteen years, and I really can't remember too many happy times. Of course, my children being born and caring for them, but where Jonas is concerned, not too many good memories. I was holding on to this marriage, this relationship that should have been buried long ago. It was dead from the start. Maybe it could have been resuscitated if we both were invested, but I see now that only I was married. "God, you have all of me. No more idol worship. You are my only God. I trust the plans you have for me. I know that you have the right person in my future."

I spent the next few days getting to know the area and visiting with Pastor Bryant--I mean Michael. He took time to answer some questions for me in the word and tell me about the wonderful church and ministry he had built. He told me about his vision for the ministry and how he wanted to really impact the community. What a wonderful plan!

My stay in paradise ends too quickly and home and routine comes way before I'm ready. The kids and I grow closer. I sit down with Gabrielle one afternoon and we just talk for hours. I tell her about finding her diary and she wasn't too upset with me. She tells me that she can see I am happier now, and she likes that I am giving her more responsibility. We even talk about Keith and how sometimes people look like answers to prayer but they are just distractions. Um, yes, he did call me, quite often. News of Jonas' indiscretion had travelled far. "Mildred, I'm here for you," he said, or rather crooned. I had to change my numbers so he would know that it was indeed over. Last I heard from Cherise, he was dating a widow from her church. She was a little disgruntled at first, but God sent her the perfect guy a year later. Now they are talking about their future together.

As for me, in time, I start sleeping in the center of the bed instead of on the right side. How's that for living? I'm not even mad that I had to switch to the left a little while later. It just goes to show how much I've grown. My words and my thoughts slowly but surely changed and were more acceptable, not only in God's sight, but in mainstream bookstores. I had to tell my story—to get it out—so it wouldn't sit in my chest and eat away at me. Who knew it would do so well?

Future Past

"Mildred, I am so amazed how much has happened since we met four years ago," exclaims Aniyah, breathlessly. "Who would have ever thought we'd be here?"

"Certainly not me," Trish answers. "This is the big time, girl!"

"I am so nervous! Look at all those people! You know this reminds me of Angela Bassett in 'What's Love Got To Do With It' just before she went out on stage at the end," I say, smiling. "All them people here to see me Ike, me," I quote badly.

"You so crazy, Mill!" Aniyah laughs. "But you are right. They are here to see you. J.U.S.T was the best thing that could have happened. It's been a blessing to me and now you are taking it to the world."

"Yes. And you are definitely my newest hero," chimes in Trish. "I have trained you well, Grasshopper. You are one of the most outspoken women I know. Truth be told, I am a little intimidated now."

"Why in the world would you be intimidated by me?" I ask. "I've only done what you guys have pushed me to do. You were my biggest support and encouragement. Of course, none of this would have happened without God."

"Yeah, but you have made this look easy. I know it wasn't, but...wow!" She says.

I think back over the time following my return from the mountains. Work was great. I had some trying times dealing with Jonas, but because of his infidelity, I was able to dissolve our marriage without much hassle. The custody and visitation was another issue. The kids live with me, but I make sure they spend as much time as they want with their dad. He's actually stepping up and handling his business. I did file for child support because I wanted to make sure he supported them, and it's only fair. I have been putting out so much, now it's his turn. I don't think he'll miss it. I was only awarded a few hundred dollars. As I've said, things have been really good. I had taken a few vacations back up to the mountains alone at first, then later on with the kids. They really enjoyed it. It helped with the healing. After my divorce, God opened my heart up to love again.

The three of us turn and peek out from behind the curtain at the mass of people, some still filing into the church. "Wow!" We say in unison.

"Well, let's pray before we run out of time." We hold hands and thank God for bringing us to this point, for blessing the conference and all the people who played a part in this night. We say amen just as I am being introduced.

"Now, I introduce to you the Hostess, MC and organizer of this great event, my wife and friend, my soul mate Pastor Mildred Bryant!"

I look down at the ring on my finger. I take a deep breath and go join my new husband onstage as the crowd applauds.

By the Way . . .

So, trust me guys, life didn't just work itself out after I got back, there was a whole host of drama. Once the DNA test came back proving that Jonas was not the father, he really started showing his tail again. Excuse me, but didn't you still cheat on me? He really took me through. He wanted full custody even though he spent little time with the kids. He told the judge about all the time he took time off to be with them. He sang a real good song, but the judge had heard that one before. So I won physical custody, but we shared legal custody. If that wasn't enough, he tried to file for child support from me. Huh? Yeah, right.

You see with my new raise and position, my up and coming social status, I was bringing in more money—not enough to ball, but enough to cover my expenses. All of which went up when we separated, but you would have thought I hit the big one. That became his "new" song. "She makes more than me!"

I'll admit, the whole thing was taking a toll on me and my faith, but I couldn't believe God would allow the foolishness to continue. I had to constantly check my heart, because, believe me Saints, I felt some kinda way! Jonas turned into a stranger to me. This was not the man I married, the man I had seen God use on many occasions. I was like, "God, Jonas is an assistant pastor. Please tell me You are not going to just stand there and keep silent!" But apparently He had a plan.

One night after Jonas kept the kids from me and wouldn't bring them back, I called him and he laid me out. He told me that I needed Jesus and some mental help. Jonas said I never did anything for him and that I was never there for him, that he was a good daddy and I was trying to keep his kids from him. I could only stand there with my mouth hanging open, listening to this nonsense. It was then that I knew for sure that I was in a spiritual battle, wrestling not with flesh, but principalities and powers. I hung up that phone and had me a good laugh, because I knew those spirits were raging because they were losing. Perhaps our whole "marriage" was to expose those demons and drive them out.

Shoot, things went so smooth for me after that. No, he didn't stop cuttin' up all the way, but I stopped reacting to it. It made Jonas so mad! He didn't even notice how it was affecting him. He was losing weight. People stopped calling him to speak. The pastors only used him for minor duties, little speaking and no preaching. They wouldn't take the title, though. It was truly an awkward time, but God worked that out. I was getting more invites out to speak so I didn't have to be at church every Sunday. J.U.S.T. took off. I had to plan impromptu getaways every month instead of quarterly because the women wanted more SPA days (spiritually powerful awakenings)—true encounters with God. So we made several trips to the mountains. That was the perfect place to host those S.P.A. days. And, we had a great pastor in the area willing to offer spiritual insight and guidance (wink, wink). I found my Boaz. Who knew? I guess Marla did. He gave me the time, attention and care that I needed. He allowed me to heal and grow stronger. And boy did he hit it off with the kids!

It's amazing how it all came together. But all things do work together...Right? Yes, it's all good for everyone. Jonas had a major health scare and it seemed to mellow him out. God healed him. He eventually apologized, repented and got himself together. Of course, it was too late for me, but I hear there is someone out there for everybody...

About the Author

Kyra Taylor is the second born daughter of a pastor who has a passion for God and the church. A dedicated mother of four, Kyra enjoys music, reading, traveling and writing poetry, short stories and articles in her spare time. She also is committed to growing her JUST, Inc. women's ministry and helping to empower other women to pursue their dreams.

If you enjoyed this story, you'll enjoy:

Ms. Understood: Re-messaging the Journey from Healing to Wholeness
Kimberly R. Taylor

An inspirational book and journal that confronts and challenges the reader to reconsider, reinvestigate and re-message the chaotic events that life sometimes brings. Part prose, part narrative, part lyrical, part rhetorical, part journal, combined to promote healing and wholeness when life leaves us wounded and uninspired.

Lisa's Dress
Kimberly T. Matthews

Will is reminded of the love he lost when he sees Lisa's wedding gown hanging in their bedroom closet. There's only one way to fix the damage he's caused to his marriage, but is he willing to do it? Can this couple win at making marriage work, proving that they can stay married and love it, or will the result of Will's infidelity and pride cost him the love of his life.

KISSED PUBLICATIONS
www.kplapublishing.com | www.kplaconsulting.com

www.ingramcontent.com/pod-product-compliance
Lightning Source LLC
Chambersburg PA
CBHW020748250626
47155CB00003B/973